Baby Emily was a warm weight against his chest, too surprised and unhappy at the moment to notice who held her.

It didn't seem to matter that Jack wasn't exactly sure how to hang on to a baby properly. Her legs kept slipping free of his grip, and he was afraid he might drop her. But the little girl leaned into his arms with complete abandon, trusting him to hold her up.

He didn't want her to trust him.

He didn't want to be holding her at all, but somebody had to do it, and at the moment Shelby couldn't. "Come on." He pitched his voice to be heard over Emi's wails and reached across Shelby's lap to open the passenger door.

Shelby smelled far too sweet as he leaned across her to unlatch the door.

Like warmed honey.

Like open air.

It was going from bad to worse....

Dear Reader,

It's summertime, and the livin' may or may not be easy—but the reading is great. Just check out Naomi Horton's *Wild Blood,* the first in her new WILD HEARTS miniseries. In Jett Kendrick you'll find a hero to take to heart and never let go, and you'll understand why memories of their brief, long-ago loving have stayed with Kathy Patterson for sixteen years. Now she's back in Burnt River, back in Jett's life—and about to discover a secret that will change *three* lives forever.

We feature two more great miniseries this month, too. Cathryn Clare's ASSIGNMENT: ROMANCE brings you *The Baby Assignment,* the exciting conclusion to the Cotter brothers' search for love, while Alicia Scott's THE GUINESS GANG continues with *The One Who Almost Got Away,* featuring brother Jake Guiness. And there's still more great reading you won't want to miss. Patricia Coughlin's *Borrowed Bride* features a bride who's kidnapped—right out from under the groom's nose. Of course, it's her kidnapper who turns out to be Mr. Right. And by the way, both Alicia and Patricia had earlier books that were made into CBS TV movies last year. In *Unbroken Vows,* Frances Williams sends her hero and heroine on a search for the heroine's ex-fiancé, a man hero David Reid is increasingly uninterested in finding. Finally, check out Kay David's *Hero in Hiding,* featuring aptly named Mercy Hamilton and enigmatic Rio Barrigan, a man who is far more than he seems.

Then join us again next month and every month, as we bring you more of the best romantic reading around—only in Silhouette Intimate Moments.

Yours,

Leslie Wainger

Leslie Wainger,
Senior Editor and Editorial Coordinator

Please address questions and book requests to:
Silhouette Reader Service
U.S.: 3010 Walden Ave., P.O. Box 1325, Buffalo, NY 14269
Canadian: P.O. Box 609, Fort Erie, Ont. L2A 5X3

THE BABY ASSIGNMENT

CATHRYN CLARE

Published by Silhouette Books

America's Publisher of Contemporary Romance

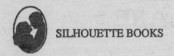

SILHOUETTE BOOKS

ISBN 0-373-07726-2

THE BABY ASSIGNMENT

Copyright © 1996 by Cathy Stanton

Printed in U.S.A.

Books by Cathryn Clare

Silhouette Intimate Moments

Chasing Destiny #503
Sun and Shadow #558
The Angel and the Renegade #599
Gunslinger's Child #629
*The Wedding Assignment #702
*The Honeymoon Assignment #714
*The Baby Assignment #726

*Assignment: Romance

Silhouette Desire

To the Highest Bidder #399
Blind Justice #508
Lock, Stock and Barrel #550
Five by Ten #591
The Midas Touch #663
Hot Stuff #688

CATHRYN CLARE

is a transplanted Canadian who followed true love south of the border when she married an American ten years ago. She says, "I was one of those annoying children who always knew exactly what they were going to be when they grew up," and she has proved herself right with a full-time career as a writer since 1987.

"Being a writer has its hazards. So many things that I see—a car at the side of the road, two people having an argument, a hat someone left in a restaurant—make me want to sit down and finish the stories suggested to me. It can be very hard to concentrate on real life sometimes! But the good part of being a writer is that every story, no matter how it starts out, can be a way to show the incredible power that love has in our lives."

For Jesse
and black magic.

Chapter 1

"Come one step closer and I'll shoot you."

Jack Cotter paused at his boss's office door.

"I'm serious, Jack." Jessie Myers put a hand on her chest. A deep, rattling cough overtook her words, and she turned away for a moment, trying to smother it. "Or maybe I'll just shoot myself," she amended hoarsely, when she could speak again. "Lord knows, I couldn't possibly feel any worse."

"For Pete's sake, Jessie, why don't you just go home? You sound like—"

"Death. I know. People have been very kindly pointing that out to me all day." Jessie pulled a tissue out of the box on her desk and blew her nose loudly. "Jack, listen to me, because I've only got enough voice left to say this once. Jerry Lawrence just walked."

"You're not serious."

"I wish I wasn't." Another cough shook Jessie's whole body. "The one witness we had—the one person who could tie Jerry to those shooters who killed the cop out in Lafayette—just turned up in a Dumpster with a bullet in his own forehead. Without that witness, we have no case. With no case, there's no point in going to trial. And you can bet Jerry Lawrence's attorney made that point loud and clear to the judge at Jerry's pretrial hearing this morning. The judge dismissed the charges, and that's that. Jerry's a free man again."

Jack swore softly. "I thought we had that witness under wraps," he said.

Jessie looked bad enough, with her eyes streaming and her nose reddened by the vicious cold she'd come down with overnight. Her grim expression didn't improve her appearance.

"I thought so, too," she said. "We had him and his family in a nice little place in Hays County, well out of the way. But for some reason the guy decided it was safe to show his face in San Antonio again. Look, Jack, what I want you to do—"

Her coughing fit this time lasted longer, and Jack was starting forward sympathetically, heading for the chair across from Jessie's own, when she held up a hand.

"Stop," she croaked. "I mean it. If you catch this cold and take it to your brothers' wedding, they're never going to forgive you. Hell, *I'll* never forgive you. You're supposed to be having a good time in the next couple of weeks, not spreading this plague across central Texas."

It was amazing, Jack thought. Everyone seemed to think weddings were occasions for universal rejoicing and celebration. He'd already been congratulated more times than he could count, and he was only the best man, for pity's sake.

Nobody seemed to consider the possibility that he wasn't wild about this change in his life.

And there wasn't a soul on earth he could say that to. His only real confidants in the world were Wiley and Sam themselves. And Wiley and Sam were far too much in love with their respective brides to understand why Jack couldn't quite share in their prenuptial bliss.

He leaned back against the doorframe, and waited without speaking while Jessie blew her nose again. When she finally spoke, her words were raspier and harder to hear.

"Remember the widow of the cop who got shot?" she was asking.

"I thought she was in the witness protection program by now."

Jessie's long, serious African-American face grew even more serious. "That's what I wanted people to think. In fact, she refused to let us relocate her—refused almost everything I offered to do for her. She wanted to find her own hiding place, and keep as much of her own identity as she could hang on to."

Jack stared. "She got a death wish or something?"

"She's a—an unusual woman. She had her own reasons for what she's done, and I respected them. But that was when it looked ninety-nine percent certain that Jerry Lawrence was going to prison until he was long past old and gray. Fortunately I made our witness promise to give me— and *only* me—an address where we could reach her when it was time for her to testify."

She reached into her purse and pulled out her bulky black date book. She slid a piece of paper out of the back pocket of the binder, then paused. "You're the only one I'd trust with this, Jack," she said slowly. "I know you're just about to start your vacation, but—"

"Come on, Jessie, spit it out." Jack pushed himself away from the doorframe. "Turning you down when you're in this state would be like refusing a deathbed request. What do you want me to do?"

Her answering smile was weak but relieved. "Get to the woman and warn her," she said.

"Why not just call her yourself?"

"She doesn't have a phone of her own. She's at... apparently it's some kind of ranch. She didn't want anyone calling her there. I know it's out of your way, and I know you're eager to get to Austin, but—"

"Don't worry about it." In fact, Jack was due at a tuxedo fitting with his brothers in Austin this evening, followed by a party hosted by some of his brothers' buddies. But it seemed possible that he would be able to fit the extra trip in, if he left Houston right away.

He didn't have to tell Jessie that he'd willingly do any favor she asked him. Hell, she'd do the same for him. They'd worked together long enough and built up enough mutual respect that they both knew it without saying it out loud.

He copied the ranch name and address on a piece of scrap paper and handed the original back to Jessie. As he slid the copied version into his wallet, it snagged on something, and he had to pull out a pile of other scrappy little notes to make room.

"Too much money, Jack?"

He shook his head. "Too many lists of things to do," he replied. "Would you believe, Sam's fiancée's mother has a deeply ingrained fear of the wedding rings going missing right before the ceremony, so she wants me to go out and buy a couple of cheapie imitations just in case I lose the real things. She's not even flying in until the middle of next week, and already she's stepping all over things."

"*Nothing* would surprise me about weddings." Jessie wiped her streaming nose and waved her free hand at him again. "Now get out of here," she said, "before you succumb to this horrible bug."

Jack stuffed everything back into his wallet, not caring what order it was in. "'I'm a goner, boys—save yourselves,'" he said. "Right?"

"Something like that. Or maybe I'm the captain going down with the ship. I feel too awful to figure it out." Jessie plucked another tissue out of the box, and added, "Tell Shelby Henderson from me that the offer of federal protection still stands. In fact, you can tell her I think she's a fool if she refuses it. Jerry Lawrence is a cold-blooded reptile, and he's never been afraid of killing."

Jack didn't need to be told that. "I've got it," he said. "*Now* will you go home and go to bed?"

"Willingly. I only came in today because I wanted to find out about Jerry Lawrence's hearing. And once I heard the news, I had an idea about driving out to see Shelby Henderson myself, but—"

"But it's hard to drive when you can't see straight. I get the picture, Jessie."

When he'd satisfied himself that his boss really was clearing her desk and getting ready to leave for home, he went back out to the open-plan office he and the other members of Jessie's current team shared. It was still early in the afternoon, but the atmosphere of Friday—or maybe of Jack's impending vacation—seemed to be affecting everyone.

"Hey, Jack." Garry O'Dette, the youngest member of the group, tossed a rolled-up scrap of paper at him from across the room. "Now that you're an expert on weddings, can you help me convince Annette to marry me? I keep telling her she's passing up a great chance to become Annette O'Dette, but she won't listen."

"Can I help it if she's got good sense?" Jack neatly deflected Garry's toss, batting the paper back across the big room with the flat of his hand. "And being a best man doesn't make me an expert on weddings, smart guy, any more than Mack's an expert on naval policy just because he's got that big boat."

"Hey, naval policy's gotta be a cinch compared with looking after a boat." Mack MacGuire, Jack's longtime colleague, looked up from his computer screen. "I'd have offered it to Wiley and Sam to use on their honeymoons,

Jack, except the damn engine's been acting up again. I swear that thing spends as much time in the shop as it does on the water.''

"That's all right. The happy couples have their honeymoon plans all lined up, I believe."

It felt harder all the time to keep that bittersweet tone out of his voice, but maybe he was the only one hearing it. None of his colleagues seemed to notice, to his relief.

"Aren't you worried about being a best man two times in one day, Jack?" Annette Caniglio was smiling at him. "You know what they say—'Three times a bridesmaid, never a bride.' "

"I'm not losing sleep over it." Sliding out from under the whole sore subject, he added, "Listen, can someone wrap up that report on Gutierrez Industries? I've got to run an errand for Jessie, and then get up to Austin."

"I'll do it. I'm in that file, anyway." Mack looked back at the screen in front of him. "Jessie going home?"

"Yeah. She was just concerned about one of her witnesses in the Jerry Lawrence case. I've got to run out to where the woman's staying, and tell her Lawrence is on the loose again."

The other members of the team shook their heads. Clearly the word about the last minute foul-up in the Lawrence case had made the rounds while Jack had been at lunch.

"Bad scene," Garry said.

"But a great way for Jack to skip out of the office even earlier," Annette teased.

Jack didn't answer her this time. How was he supposed to explain to his well-meaning associates and friends that an essential part of his world was going to come to an abrupt end a week from tomorrow? Or that he didn't know what he was going to do when it was gone?

He was scowling at nothing in particular as he headed for his own desk. He was going to have to figure out some way to get a smile onto his face by the time the happy event rolled around, he thought. But at the moment, smiling was more than he could manage.

And he wasn't going to have to smile at Jessie's reclusive witness, thank God. All he had to do was deliver a message and hit the road for Austin. Compared to grappling with his own mixed feelings, Jessie's request seemed blessedly simple and straightforward.

Ignoring the wedding-related banter still peppering the office air, Jack sat down at his desk and started getting ready to go.

Shelby had no contact with the guests. That had been one of her conditions; she didn't want to find herself someday running into a visitor who would look at her and say, "Didn't you use to live down in Lafayette?"

But even though her work on the ranch was confined to cleaning the cabins and helping in the kitchen and laundry, she'd spent enough time watching the new guests that she could tell at a glance which of them had potential as riders, and which didn't.

This one definitely didn't.

Shelby paused at the window of the laundry cabin and watched the awkward teenager bouncing across the yard on board old Leo. Leo was one of the ranch's most docile horses, yet even he was looking impatient with the thumping and shifting of the human on his back. In fact—

What would it be like to live without this constant watchfulness, she wondered, this nonstop search for anything that might constitute a threat? She could feel it kicking in as Leo veered away from his rider's attempt to control the reins, and began trotting purposefully toward the other side of the yard.

The other side of the yard was where the kids were playing. Shelby had been keeping an eye on the red hat she'd clapped onto Emi's blond head, watching her daughter even though she knew the baby was perfectly safe with the teenagers who were looking after her.

Now, though, Leo's piebald bulk came between her and her child, and Shelby's chronic wariness flared into unease. Quickly she dried her hands and stepped out into the yard.

The young rider was hauling back on the reins, ignoring the shouted advice of the teenage babysitters—experienced riders all—to go easy on him. Leo was good-natured, but he hated to have his mouth pulled. Shelby's heart picked up a beat as she watched him starting to stamp his hooves angrily on the hard-packed earth.

She was halfway to the circle of kids in the sandbox when Leo decided he'd had enough.

She heard him snort, and saw his forefeet come up slightly off the ground. His passenger yelled, and someone from the paddock started running toward them. By now Shelby was running, too, because Leo's thudding hooves were taking him closer and closer to the sandbox.

She saw the teenagers urging the smaller children out of the way, but all the common sense in the world wasn't going to be enough to convince her that Emi would be all right if she wasn't there to see to it herself.

The panicked rider was trying to climb down from Leo's back now, she noticed fleetingly. It was further unsettling the horse, making him jumpier and more unpredictable. If somebody didn't take him in hand soon—

It happened almost too late. She didn't see exactly where the dark-haired stranger had come from. She made a final dash for the sandbox and scooped Emi out of the arms of the teenage girl who held the baby, just as a man sprinted toward Leo and caught his bridle. The big animal was pivoting toward the knot of children, shaking his head, but the man held firm to the leather strap, reaching up his other hand in a gesture that was both firm and calming.

"Whoa there," she heard him say, and hoped Leo could recognize, as she did herself, the note of authority in the man's deep voice. "Take it easy, big guy. No need to get all cranky."

Leo disagreed. He was still snorting, trying to shake his head free, but the stranger hung on to the bridle until Rudy ran up from the paddock and took over. The ranch hand eased the rider out of the saddle and led Leo away while treating the inexperienced guest to a lecture about not riding away from the group without permission.

It had all happened so quickly that Shelby wasn't quite sure how she'd gotten from rinsing the cookhouse curtains to clutching her baby daughter on the other side of the ranch yard. Her heart was still pounding hard as she lifted Emi's red cap and smoothed the white-blond baby hair that was so much like her own.

"And you didn't even notice anything was wrong, did you?" she said. "Honestly, Emi, the world could fall to pieces around you and it wouldn't bother you a bit."

Shelby kissed the top of the child's head and put her hat back on, then noticed in her automatic once-over that her daughter had managed—again—to unsnap both sides of her denim rompers in the sandbox. Her pant legs, not to mention her diaper, were doubtless filled with fine sand by now.

"And while we're on the subject of things falling to pieces—" she began.

"Ms. Henderson?"

She'd already forgotten the dark stranger's presence. In the back of her mind, she'd assumed he was some new guest, someone experienced around horses, judging by the way he'd handled Leo. But to hear him speaking her name—

"Ms. Shelby Henderson?"

Shelby went still.

They'd found her.

And she hadn't been ready for it.

Her heart slammed into her chest wall, making it suddenly hard to breathe. She clutched Emi tighter, until her daughter started squirming in her arms.

The man was tall, at least six inches taller than Shelby's five foot six. His hair was dark. So was his skin, tanned bronze by the sun. His eyes, when he pulled off the sunglasses that had hidden them, were dark, too, a deep, bottomless brown quickened by an obvious intelligence and fringed by astonishingly thick and long black velvet lashes. His clothes were casual but stylish, a brown linen jacket over a tan T-shirt and trousers.

He didn't look like a killer. But Shelby wasn't about to take chances, not with Emi in her arms, a yard full of people watching and everything in her life at stake.

Without answering the stranger's question, she turned and headed for her cabin.

"Wait a minute—"

Her abrupt about-face had taken him by surprise, which was what she'd intended. By the time he started to follow her, she was halfway to safety.

The staff cabins were ranged over the hill behind the ranch. Shelby had the last one in the row, a one-bedroom log building with a small porch and a double lock on the door. Her plan was to get inside, lock the door, deposit Emi in her playpen, and grab the police-issue revolver she'd kept after Emilio's death.

She hated having the gun around, hated the idea of ever using it.

But not as much as she hated the idea of her safety—or her daughter's—being threatened.

She didn't quite make it to the cabin steps by the time the dark stranger caught up with her. She could hear his city shoes hitting the hard-packed dirt behind her, cutting in over the quieter steps of her own well-worn sneakers.

When he put a hand on her elbow, she whirled to face him.

"Don't you touch me!"

He raised both hands in the air. "Ms. Henderson, I'm not one of the bad guys. I work with Jessie Myers. I'm with the FBI."

Shelby took a step back from him. The touch of his skin on hers had been disturbingly close, disturbingly intimate.

It made her realize how long it had been since she'd let a stranger get close enough to touch her.

And how leery she was of any kind of closeness with anyone except Emi. She didn't want any of the things that were involved in getting too close to people—and she didn't want anything at all from a man who worked for the FBI.

"Yes?" She held his dark gaze, challenging him to do the talking.

"Jessie would have come herself, but she's sick. Caught a killer cold from her sister's kids."

His brown eyes flickered to the baby in Shelby's arms. She couldn't be certain, but she thought there was something impatient, almost disapproving, in his glance.

"And you are—?" She let the sentence hang in the air between them.

"Jack Cotter. Special Agent, out of Houston." He reached into his jacket pocket and Shelby stiffened, then relaxed as he handed her an official badge in a leather cover. "I'd have pulled that out right away, but I figured you'd rather I didn't do it in the middle of all those people."

His discretion surprised her. And so did the fact that as soon as he'd pocketed his badge again, he put his hand back on her elbow and started to steer her toward the cabin at the end of the dirt path. Shelby resisted, but his grip was firm, his pace steady and determined.

"I told you—"

"Look, Ms. Henderson, I don't have a lot of time. I have to be somewhere at six o'clock. And this is important."

She managed to shake him loose as they climbed the cabin steps. "Wait outside, then," she said.

She wished she could erase the lingering pressure of his fingers against her forearm as she went into the living room and settled Emi in her playpen. She didn't like being muscled around, or having her privacy invaded like this. She didn't like the unsettled feeling she'd had while looking into Jack Cotter's eyes.

Nothing about the situation pleased her. And when she went back out to the porch she planned to make that clear to Special Agent Jack Cotter.

But she didn't get the chance.

"Are you expecting company?"

Cotter's voice was a rich buzz, a deep baritone that a woman might very easily enjoy listening to. He was an attractive man—in the few confused moments before she'd walked out of the stable yard Shelby had noticed the teenage girls around them eyeing him with open fascination.

It was his voice that caught her attention now, and she didn't hear the warning note in it quite soon enough.

"I'm never expecting company, in case you hadn't figured that out by now," she said over her shoulder as she put Emi's current favorite toy—a set of brightly colored plastic rings—into the playpen with her daughter. "I came here because I didn't *want* company. I wanted to get away from everybody who ever knew me. And Jessie Myers promised me that she would respect that. I'm not pleased to find that not only did she share my address with you, but—"

"I mean, are you expecting company other than me?" he cut in abruptly, and this time Shelby heard the tension in his voice. "Because if you're not—"

"What are you talking about?"

Jack Cotter had stayed on the porch, and Shelby joined him there now. If this was some kind of trick—if she'd let her guard down too soon—

At first she couldn't see what he was looking at. But then a pair of heads came into view, walking purposefully up the path toward her cabin. A big prickly pear hid them for a moment, but then they emerged again, heads down, treading carefully, as if unfamiliar with the rough outdoor terrain.

"You know them?" Jack Cotter's voice had gone low.

"No." Shelby was already stepping back into the cabin. "Do you?"

"They're not our boys, if that's what you're thinking." He came inside after her, and this time Shelby didn't argue.

Jack Cotter's sudden arrival had caught her by surprise. And there was something about him—his intelligent dark gaze, maybe, or his air of trying to take command, or maybe just some kind of restlessness that she sensed in him without knowing where it came from—that Shelby found unnerving.

But these two men—silent, hard-faced, purposeful—scared her.

She'd have given a lot to be proved wrong, to have the two strangers turn out to be new guests or repairmen arriving to fix her ceiling fan. Just before she got the door closed, though, she had grim proof of why they'd come here.

"That's her!"

It was the taller man who spoke, the shorter one who moved. Shelby saw him reach inside the pocket of his blue jacket.

Saw the glint of the late afternoon sun on metal.

Saw—slowly, agonizingly, as though the world had just slipped into slow motion, carrying her with it—the concentrated, merciless squint on the gunman's face as he took aim.

And for one endless, horrible moment, she found herself looking at the light glinting off a long-barreled revolver, staring at death and utterly unable to move.

Chapter 2

Jack Cotter's big body slammed into her, knocking her back into the living room.

"Grab the baby!" She heard the words as she was scrambling to get her balance, already heading for Emi's playpen.

It was happening too fast.

Shelby had been afraid of this moment for what felt like forever. At least a thousand times she'd rehearsed in her own mind what she would do if Jerry Lawrence found out where she was. She'd known it was a possibility, ever since the night almost two years ago when she'd clasped her husband's dead body in her arms and realized that the two men she'd seen in the kitchen doorway had killed him—and that they might very well decide to kill her, too.

But in her imagination, she'd always been in charge of the situation. There'd been no invisible hand clutching at her throat, stopping the air from reaching her lungs. And no oversize FBI agent in her way.

There wasn't time to argue with him. As she reached into the playpen and lifted Emi into her arms, Shelby heard a fast, high-pitched whine and a splintering impact as something hit her front door, hard. She'd barely had time to process the idea that it was a bullet when a second one followed, bursting through the wood in almost exactly the spot where she and Jack Cotter had been standing just seconds before.

It was really happening. Someone was trying to kill her. In spite of all her planning for this moment, Shelby was still having a hard time catching her breath, or making her muscles do what she wanted.

But Jack Cotter was grabbing her attention again, clasping her shoulder with one broad hand. "Is there a back way out of this place?" he was demanding.

And that was enough to do it. Shelby held Emi close, shut off her racing imagination, and forced herself to recall the careful plans she'd made.

"Through the bathroom," she said. "That way."

When she'd pictured this scene, Emi hadn't been squirming quite so energetically in her arms, and her attention hadn't been divided between the pursuers behind her and the big man who was shouldering his way into the bathroom ahead of her. But she still had enough presence of mind to lock the bedroom door and pocket the key. On her way past the hall closet she grabbed the bag she'd kept packed ever since she'd first arrived at the ranch.

"Here," she said to Jack Cotter, thrusting the bag at him. "Go out through the shower."

There was a big window on the other side of the shower enclosure. Shelby had identified it as her escape route the day she'd moved into the cabin. She deliberately left the bathroom door ajar—she wanted the gunmen to think they were hiding in the bedroom, after all, not the bathroom—and took a fleeting moment to be grateful that while Jack Cotter might be a distraction, he was also quick, and smart.

He'd figured out immediately how to open the window behind the shower curtain. By the time Shelby heard the awful sound of another bullet hitting the front door, followed by a crash as the wooden door slammed against the inside wall, she and Jack were on their way out.

"Close it behind us." She spoke as quietly as she could while clambering over the windowsill with her daughter held tightly against her chest. The baby was beginning to protest now, and Shelby wanted to be clear of the cabin before Emi started to raise the fuss she was capable of.

"Got it." Jack Cotter pushed the window shut and slung the padded bag over his shoulder. "Which way?"

"Up. Then down."

She didn't waste breath describing the path that snaked upward behind the cabins, then cut back down toward the horse barn. It was hard enough just keeping hold of Emi while scrabbling for footholds on the steep hillside.

Behind her, she could hear more shots being fired, and guessed that her pursuers were blasting their way through the bedroom door, expecting to find her cowering inside. Well, she'd never been the cowering type, but she wasn't any too far ahead of the two gunmen, either. Trying to fight off the tight feeling of panic in her chest, she pushed herself to run a little faster, keeping up with Jack Cotter's pace.

They'd almost reached the split in the path when things started to go wrong.

She could hear shouting voices from back at the cabin. That wasn't so bad—it probably meant that the two strangers had discovered they'd been duped, but Shelby had cut several false paths behind the cabin, and her attackers would probably use up a little time trying to decide which one to take.

The problem was that the shouting distracted her from the rock-strewn ground underfoot. And before she knew what was happening, her old, smooth-soled sneakers had gone out from under her in a shower of loose gravel, sending her sliding off the side of the steep path and into a tangle of mesquite and prickly pear.

She managed to stifle her own gasp of pain and surprise, but Emi's voice was raised immediately in a wail of protest. And as Shelby tried to lift the baby out of the sharp branches they'd landed in, her feet slipped again. Trying to keep Emi clear of protruding sticks and cactus leaves, Shelby half turned, putting her right arm out instinctively to break her fall.

She could feel the impact of it going all the way through her.

The pain took a second or two longer. But once it started, dull at first, then sharp and hot, centered in her right wrist, she knew she'd done some serious damage.

"Come on—we've got to keep moving."

Jack Cotter was standing over her suddenly, reaching for the baby. Shelby kept a tight hold of the child with her left arm, lifting up her right so that Jack could help her to her feet.

A jolt of pure agony shot all the way along her arm.

This time she couldn't suppress her own startled cry. She'd sprained something, she thought, if not broken it.

And this was definitely *not* a part of her great escape plan.

Neither was letting a near-stranger take her daughter, but at the moment she couldn't see a better choice. She eased Emi into Jack Cotter's waiting arms and clambered to her feet, trying to ignore the pain stabbing through her right wrist.

"We don't have a lot of time here." Cotter's voice was grim, all traces of its earlier old-brandy smoothness gone.

"I know. It's this way."

They'd almost reached the fork in the path. Emi's frightened crying had broken off abruptly the moment she'd found herself transferred to a stranger's arms, but

Shelby knew it might be only a matter of seconds before the baby started wailing again, giving away their position with deadly accuracy.

If they could just reach the shed by then....

"Mind telling me where we're going?"

Ahead of her, Jack Cotter's voice was deep and low. Shelby fought to keep her own voice soft but audible as she answered him. "There's a pickup truck. Take the left fork when we get to the bottom."

By the time the rocky path leveled out, Shelby could hear heavy crashing noises on the hillside above them. The two gunmen were on their trail again, getting closer all the time.

She hated to do what she had to do next. There were people all over the ranch property, staff and guests and children, and Shelby's stomach churned at the idea that she might be putting any of them in danger.

But the danger was here, whether she wanted it or not. And the safest thing she could do was get out of the way and hope to heaven her pursuers would give up when they realized she was gone.

Praying that her plan would work, she reached for the padded bag that was bumping against Jack Cotter's hip with every stride he took. Using her left hand was awkward, but she managed to pull out the spare baby shoe she'd stuffed into the bag's outer compartment, and tossed it onto the path leading down toward the stable yard.

"What are you—" Jack Cotter half turned to look at her.

"Never mind. Just keep moving."

The shed was half-hidden in a clump of live oak trees. As Shelby ducked under them, she heard Emi starting to whimper, and turned to hold her arms out for her daughter.

"You'll have to drive," she told Cotter. "The key's in the ignition."

He was already handing her the baby and pulling open the rickety wooden doors at the other end of the shed. There were wooden blocks under the truck's wheels—the steep incline below the shed had seemed like a godsend to Shelby when she'd first located this place—and Cotter seemed to realize immediately what to do.

For a moment—one brief moment—she was glad he was here. Pain spurted along her arm again as she supported Emi's weight, and she knew she wasn't going to be capable of shifting gears in the old pickup truck.

If she'd been alone—

If Jack Cotter hadn't been here—

This had always been a plan of last resort, and she'd hoped she wouldn't have to use it. Under the best of conditions, she'd known it wouldn't be easy to drive the old truck on her own while keeping Emi safely buckled in and wedged next to the padded shoulder bag. But now, with one hand out of commission and the air catching in her throat every time she tried to breathe—

She shoved those thoughts aside and scrambled up into the passenger seat with Emi in her arms, gritting her teeth against the ache in her wrist. She watched Jack Cotter kicking the wooden blocks out from under the tires as she pulled the truck door closed behind her. The vehicle began to roll slowly, and for a split second Shelby was afraid Jack wasn't going to get into the cab in time.

But there was something effortless and efficient about the way the man moved. He seemed to know exactly how to gauge time and distance to get where he wanted to be. By the time the truck had cleared the shed, he was behind the wheel, stepping on the clutch and maneuvering his long legs to fit into the space behind the dashboard.

"Let it roll," Shelby said. "At least until we're clear of the—"

"I've got it."

He spoke without looking at her, and Shelby felt unexpectedly as though she were tagging along on Jack Cotter's adventure, instead of the other way around.

Her gratitude of a moment ago was mixed with resentment at the way this man had landed in the middle of her life and taken it over. And other, darker thoughts were starting to creep in now that she was starting to think again.

She didn't like the timing of this—the arrival of the two gunmen right on Jack Cotter's heels.

She didn't like the way his presence seemed to fill up the truck cab, or the way his handsome profile kept drawing her eyes, catching her attention at a time when she needed to keep her wits as sharp as they'd ever been.

She didn't like any of it.

And she was going to tell him so, just as soon as they were safely away from here. But for now there was nothing she could do except try to calm Emi's whimpering and silently urge the truck forward as it carried them faster and faster down the hill and out of danger.

The thing was only firing on three cylinders.

There was a rusted-out place in the floor of the cab. Jack could clearly see the road skimming by, disconcertingly close to his right foot.

He didn't have the foggiest idea where they were, or where this road led.

And those were just the problems he was allowing himself to think about. As for the rest of it—

Jack scowled and shifted down another gear as he urged the old truck toward the crest of another hill. "Jessie didn't say anything about you having a baby with you," he said.

"Jessie didn't know."

Normally Jack never let himself get involved in anything he hadn't checked out in advance. He was well-known in the Bureau for insisting on full briefings, access to the case files, everything he could get his hands on before he went out in the field.

He knew next to nothing about this case. Or about this woman.

It wasn't a feeling he enjoyed.

The baby in Shelby Henderson's arms was wriggling like a puppy now, trying to get free. Shelby had had to raise her voice to be heard over the child's whimpering, and it put a hard edge to her otherwise light, husky tones. Jack had noticed that right away: her pleasant, throaty voice hadn't been meant for sharpness. Or suspicion. Or any of the things he'd been hearing in her words since he'd shown up at the ranch.

He'd noticed a lot of other things about her, too.

Like the wariness that seemed to be a permanent fixture in her wide hazel eyes. And the way her slender shoulders seemed permanently tensed, ready to jump if she was threatened.

He'd noticed that her pale gold hair didn't seem to want to stay in the ponytail she wore. It looked as though it wanted to be loose over her shoulders. And as though it would feel like silk against a man's hands.

Her body was so slight that at first impression she seemed almost girlish. In those faded jeans, with a light blue shirt knotted around her waist and rolled up above the elbows, she looked more like a cowgirl than anything else, easily a part of the rugged hill country landscape around them.

Except for the wary look in her eyes.

And the tight way she held herself.

Jack cudgeled his brains to try to recall what he knew of Shelby Henderson's case. She'd been married to a police officer—maybe a police chief?—in a tiny town in the southwest part of the state. The man had been shot about a year and a half ago, Jack thought, maybe a little more.

He wasn't any good at gauging children's ages. The blond baby in Shelby's lap was no newborn infant, but it didn't seem to have reached the walking stage, either, judging by the unsteady way it was clambering around looking for its footing.

If it was a year old, it could easily be the child of the cop who'd been shot. If it was much less—

"I didn't go out and sleep with the first cowboy I met after Emilio was killed, if that's what you're wondering." Shelby's voice cut pointedly into his musings. "Emily is my husband's child."

Usually Jack was good at hiding his thoughts. Either he was being transparent about this, or Shelby Henderson was even smarter than she seemed to be.

Both options made him uneasy.

"How long have you had that escape route planned?" he asked.

"Ever since I got here."

The packed bag, the false trails, the baby shoe tossed onto the wrong path to mislead the two gunmen—it had all been slick, as slick as anything Jack could have come up with himself.

And that puzzled him.

"You know," he said, "you're obviously a pretty sharp lady."

She didn't answer, just gave him a quick sideways look out of those half green, half brown eyes before dipping her head back toward the baby.

"Then why the hell didn't you go into the witness protection program when Jessie offered you the chance? Why put yourself—not to mention your kid—at the kind of risk you were running just now? I don't get it."

"Don't you?"

Her reply was sharp, and half-buried in a loud protesting squawk from baby Emily. The infant was making a determined effort to get out of her mother's lap, and Shelby had to shift her weight to the right to hold her daughter steady.

It wasn't until she moved that Jack noticed how awkwardly she was holding her right arm. Or the angry swelling at her wrist, contrasting strangely with her fine bones and delicate coloring.

Oh, Lord, he thought, and dragged a hand through his hair. This was *not* what he'd bargained for when he'd agreed to do a favor for Jessie. He'd been planning to deliver a simple message, for heaven's sake, not get involved with a woman who was on the run for her life.

With a child.

And one arm that didn't work.

Jack shifted gears as the truck topped the hill and started down the long curve on the other side. The scenery below them was spectacular—scarred, wind-carved mountains half-covered with scrubby trees and overlooking river valleys that must have been old a million years ago. But at the moment Jack's thoughts were focused entirely on the present.

"How bad is your wrist?" he asked.

"It's fine."

A *stubborn* woman on the run for her life, he amended. Possibly even a crazy one. Who else but a crazy person would refuse help when she so clearly needed it?

She was reaching into her bag now, pulling out a bunch of big plastic keys on a ring. That seemed to please the baby, who immediately stuffed one of the keys into her mouth. Without the fussy noises Emily had been making for the past half hour, it was suddenly much quieter inside the truck cab.

"We need to get to a phone." Shelby Henderson's words were distinct and clipped.

"I agree. We need to contact Jessie, see how she wants to handle—"

"*You* need to contact Jessie," she corrected him smoothly. "And didn't you say earlier that you had to be somewhere? You're going to need to figure out a way to get yourself there, because I need the truck myself.''

Jack almost laughed. She actually seemed to be serious. "How exactly were you planning to drive it?" he demanded.

"We'll find a drugstore. An elastic bandage will take care of this."

"You need a doctor. And a splint, at the very least, if not a cast."

"I told you, my wrist is—"

"Already the size of a Georgia peach. And working on becoming a grapefruit, unless I miss my guess. It must hurt like hell."

It wasn't sympathy that was prompting his words, Jack told himself. He was just testing her, seeing how far that stubbornness of hers would take her.

Still, he couldn't hold back a twinge of pity as he watched Shelby tentatively probing the inflammation around her wrist. He saw her wince, and recognized the slight hunching of her shoulders as an attempt to block the pain.

Damn it, she looked so fragile, so small. Her sun-bleached blond hair was nearly as fine and pale as her baby's. She looked as though she didn't eat enough square meals, as though she worried too much, as though that soft pink mouth and those intelligent hazel eyes had been meant for more laughter than they'd seen in the recent past.

When she turned her eyes on him again, though, there was nothing but defiance in her gaze.

"I suggest you deal with your own problems, and leave me to deal with mine," she told him. "And the first problem *I* need to tackle is figuring out just where the heck we are."

It was a good question.

Jack had let the truck coast silently to the bottom of the hill below the shed before popping it into gear. Since then he'd been following his nose, turning toward the sinking

sun whenever he could, trying to put enough distance between them and the ranch that there was no danger of running into those two gunmen around the next bend.

He figured they were safe by now. But the region was
crisscrossed by hundreds of little farm roads like the ones
they'd been traveling on. And Jack didn't know the western end of the hill country at all.

"We should have hit a main road by now," he said,
speaking to himself as much as to Shelby Henderson.
"We're not just going in circles—we've been heading west
almost since we left the ranch. In which case—"

"We're lost."

"That's pretty much the size of it."

"Oh, God."

It was the first sign of weakness he'd seen in her since
that first, unmistakable bolt of fear when he'd spoken her
name back in the stable yard. He couldn't see her eyes this
time—she'd turned her head again to retrieve the plastic
keys as Emily hurled them onto the dashboard—but the
quick tremor in her voice betrayed her.

In spite of her brave words, Shelby Henderson was
scared.

And that didn't make it any easier for Jack to decide
what in hell he should do.

"Look, Shelby, there's something you should know." He
slowed the truck as they negotiated a sharp bend at the
curve of a river. Tall cypress trees lined the river's route,
their bare winter branches momentarily diffusing the low
rays of the setting sun. "Jerry Lawrence is out of custody
as of this morning. We lost the only witness we had to link
him with the men who shot your husband."

"What do you mean, you lost him?"

He was surprised by his own reluctance to say the words.
"He was killed. Shot."

"Did you people lead the killers to him, the way you led
them to me?"

Jack almost laughed. Her question was the last thing in the world he'd expected. She was supposed to express surprise, and dismay. She was supposed to realize what a tight spot she was in, and enlist Jack's aid in figuring out what to do next.

She wasn't supposed to snap at the hand that was trying to help her.

"That's ridiculous," he said bluntly.

"Is it? How else do you explain the fact that Lawrence's men showed up right after you did?"

They were out of the shade now. Even through his sunglasses Jack had to squint into the low rays of the sun. "Look, lady," he said, "I'm not the bad guy in this. The FBI is on *your* side, all right?"

"The FBI couldn't do anything to save my husband's life. Why should I believe you'll do any better with mine or my daughter's?"

Jack wished he knew more about this case. If he'd had a few more facts at his fingertips, maybe he'd have been able to counter that angry, determined sound in Shelby Henderson's voice.

But this had been Jessie's project, not his. He was just picking up the pieces, and he wasn't very happy about it. "Well, those two guys didn't follow me out here, if that's what you're thinking," he told her.

"Are you sure about that?"

In fact, he'd checked his mirrors religiously all the way out from Houston. It was pure habit, an ingrained reflex after seventeen years in the business. "Yes, I'm sure," he said. "Lawrence must have had you traced some other way."

"How?"

"There are lots of ways to find people. Employment tax records—"

"I don't get paid. I work for room and board—*worked* for room and board, I mean."

"Car registration."

"I don't have a car."

"Baby immunized?"

"Under another name."

"And Henderson—"

"Is my own name. But it's not on any official records connected with the ranch. I made sure of that."

She was thorough, he had to give her that. Jack searched his memory for what his brothers had told him about locating missing persons. After all, that was one of Cotter Investigations's specialties.

"How did you wind up at the ranch?" he asked finally.

"It's owned by friends of friends. They agreed to help me out."

"Then that's probably how Lawrence's boys found you. If you're really looking for somebody, you go through all their known acquaintances."

"But they wouldn't tell—"

"They wouldn't have to. There are ways to get around people. You 'accidentally' bump up against them in a diner, for example. You get to talking about how you and the wife are looking for a nice quiet place to rent for your vacation this year—somewhere really off the beaten track. And if you find that one of your subject's friends knows about a nice quiet place like that—the kind of place that might be perfect for hiding out—you go and check on it."

"The timing is too perfect. First you show up, and then—"

"Jerry Lawrence wasn't doing a lot of business while he was in custody. There were people making sure of that. So even if his hired hands had traced you before now, they wouldn't have done anything about it, because Jerry wasn't around to give orders. But now that he's free—"

He didn't finish the sentence. Shelby Henderson was clearly smart enough to figure it out for herself.

But she was still refusing to see sense.

In fact, she didn't even seem to be listening to him anymore.

"Look," she said, leaning forward on the seat. "We're coming to something."

Three things happened all at once.

Jack caught sight of a cluster of low buildings up ahead, shadowy in the lowering sun.

Shelby Henderson reached out her right hand to point.

And the baby decided to stand up.

The child had been playing contentedly with the plastic keys, but now, maybe stirred by her mother's movements, she pushed herself free of Shelby's restraining left arm and got her feet under her. One small hand had latched on to Shelby's hair by the time Jack noticed what was happening.

Instinctively he eased up on the accelerator, trying to keep the jouncing of the truck to a minimum. But Emily was too quick, and Shelby's one arm wasn't enough to hold her back. Before either of the adults could catch her, the baby had launched herself upward and lost her footing.

"Emi—"

Shelby's cry was sharp, and so was Jack's muffled curse as he reached out his own right arm to steady the child. He got two fingers hooked into the back of her denim playsuit, but the momentum of her fall carried her away from him, toward the dashboard.

At the same moment the truck went over a bump. It shook loose what was left of Shelby's grip, and left her grasping urgently for her daughter. Her left hand managed to break the impact of Emi's head against the dash, but her right hand hit the hard red plastic, too. Jack heard her palm slap hard against the surface, and her sudden cry as her wrist took the force of the blow.

With another muttered curse Jack swung the wheel to the right. Emi was wailing now, frightened by her fall and perhaps by her mother's yelp as well. And Shelby was gasping, her face pale under her tan.

"Hang on to her if you can." He said the words grimly as he shifted gears and brought the truck to a stop on the shoulder.

"It's—okay." Shelby spoke around a sharp inhalation.

Jack scowled and reached for the baby. "Stop giving me that stuff, all right?" he said. "You're *not* okay, and you're not making things any easier by pretending you are."

Baby Emily was a warm weight against his chest, too surprised and unhappy at the moment to notice who held her. It didn't seem to matter that Jack wasn't exactly sure how to hang on to a baby properly. Her legs kept slipping free of his grip, and he was afraid he might drop her. But the little girl leaned into his arms with complete abandon, trusting him to hold her up.

He didn't want her to trust him.

He didn't want her to be here at all.

He didn't want to be holding her, but somebody had to do it, and Shelby couldn't. She was still fighting to get her breath, still blanched under the sun-kissed gold of her skin. Her eyes looked wider than ever, and her shoulders, although she was obviously trying to square them against the pain, looked impossibly fragile.

"Come on." He pitched his voice to be heard over Emi's wails, and reached across Shelby's lap to open the passenger door. "Let's see what this guy's got in the way of first aid. And there's got to be a phone around here somewhere."

It was going from bad to worse.

Shelby smelled far too sweet as he leaned across her to unlatch the door.

Like warmed honey.

Like open air.

Jack tried his best not to notice it, but her beguiling scent had wrapped itself all around him before he'd even realized it was happening.

He relied on his head to keep him out of trouble in his life. And out of entanglements that might lead to trouble.

But his head had nothing to do with what was happening here.

It was his body that was responding to Shelby Henderson's nearness, and to the weight of the small, trusting creature he held in his arms.

This was good, his body told him. This was earthy, it was real.

The baby's crying was real. And vital. And alive.

A strand of Shelby's fine blond hair touched his face as he pulled back on the door handle. The lightness of it astonished him. The woman's strength and fragility—that fierce spirit contained in such a slight, feminine frame—astonished him even more.

For one long moment Jack stopped thinking and just let himself slide into the sensations that surrounded him.

The perfume of talcum powder and a baby's skin.

The pale gold halo of Shelby Henderson's hair.

The sudden sense of being in the middle of something urgent, something vibrant, something that touched pieces of himself he usually kept tightly under wraps.

Something he hadn't even suspected might be missing.

The thought shook him. He blinked and drew back toward the driver's door, not at all certain what had just come over him.

You're working on a case, Cotter, he told himself firmly. *You're doing Jessie a favor. That's* all *you're doing.*

He'd brought the truck to a halt in front of the first of the buildings, which seemed to be a combination gas station and general store. He got out of the truck cab and managed to get Emi settled on one hip while he waited for

Shelby to join him. Just as hard as he could, he willed his senses to calm down so his brain could get back to work.

But his nerves were still jangling from the sight of the baby careening toward the dashboard. And his heart was beating hard at the remembered sweetness of warmed honey and fresh country air. At the closeness of a slender, stubborn, mystifying woman. At his sense that there were many things bottled up inside Shelby Henderson, held inside by too much fear and caution and responsibility.

He didn't want to shoulder any of that responsibility. This wasn't even his case, for crying out loud. It was Jessie's file, and Jessie's problem. Jack wasn't even supposed to be here. He was supposed to be in Austin right now, getting his tuxedo fitted.

So he could help his brothers march down the aisle and out of his life.

He scowled and stalked toward the building with Emi still riding his hip and sobbing. Whatever else was in store for him today, he thought, he might as well get it over with.

Chapter 3

"Oh, Emi, *please* try to settle down, honey. I'll be there just as soon as I can."

The whoosh of running water at the tiny bathroom sink blended with Emi's steady sobbing from the crib in the other room. Shelby's head felt as if it were filling up with noise. She leaned a little lower to submerge her whole forearm in the icy water, and clamped her back teeth together as the cold of it knifed through her.

"I know you're hungry. I know your diaper needs changing. But I can't do anything until I can use this arm. If you can just hang on—"

It was ridiculous, asking a crying infant for patience, Shelby knew. But sometimes the sound of Shelby's voice could calm Emi down.

It wasn't working tonight.

The cabin was so small that the noise seemed to fill every corner of it. With the double bed, one old upholstered chair, a bureau, and the ancient wooden crib the owner had unearthed from somewhere, the place was packed to the walls, and Emi's wailing made it seem even more crowded.

At least it was clean. The green carpet on the floor was worn but spotless, and the white curtains over the two big windows seemed to have been recently washed and ironed.

Just a few hours ago, Shelby herself had been washing curtains, standing in the laundry cabin back at the ranch and wondering whether it was time for a trip into town to get more diapers.

And now—

She shook her head, and jumped a little as the cabin door opened suddenly.

If the cabin had seemed full before, Jack Cotter's big, dark presence seemed to overflow it. He was frowning as he stepped through the door and set a paper grocery bag down on the bureau.

"He says he doesn't have a hot plate." He didn't meet Shelby's gaze as she cranked off the tap and looked out at him. He hadn't really made eye contact with her, she'd noticed, since they'd stopped at the gas station in front of these cabins. "Best he could do was this."

He held up an immersion heater. For a moment Emi paused in her wailing, her attention caught by the coiled wire gadget dangling from Jack's big hand. But since the device didn't seem to offer much in the way of either play value or food content, she quickly gave up hope, and lifted her voice in frustration again.

"Is the ice helping any?" Jack Cotter raised his voice, too, so Shelby could hear him over the baby's cries.

"I think so. It's numbing the pain, if nothing else."

He snorted. "So you *do* admit to feeling pain," he said. "I guess we're making progress."

Shelby wasn't so sure.

They'd at least discovered where they were, and had agreed that the isolated spot was far enough away from the ranch that there wasn't much chance of the two gunmen stumbling on the spot by accident. Still, Jack had parked the old red pickup behind the cabin, well out of sight of the road.

He'd rejected the idea of renting two cabins. "First of all, I've only got enough cash for one," he'd said, "and I don't want to use a credit card in case Lawrence's people have some way of tracking it. And anyway, we're less noticeable this way. Just a traveling couple with a baby, stopping for the night."

Fortunately the elderly owner of the cabins hadn't seemed to notice that the male half of the traveling couple was avoiding his companion's eyes at every opportunity. Or that neither of them had any luggage besides the big padded bag in the cab of the truck.

All of that qualified as progress, Shelby supposed. But personally, she wasn't going to be happy until she knew she could use her right arm again. And in spite of the bag of ice Jack had brought from the grocery store behind the gas station, she wasn't sure that was about to happen anytime soon.

"Let me see it." Jack Cotter was threading his way across the cabin floor, sidestepping the crib.

"There's nothing much to see." She stood up a little taller, as if straightening her spine might guard against the effect of his big, masculine presence in the cramped space of the bathroom.

It didn't. He shouldered his way in and stood next to the sink, one broad palm extended. It was like being cooped up with a bear, Shelby thought. He was too strong, too dark, too forceful, too much of a stranger to her. He wasn't who she wanted right now.

But she was stuck with him. And judging by the look on his handsome face—serious, watchful, almost grim—he wasn't much happier about the situation than she was.

She didn't pull her arm out of the water right away. "I don't think it's broken," she said.

"Would you know what it would feel like if it was?"

"I broke my ankle falling off a church roof once. I think I'd recognize a broken bone. And I don't think that's what this is."

His lips tightened a little, and Shelby found her eyes drawn to the firm line of his mouth. There was a slight upward lift at the corners of it that hinted at laughter and sensuality and a hidden host of things he seemed to be keeping tightly under control. At close range like this, it was easy to believe that there was a lot more going on inside Jack Cotter than he let people know.

It was possible to picture that sensuous mouth tilted in a smile.

Or softened by desire.

It was easy—surprisingly, unnervingly easy—to imagine what Jack Cotter's lips would feel like against a woman's skin. Against Shelby's skin.

And how his deep voice would sound murmuring tender words against her ear. He had a beautiful voice, she thought, a voice as smooth as warm brandy, made for caresses and confidences.

"Let me see it anyway."

Shelby blinked. How on earth had she let herself get sidetracked so far, and so fast? The man was here to look at her sprained wrist, for heaven's sake, not to whisper sweet nothings in her ear.

And his voice was anything but caressing at the moment. He sounded blunt, impatient, even reluctant. He didn't want to be here, she thought. He was just performing a duty, and not a very pleasant one, at that.

Carefully she lifted her arm out of the water and let him touch it.

And instantly all the fantasies she'd just subdued came rushing back into her mind again.

It wasn't so much the feeling of his fingertips against her skin—her wrist had been numbed by the ice water, and at first she could barely feel his touch. It was more the way his strong, tanned fingers looked against her fairer skin, and the astonishingly gentle way he held her.

It was hard to reconcile his hard, athletic body with the lightness of his touch as he ran his hands over her swollen wrist. *This means nothing,* Shelby told herself, but it was impossible not to look at the way his fingers moved across her skin, impossible not to wonder where Jack Cotter had learned to be so gentle with a woman.

"This is probably going to hurt."

He still wouldn't look right at her. Shelby could see the black fringe of his lashes masking his eyes as he examined her wrist. The faint stubble along his jawline was darker now, and his nearly black hair had fallen forward across his forehead, making him look a little more rumpled, a little more approachable than he'd seemed when she'd first set eyes on him.

But he clearly didn't want to be approached. He wanted to get this over with. Shelby swallowed, feeling almost glad for the twinges of pain that were starting to make themselves known again, and said, "What are you going to do?"

For what felt like a long moment he just held her forearm, the way he might hold an injured bird. Shelby found herself breathing a little faster, wondering why the tight line of his lips had loosened now. His palm under her elbow was sure and smooth, his touch featherlight.

But his voice was grim. "I can't—I *have* to make sure this isn't broken before I feel all right about wrapping it up. I'd insist on taking you to a doctor—"

"I wouldn't go."

"—even if you said you wouldn't go, except that our buddy out there at the gas station tells me there isn't one anywhere close. And the nearest hospital is halfway to San Antonio. So you're stuck with me and what I remember from my first aid training."

It wasn't pleasant. By the time his careful fingers had thoroughly probed the inflammation at her wrist, Shelby's whole arm felt alive with pain, and her sensual fantasies about Jack Cotter had been safely obliterated for the moment.

"Sorry—I'm being as fast as—"

"Don't talk, Jack. Just do it, all right?"

One strong, cautious forefinger pressed down on the bone at the curve of her wrist, and Shelby almost yelped.

For a brief second his eyes met hers. "You can kick me in the shin, if it'll make you feel better," he said.

"Don't tempt me."

But she didn't have a lot of strength left over for kicking. And Emi's crying had steadily increased in volume as she watched her mother and Jack becoming engrossed in some mysterious activity that clearly had nothing to do with either food or clean diapers. By the time Jack pronounced himself satisfied, and wrapped Shelby's wrist securely in the elastic bandage he'd bought at the store out front, Emi was hitting high notes that would have made an opera star proud.

"I'm coming, honey." Shelby pushed her disheveled hair back with her left hand, aware for the first time that she'd broken into a sweat. "It's all right."

"Is it?"

She was starting for the living room when Jack asked the question, and it caught her by surprise. After that quick shared glance, he'd kept his eyes down again, but now, as she pushed past him, he suddenly looked up at her.

What she saw in his face wasn't what she'd expected.

His touch had been so gentle, so efficient. But his dark eyes held neither gentleness nor efficiency.

They looked uncertain.

And hungry.

And scared.

Shelby stopped moving. It was like seeing her own feelings in a mirror, she thought. It was like looking into a stranger's face and watching her own inner turmoil reflected there.

And that was crazy.

The whole thing was crazy. Her heart was beating fast again, and she wished she'd kept moving instead of pausing so close to Jack Cotter. Her left hip was touching his thigh, and she could feel the rock-solid muscle of him through his tan linen trousers.

The bathroom was too small. There was no way to escape the clean, masculine smell of Jack Cotter's skin. Or the swirl of emotions in those bottomless brown eyes.

There was no way to sidestep his touch when he lifted one hand and smoothed back a strand of hair that had stuck itself damply to her face. "If you mean it's all right because it's a sprain, not a break, you're right," he said. "But damn it, you look so pale—" He paused, and Shelby had the feeling he was talking to himself more than to her as he added, "I wish there'd been some way to do this without hurting you."

Shelby felt something quivering inside her, something that was aching for both the sensuality and the simple human comfort in Jack Cotter's touch.

This shouldn't be happening, she told herself. It was the wrong time and place to be responding to a handsome man she barely knew. And comfort was a dangerous thing for a woman in her position. It could only make her weaker, and she needed to be strong more than she'd ever needed it before.

But somehow she couldn't make herself step away. She found herself staring with fascination at the slow curve of Jack Cotter's lips, at the faint shadow of beard along his jaw, at the deep bronze of his skin.

"It'll be better now." Her voice sounded breathless. She wasn't sure he'd even heard her over the mounting wail from the other room.

Oh, Emi, she thought, *please be quiet, sweetheart. Please let me have two minutes of silence to figure out what's happening here.*

But there was going to be no chance for silence until Emi was changed and fed. And Shelby had made her daughter wait long enough already. She cleared her throat, and spoke more briskly this time.

"Thank you—for wrapping me up. I don't think I could have managed it on my own."

Jack Cotter seemed to hear her unspoken hint. He stepped back against the wall, leaving the doorway clear.

But he didn't lower his hand, not yet. His knuckles still grazed her cheek, and his eyes held hers in a way that was altogether too pleasurable, and far too provocative.

His thumb came up to touch the tip of her chin, and once again Shelby was caught by the gentleness in him, the slow tenderness that was so much at odds with what she'd seen of his working self. She felt him tilting her face up slightly, felt her breathing quicken a little more, and wondered what he was seeing in her parted lips, her wide-open eyes.

"Jesse was right," he said. "You are an unusual woman, Shelby Henderson."

She tried hard to tell herself that this was all wrong.

She was just reacting to the fear of this afternoon, and the long months she'd spent worrying on her own about her future and her daughter's.

It had just been too long since she'd had anyone to share her troubles with. That was all. That was why the idea of a big, strong set of shoulders to lean on was so tempting now.

But the more her breathing quickened, the more she had to admit it wasn't just Jack Cotter's shoulders that suddenly seemed so enticing. It was all of him—that hard athlete's body, that sensuous mouth, those dark, hungry eyes.

She hauled in a deep breath and pushed the rest of the way past him into the main room. Jack Cotter watched her until she'd lifted the padded bag up onto the bed, then he followed as far as the crib and hoisted Emi out.

"Can you manage?" He had to speak loudly to be heard at all.

"Oh, sure." She could feel Jack's gaze on her, but this time it was her turn to avoid eye contact. "If you think I'm unusual now, wait'll you see me diaper a baby with one hand behind my back."

She had to make it into a wisecrack, because doing anything else was just too unsettling. And Jack Cotter seemed just as unsettled as she was. He waited until he saw that she was capable of unfolding a diaper on her own—awkwardly, it was true, but well enough to get the job done. Then he muttered something about having to make a phone call, and stalked out of the cabin as though there was a pack of furies—all screaming blue murder and needing clean diapers, no doubt—snapping at his heels.

"You all right, little brother?"

Jack couldn't think of a good answer to Wiley's question.

Yes, he was all right, in the sense that he'd gotten away from two professional shooters without picking up any holes in his hide in the process.

He'd accomplished his assignment and then some. He'd carried Jessie's message to Shelby Henderson, and had gotten her out of the line of fire without any holes in *her* hide, either.

He'd found Shelby and her baby a place to stay, although he still wasn't sure how he was going to handle the fact that there was only one bed in the cabin they'd rented.

And it wasn't as though he was completely on his own in this business. He had the resources of the Federal Bureau of Investigation at his fingertips, after all, just as soon as he could reach anybody on his team to enlist some help.

But other than that, things were a mess.

"Yeah, I'm all right," he growled into the receiver. "Look, Wiley, I don't know when I'm going to get back to Austin, so fitting that suit—"

"Can wait until you've got this witness of yours on ice." Wiley chuckled. "I've got news for you, bro. Even if your pants are a bit baggy around the ankles, you're *still* not getting out of this wedding party."

"I never said I wanted out."

I just never wanted in...

This must be the theme of the week, Jack thought. Much as he liked his two prospective sisters-in-law, he didn't really want to help his brothers get married. He hated the thought of losing what he and Wiley and Sam had built up together, the loose but essential family unit that the Cotter brothers had shared ever since the three of them had been reunited ten years earlier.

And he didn't want to be at the western end of the Texas hill country now with a woman and baby who seemed to be on somebody's death list.

Especially *this* woman...

He could hear the deep, amused-sounding rasp of his brother Sam's voice in the background, and then Wiley came back on the line. "Sam wants to know if she's pretty," he said.

Jack scowled. Pretty?

Pretty was the wrong word for Shelby Henderson.

She was—troubling. That was the term for it.

Everything about her troubled him. Her quickness. Her spirit. The baby blond halo of hair, so soft-looking that he couldn't look at her for long without wondering what it would feel like if he slid his hands into its golden depths.

The pink rosebud of her mouth. The slim, fine bones that made her look as though a good southwest gust of wind would knock her right off her feet.

Why the hell had he given in to the urge to touch her? It was utterly unlike him, unlike anything he'd ever done in his career. He'd had his hand raised before he'd even realized he was reaching toward her. And once he'd felt that rapidly beating pulse where his knuckles grazed her temple, he'd been powerless to stop.

He'd hurt her, and he couldn't stand the thought of it.

He closed his eyes now, remembering the silk of her skin under his fingers. If she hadn't had the sense to move away, he'd probably still be back there, touching her, finding out what she tasted like, how she sounded when a man found the way to please her, discovering whether he was right about the promise of hidden sensuality that lay somewhere inside Shelby Henderson.

Slowly he became aware that he was gripping the receiver until his knuckles were tight. And Wiley was still waiting for an answer.

"Tell Sam his head's getting soft," he said gruffly. "I *knew* getting married was going to have both of you seeing hearts and flowers everywhere you looked."

Wiley chuckled. "You'd be surprised what a lovely sight it is," he said. "Well, enjoy yourself, Jack. And get back up here as soon as you can."

That wouldn't be until he'd raised some backup, Jack thought, as he hung up the phone. He'd had no luck with Jessie's beeper, but no doubt she'd just turned it off so she could crawl into bed and sleep off the bug she'd caught. Mack MacGuire, the FBI answering service informed him, had gotten his boat into the water sooner than expected, and was now cruising the high seas, far from a phone. Garry O'Dette was in transit to a family reunion in Louisiana, and nobody knew where Annette Caniglio was at the moment.

"Justice never sleeps," Jack muttered as he left the phone booth outside the gas station. He'd left messages for everybody, saying he needed a hand and would call back in a couple of hours. For the moment it was all he could do.

The baby looked lopsided.

And she was still crying.

A small tornado appeared to have passed through the room since Jack had left it an hour earlier. He'd taken his time getting back here, stopping at the store before it closed and picking up some adult food to supplement the milk and juice and baby food he'd bought earlier. Then he'd checked out the territory around them, hiking as far as the river that bordered the back end of the property.

In the dark of the winter night, the river seemed to be rushing somewhere in a hurry, murmuring to itself as it flowed toward the southeast. Jack could hear tree branches clacking over his head, and the quick, quiet rustling of the dried grasses on the other bank.

It should have been a peaceful spot. But Jack was in no mood to enjoy it. He walked along the river's edge just far enough to satisfy himself that there were no roads or tracks approaching this place from the rear, and then he started back toward the cabin.

He could hear the baby's cries as he got closer to the little building. By the time he'd climbed the two wooden steps leading to the door, it was clear that Emily wasn't much happier now than she'd been when he'd left.

And the room was a shambles. There seemed to be towels, pillows, toys and clothing everywhere. Shelby was sitting cross-legged in the middle of the bed with a jar of baby food held cautiously in her right hand. With her left she was trying to spoon food into the baby's mouth while heading off Emi's attempts at escape.

She looked over her shoulder as Jack came in. "You know," she said tiredly, "until this moment I never appreciated what a brilliant invention the high chair really is."

It took him a moment to figure out that she'd propped all four of the pillows against the headboard and tried to wedge Emi into the middle of them. As a restraining device it left a lot to be desired. Emi kept flinging her little body sideways, rolling over, protesting in a way that seemed to have become purely habit by now.

The reason she looked lopsided was that her diaper was crooked, he realized. Despite her brave words, Shelby must have had problems managing with just one good hand.

"Maybe she's not hungry," he suggested.

"Emi's *always* hungry." Shelby made a face. "She's just too hungry to eat, and too tired to go to sleep. She's all disoriented, and she doesn't even know why. Do you, sweetie?"

Emi refused her mother's overtures, pushing away the spoon with one flailing hand.

She was getting red in the face from so much crying, Jack thought. Even so, she was still a beautiful child, with her mother's pale gold hair and a pair of the most incredible velvety near-black eyes. As she turned those tear-filled eyes on Jack now, he felt his heart being tugged toward this small, unhappy scrap of humanity.

And he resisted it just as hard as he could.

"Maybe if you tried putting her in the crib—"

"I've tried. She just gets louder."

He could hear the frustration in Shelby's voice. She pushed a long blond strand back behind her ear, and Jack looked away quickly. He didn't want to remember what it had felt like to touch her hair, her skin.

He didn't want to get any more involved with Shelby Henderson and her baby than he already was.

It was hard to stay uninvolved when the cabin was so small and the baby's belongings seemed to have taken up every square inch of it. Jack lifted Emi's denim rompers and a stuffed doll out of the chair before sitting down. How was it possible, he wondered, that all this stuff had come out of that single padded bag?

"I called the office." He tried to make his voice as businesslike as he could. This was routine, he told himself. He was updating a witness on the progress of the case. This was the way things were supposed to work. "Nobody was around, but I left messages. By morning, at the latest, somebody'll be on this."

"You mean Jessie Myers?"

"If she can get out of bed. If not, it'll be someone else on our team."

He saw her slim shoulders rise and then settle in a quiet sigh. "I wish there was a way to do this without bringing in the entire federal government," she said.

Jack raised his hands and clasped them behind his head. This was better, he thought. This was work. This, he was equipped to handle.

"What do you have against the witness protection program, anyway?" he asked her. "It's set up specifically for people like you."

"No, it isn't." Her eyes flashed green at him. "You don't know my circumstances. So please don't presume to make decisions on my behalf."

"Enlighten me, then."

"I'd be happy to, if I wasn't in the middle of trying to—" She broke off abruptly, frowning. "Listen to that," she said.

Jack straightened in the chair. All he could hear was the slight breeze in the live oaks outside the cabin. Had he missed something, some faint signal that they weren't as safe here as he'd decided they were?

"What?" he demanded. And then it struck him.

Emi wasn't crying.

For the first time since they'd arrived, there was actual silence in the cabin. Jack met Shelby's puzzled gaze, then looked at the baby.

Who was looking at *him*.

There was no doubt about it. Emi's little legs were splayed in front of her, and she was leaning forward on her hands as though she'd caught sight of something absolutely riveting.

The "something" seemed to be Jack. She was staring at him with her round, velvety, near-black eyes, utterly transfixed.

"She's never seen a male adult before, is that it?"

He wished he could grab the words back as soon as he'd said them. Of course Emi had seen male adults—but the significant male in her life had been shot to death before she was even born. She was missing a father, thanks to Jerry Lawrence, and Jack's comment had been tactless, to say the least.

But Shelby seemed too grateful for her daughter's silence to take offense. "Who knows?" she said. "She gets these fixations sometimes. Last time it happened, it was one of the nanny goats at the ranch. So don't feel too flattered."

He tried.

He did his best not to meet Emi's big round eyes, not to feel the intense scrutiny of her innocent gaze. But it was hard.

How was he not supposed to feel flattered, when a baby who'd been crying inconsolably for the past four hours suddenly calmed at the sight of him? In spite of all his efforts to stay aloof, Jack was starting to feel as though he'd just won a medal for something.

In fact, he *had* won medals for various things over the course of his career. It hadn't felt nearly as good as seeing the slow beginnings of a smile on baby Emily's face.

The smile, when it finally blossomed, transformed her. Suddenly she was more beautiful than anything Jack could imagine, with that gleeful look in her deep velvet eyes and a pair of dimples in her cheeks that any man with an ounce of sense would cheerfully have walked a hundred miles to catch a glimpse of.

She was pointing at him, extending one pudgy forefinger.

"Dja," she said clearly.

"Hey." Jack couldn't believe it. "She's saying my name," he said.

"She doesn't *know* your name. It's just a sound to her."

Jack didn't believe it. There was such a knowing look in Emily's dark eyes—she *must* have spoken his name on purpose.

As if to prove it, she did it again. "Dja," she said. This time it sounded like an order.

"What do you think she wants?"

He couldn't take his eyes off Emi's face. He'd never spent any time with real, live babies, and the few he'd encountered had been tinier than Emi, little wrinkled creatures whose facial expressions, their parents had assured him, were probably due to gas rather than to any actual thought processes.

But this was different. Emi obviously had something on her mind. And whatever it was, it obviously involved Jack.

"Dja," she said, a third time, and started to crawl toward him across the bed.

"I think she wants *you.*" Shelby didn't sound completely pleased about it, but she didn't argue, either. Maybe when you'd been trying to placate a crying baby for hours at a stretch you went along with whatever seemed to work, Jack thought.

And Jack seemed to be the solution now.

He made one last effort to keep himself aloof, but it was doomed before he even began.

He knew this was a bad idea.

It went counter to all the rules about getting too friendly with witnesses, not to mention Jack's own rules about keeping his feelings from getting too tangled up with other people.

But the people he'd been trying to stay clear of had been adults. He'd never had to deal with a designing baby before.

If he had any sense at all, he would walk out of here right now. He would inform Shelby Henderson that he, personally, planned to sleep in the front seat of the pickup truck, and that feeding and otherwise caring for the baby was her job, not his.

But all that good, straight, common sense had disappeared like morning mist by the time Emily reached the edge of the double bed. She clearly intended to keep right on going until she got to Jack, and Shelby made a quick move to set down the food and the spoon and keep her daughter from crashing to the floor.

Before she could get there, Jack had already scooped Emi up in his arms and swung her into his lap. When she gave a delighted laugh and said his name again, he gave up on common sense. What did common sense have to offer that could compete with the smile of a baby who'd decided you were just about the most wonderful thing in the known universe?

By the time she'd beamed at him from close range and turned around to poke one stubby baby finger into his chin, Jack Cotter was a man head over heels in love.

Chapter 4

Shelby wasn't sure she liked this.

It was one thing to accept Jack Cotter's help because she'd had no way of getting away from the ranch on her own. Or to admit that he'd been able to do a better job of wrapping the elastic bandage around her wrist than she'd been able to do by herself.

But this was different.

She leaned back against the headboard and listened to him start to sing "The Yellow Rose of Texas" for the umpteenth time. He'd gotten all the way through "Ninety-Nine Bottles of Beer on the Wall" an hour or two ago, to Emi's delight. And he seemed prepared to go on singing all night, if that was what it took to lull the baby to sleep.

His voice was like the rest of him, Shelby thought. It was dark and smooth, with the buzz of authority running through it. It was a very easy voice to listen to.

And that made it very difficult to forget how it had turned rough and uncertain when he'd spoken her name during their encounter by the sink. His facade had opened up a little then, and she'd seen in his eyes—and heard in his voice—a kind of ragged honesty, an unsuspected longing, that didn't fit at all with what she'd seen of Special Agent Jack Cotter so far.

She didn't like that, either.

She was supposed to be concentrating on getting safely away from here, and finding some kind of new home for herself and Emi. She didn't have time to wonder what buried hungers lay beneath Jack Cotter's handsome exterior. The man was an intruder, part of a world Shelby never wanted to get close to again.

And now he was captivating her daughter.

There was no doubt about it. Emi was entranced by anything and everything Jack did. She'd cooed with approval all the way through his dramatic reading of *Pat the Bunny*—four times. She'd happily swallowed her dinner when he'd finally offered to feed her, after Shelby had tried again and been rejected. She'd even started to nod off a couple of times, but whenever Jack set her down in the crib she'd immediately come to life again and starting weeping to be picked up.

Turning the lights out hadn't helped.

Tiptoeing out of the cabin had only made her howl louder.

Silence hadn't worked.

Nothing had worked.

It was nearly 2:00 a.m., and what Emi apparently wanted was for Jack Cotter to go on entertaining her until the sun came up.

"You know," Shelby said, as he came to the end of "The Yellow Rose of Texas" another time, "I had you pegged as the kind of man who doesn't like children."

"Oh?" The syllable was uncommunicative.

Shelby didn't let him shrug it off. She was happy to know that there was *something* in the world that would make Emi happy tonight. But she wasn't pleased by the way this near-stranger had intruded into the close world she shared with her baby daughter. They were a family, the two of them. And Jack Cotter was no part of that.

"When you carried her in from the truck this evening, you looked like you thought she was a ticking bomb or something," she told him.

He shrugged. "I just don't have a lot of experience with kids, that's all," he said.

"Then why—"

"Listen, I've got an idea." He cut her off deliberately, as though he saw where her questions were heading and he didn't want to go there. He'd been sitting cross-legged on the floor with Emi in his lap, but now he picked her up and sat down on the bed with her.

The sight of him—of his big, sun-bronzed hand splayed against the fresh white of Emi's nighttime T-shirt—startled Shelby. Her baby looked so little all of a sudden, cradled against Jack Cotter's broad shoulder with her face turned against the open collar of his tan shirt.

Damn it, Emi should have had a father to cradle her like this, to walk with her on those nights—like tonight—when sleep just wouldn't come.

If Jack Cotter's colleagues had done their jobs, Shelby's child might *have* a father. And Shelby might still have a home. She stiffened her heart against the protective way Jack was easing Emi down among the pillows, and tried to recall what it was he'd just been saying.

He'd had an idea. That was it. "Well, I ran out of fresh ideas hours ago," she admitted. "So anything you can come up with—"

"I think she just needs a bedtime story."

"How many more times through *Pat the Bunny* do you think you can stand?"

"No, I mean a real story. I've been noticing—when you and I are talking, she seems quieter. Like the sound of our voices lulls her."

Shelby had noticed it, too. But she'd had a hard time knowing just what to say to Jack Cotter since their surprising encounter in the bathroom. And so there hadn't been much conversation for Emi to be lulled by.

That, apparently, was what Jack planned to change. "It probably doesn't much matter what we're saying," he told her. "If we just keep talking, maybe she'll get drowsy and fall asleep."

Shelby didn't really want to talk to this man. He called up so many conflicting feelings in her that she'd have been just as happy having nothing to do with him. Especially now. Especially when her life was in such turmoil already.

But they were stuck with each other, at least for tonight. And the idea of Emi actually dropping off to sleep sometime before dawn was a powerfully enticing one.

"It's worth a shot," she conceded.

"All right." He leaned back against the headboard on the other side of the baby, giving Emi his hand to play with. She began pulling all his fingers in turn, laughing when Jack waggled them up and down. "You start," he added.

"Me? I've got nothing on my mind right now that even remotely resembles a bedtime story." And what she *did* have on her mind—thoughts of Emilio, and of those gunmen this afternoon, and of how to move farther away from Jack Cotter on the double bed without being too obvious about it—were hardly bedtime fare.

But he wasn't going to let her off the hook. "Well, dredge one up from somewhere, then," he said. "What about the time you fell off the church roof and broke your ankle? Tell me about that."

"Oh, Lord." Shelby put her face in her hands. "I knew I was going to regret saying anything about that."

"Where did it happen?"

"In my hometown."

"Which was—"

"In east Texas."

"I've spent a lot of time in east Texas. I probably know—"

"I doubt it. It was a tiny little place. Nobody's ever heard of it."

"You make it sound like you're guarding a state secret."

She wished his voice wasn't so close to her. She could hear the amusement in it, along with what sounded like genuine interest.

Well, she didn't want the FBI getting interested in her again. The first time had been bad enough; she couldn't risk her life falling apart on her a second time.

"If I'm telling this story," she said pointedly, "I'll tell it my own way. All right?"

He raised his free hand. "Fair enough," he said.

"I was the minister's kid," she said. "The minister of the church I fell off of, I mean."

"Only child?"

She glared at him.

"All right," he said. "I'll shut up."

She believed him. But there was something in those intelligent dark eyes of his that told her he wasn't going to stop wondering about her.

It was unsettling. Shelby cleared her throat, and went on.

"I was thirteen, just about to turn fourteen," she said. "My father was due to retire in a few months, right after Easter. Of course, I'd known for a long time that that was going to happen."

She remembered the calculating look in Jack Cotter's eyes as he'd tried to figure out Emi's age. Was he doing the same thing now, subtracting her age from her father's and speculating about what it had meant to have a father already in his fifties when she was born?

Well, let him speculate all he wanted. He wasn't likely to guess the real circumstances of her birth. And she wasn't going to enlighten him.

"What I *didn't* know," she said, "was that he and my mother had decided to move up North after he retired. My mother's family was from Virginia, and she'd been following my father from one parish to another ever since they'd graduated college, with the understanding that eventually they'd get back to what she considered home.

"Unfortunately, *I* considered Texas home. I always have. Even then, I hated the idea of leaving it. So when my parents told me they'd bought a house in Delaware and we'd be moving at the end of the school year, I threw a fit."

Jack Cotter raised one dark cyebrow at her.

"You said you'd shut up," she reminded him.

"Did I say anything?"

"You implied it."

He rubbed a hand along his now heavily shadowed jaw. "Well," he said slowly, "if I'm going to get in trouble whether I say anything out loud or not, I might as well make the point that you look to me like a woman who, having decided to throw a fit, would throw a darned convincing one."

"Thank you."

She didn't want to be smiling at him. She didn't want to feel warmed by his obvious interest in her, by the way he was watching her as she told her story. She wanted to keep her distance, but for some reason it had suddenly become more difficult to do.

He'd let her know, with one eloquently raised eyebrow, that he enjoyed—even empathized with—her occasional flashes of spirit.

It was something that hadn't happened to her often in her twenty-nine years of life.

Certainly her adoptive parents hadn't found it very amusing when she'd informed them she had no intention of moving to Delaware. "I loved where we lived," she said. "I knew everybody there, and everybody knew me. I *be-*

longed.'' She heard the fierceness enter her voice over the word, and tried to get back to a more neutral tone.

''Thirteen isn't an easy age for a girl, any girl,'' she said, dropping a hand onto Emi's blond head as the baby sat, still absorbed in examining Jack's fingers, between the two adults on the bed. ''And the idea of being uprooted was more traumatic than my parents seemed to understand. They kept assuming I would come around, until it came right down to the day of my father's sixty-fifth birthday.

''Almost the whole town was there, not just our congregation. There was a big party on the church lawn, and presents, and speeches. And it wasn't until they were getting ready to take the official picture of my parents with the whole parish around them that somebody figured out where I was.''

''The roof.''

There it was again—that deep note of something more than just amusement. He sounded as though he'd instinctively known what her response would be.

As though he admired her for doing what she'd done.

As though he might very easily have done the same thing himself.

Shelby shook off the feeling of unexpected affinity, and went on. ''Right,'' she said. ''I'd gotten out through the bell tower and somehow—I'm still now sure how I did it—climbed halfway along the ridgepole. The lawn looked like it was miles away, and all the people were so tiny.''

''And so pleased with you, too, I bet.''

Shelby rolled her eyes. ''Well, if any of them were pleased to begin with, they certainly weren't after I managed to get to my feet and shout down that I wasn't going to budge until my parents agreed to let me stay in Almagorda.'' She'd spoken the town name before she remembered that she hadn't intended to let Jack Cotter know anything significant about her past.

But the smile in his eyes had disarmed her somehow. And she hadn't expected it would feel so good to share this old story with someone who seemed to understand it.

"Getting to my feet was my big mistake," she said. "The pitch of the roof was too steep to stand on, and after I'd had my dramatic moment I found I couldn't keep my feet under me. And I couldn't get enough control to sit down again, either."

"I can see it coming."

"Everybody could. There was this big gasp from the crowd and then all of a sudden I was sliding down the roof and the lawn was getting bigger and bigger in more of a hurry than I would have liked."

Jack's handsome face wrinkled in sympathy.

"I managed to catch hold of the gutter on the way past— otherwise I would have broken more than my ankle, if not killed myself outright. But it was still painful enough, and I had a steel post in my leg for nearly a year while the damage healed. It still hurts a bit, when the weather's damp."

She raised her left leg and flexed the ankle, circling one sneaker-clad foot in the air.

And immediately she wished she hadn't.

There was something far too interested in the way Jack Cotter followed the gesture. And his eyes, when she turned her head to look at him, were steady and watchful.

And meltingly deep and dark.

"So, did you end up moving to Delaware?" The question was slow, as though he wanted to frame it in a way that would guarantee an answer.

Of course he does, Shelby tried to tell herself. *The man's a federal agent. Asking nosy questions is his business.*

She answered him anyway. For some reason, it had felt good to unload that old story on someone; Shelby wasn't certain she'd ever done that before, even with Emilio. And she wanted to finish it.

"Yes, we moved to Delaware," she said.

"Did you ever get used to it?"

"No. I came back at the first possible opportunity."

"Which was—"

"When I went to teachers college. I haven't left Texas for any appreciable length of time since. End of story."

It wasn't, of course. She was smack in the middle of the story right now, with a whole lot more unanswered questions hanging over her than the ones Jack Cotter had asked.

She'd figured she'd gotten far enough away from Lafayette after her husband's death that his killers wouldn't be able to track her.

But she'd been wrong.

Was she going to have to go even farther next time? Was she going to have to abandon everything she knew, all the places she loved, and start a whole new life?

It was what she'd been trying so hard to avoid. And there must be a way to keep avoiding it, if she just thought hard enough about it.

She wanted to avoid Jack Cotter's next comment, too, because she had a pretty good idea what it was going to be.

"Shelby—"

She cut him off. "Forget it, Jack. I don't want to talk about the witness protection program, or the FBI, or any of that. It's not my idea of a bedtime story."

He snorted. "Fair enough," he said. "It seems to be working with Emi, though."

He was right. Her fractious daughter had gradually been relaxing while Shelby and Jack talked, until her little head was leaning back against the pillows piled at the head of the bed. Shelby stroked the baby's fine blond hair with her left hand, and leaned forward to check whether Emi's eyelids were drooping yet.

They were, but not quite far enough. As soon as silence fell between the adults on either side of her, Emi's head wobbled upright again, and she whimpered in protest against the lull in the conversation.

"Whoops." Jack looked down. "Spoke too soon. I think we're on the right track, though. We just need to keep talking."

"It's your turn, then. Tell me—tell me how you know so much about horses."

"What makes you think—"

"I saw the way you got old Leo under control this afternoon. It's obvious you've spent some time around them."

Had it really only been this afternoon that Shelby had been placidly rinsing curtains in the laundry house, looking forward to a weekend with nothing more momentous in it than a trip to town to buy more diapers? It seemed impossible now.

It seemed equally impossible that she was stretched out on a double bed next to Special Agent Jack Cotter as though they were old friends instead of uneasy and very temporary allies. But that was what was happening, and Shelby was getting too tired to fight it.

"I spent part of one year on a ranch when I was a teenager," he was telling her. "I didn't get along particularly well with the other kids, so I spent most of my time helping out in the stables. I never really—"

"Wait a minute. Back up." In spite of herself, Shelby couldn't help interrupting. "What other kids? Was this a camp or something?"

"Not—exactly."

"A school?"

"No." He didn't offer anything more than the single word.

And that wasn't good enough for Shelby. "Come on, Jack," she said. "I answered *your* questions, even after I told you I wasn't going to. So what gives? Is there some dark secret about why you were on a horse ranch?"

"No." He'd leaned back again, and clasped his hands behind his head. His gaze was focused straight ahead of him, as though he were seeing things far in the distance. "It was just one in a long series of foster homes, that's all. I don't usually talk about it—about any of them.''

''Where were your parents?''

''Look, Shelby, maybe we should switch to—''

She shook her head. She knew this trick. She'd used it herself any number of times. When someone got too close to a painful subject, it was easier just to slide out from under it and start talking about something else.

For some reason she didn't want to let Jack Cotter pull the same stunt on her.

Was it because he'd managed to make her confide in him when she hadn't planned on doing any such thing? It must be, Shelby thought. Turnabout was fair play—that's all that was going on here.

It couldn't possibly have anything to do with the faint, forlorn echo she'd heard in his voice just now. Could it?

She didn't stop to look too deeply into it. Somehow she just wanted to know more about Jack Cotter, without having any idea why.

''Where were your real parents?'' she repeated, half turning to look at him.

He met her eyes, then shifted his gaze away again. ''My father took off when I was nine,'' he said.

''And your mother?''

''Wasn't very good at the job. She gave up my brother and me to foster care when I was about twelve.''

She hadn't expected this. His words were surprising in themselves, but the twist of sympathy she felt inside was strong enough—and sharp enough—to silence her for a long moment.

When she spoke again, her words were as slow and careful as Jack's had been not long before. ''It's not easy, is it?'' she asked. ''Knowing you're not wanted, I mean.''

''How would you—''

"I know." She didn't want to explain her insight. She just wanted to offer it—unapologetically and unconditionally—and let it go at that.

Jack was scowling now. Somehow his face got more open when he frowned, instead of closing down. When he wanted to keep you at arm's length, Shelby was coming to realize, he put on that steady, competent-looking, I'm-in-charge-here expression, the one that had irritated her so much when she'd first seen him.

When he frowned, though, that facade seemed to dissolve. And Shelby's glimpses of the man behind it weren't anything like she'd expected them to be.

"Tell me about your brother," she said.

"When I asked *you* whether you had any siblings, you wouldn't answer me."

"Jack." She pointed to the drooping blond head between them. "I think Emi's almost asleep. Let's not blow it now, okay?"

He was still frowning, but she thought it was exasperation, not hostility, that she could hear in his deep voice now. "That's a cheap shot, lady," he told her. "However, much as I like your daughter, I really don't want to sit up with her *all* night. So you win, this time."

Shelby had almost forgotten her earlier resentment about the way Emi had claimed Jack as her own. And she didn't get a chance to figure out how he'd managed to sneak past her defenses so easily.

"Actually, I have two brothers," he was saying.

"But only one got sent to foster care with you."

He nodded. "Wiley and I stayed with our mother until she was in too rough shape to look after us," he said. "My little brother Sam took off with our father when he left."

"Good Lord."

"I know. It's not exactly a Hardy Boys adventure, if that's what you were after for your bedtime story."

"I wasn't complaining, Jack. It just—it couldn't have been an easy way to grow up, that's all."

"Oh, it wasn't. Not even close."

She wished she hadn't spoken. Or that she'd been safely across the room from him before uttering the words. Or that she hadn't been looking right at him when his mouth slanted into a grin.

Once she'd seen it, though, it was impossible to look away. Against the late-night stubble on his jawline, the sudden white flash of his smile was unbearably sexy.

And unexpectedly beautiful.

He should smile more. She'd had the same thought earlier, but it hit her harder now. There were faint lines at the corners of his eyes that creased easily when he grinned. His face softened, too, and his voice—as if it weren't already pleasurable enough to listen to—got even richer, until the seductive buzz of it threatened to make Shelby forget all about the topic at hand.

Brothers. With an effort, she dragged her mind back to their conversation, and her eyes away from the dark glint of amusement in Jack Cotter's face.

"Did you lose track of your little brother after he and your father left?"

Surely the question was safe. With luck, it might even annoy him, and that sexy sparkle would leave his brown eyes.

When it did, though, it was replaced by a pensive look— almost an echo of that forlorn note of a moment ago—that affected her nearly as strongly. Damn it, what was wrong with her that she couldn't remember for two seconds at a time all the very good reasons why she shouldn't be interested in this man?

"We got back in touch about ten years ago," he said. "Wiley had gotten into private investigation by then, and I'd joined the FBI. Wiley managed to track Sam down finally, and to talk him into joining Cotter Investigations, the family firm. They both live in Austin now.''

''You don't seem very happy about that.''

''I am. I—value my brothers a great deal.''

''Are they married?''

''Not yet.''

Bingo. She didn't know exactly what she'd hit, but it was something important, judging by the way his face settled back into that calm, unruffled expression.

''What do you mean, not yet?'' she prodded.

''They're getting married next week. Next Saturday.'' The words were so neutral that Shelby *knew* there was something hiding underneath them.

''Saturday is Valentine's Day,'' she mused.

''I know. Pretty sentimental for a couple of good old Texas boys, wouldn't you say?''

''Why don't you want them to get married?''

''I didn't say that.''

''No, but it doesn't take a genius to figure out—''

''Look, Shelby, this is going nowhere. Why don't I regale you with stories about my horse-riding youth, since that's what you wanted to know? With luck this baby of yours will be sound asleep sometime before I finish, and we'll both be able to get some sleep ourselves.''

She knew when she'd been shut down by a master. There were going to be no more revelations from Jack Cotter tonight. Yet the things they'd shared with each other so far had obviously touched both of them in surprising ways. As a result, Shelby wasn't sure there was going to be much sleep, either.

It turned out she was wrong about that. Jack started into a long tale about a trail ride he'd been on with a couple of old ranch hands who'd had a falling-out somewhere along the route and had ridden off in opposite directions, neither of which was the way back to the ranch where Jack was staying. The story went on and on, eventually involving a thrown horseshoe, a blacksmith named Arnie, and a chunk of military real estate that Jack had managed to wander onto without realizing it.

That was how Shelby felt at the moment—as though she'd found herself in some kind of "three for the road" adventure without having planned to be here. It was disorienting.

And tiring. By the time Jack's horse was shod again, her eyelids were at least as heavy as Emi's. When they reached the part about the military testing range, she wasn't completely certain whether she was listening to the story or dreaming it. She kept seeing herself at the wheel of the beat-up red pickup truck, bumping across the potholes of a flat, arid piece of Texas desert.

She was trying to drive slowly, so the bumps wouldn't wake up the baby. But the truck kept shaking, shuddering as it hit each new crater in the hard-baked desert earth.

She tried to burrow deeper into sleep, tried to absorb the bumps into her body instead of letting them jar her. But it wasn't working. Her whole frame was being shaken, gently, regularly, annoyingly.

"Shelby."

His voice at her ear was so pleasant that at first it seemed like a part of her dream. And it was a lot more enjoyable than the part about the potholes and the blacksmith. Shelby murmured wordlessly and snuggled deeper into the bed.

"Shelby, you're going to be on the floor in about two minutes if you don't turn over."

She hadn't realized she'd fallen asleep, or that she'd managed to get within inches of the edge of the bed. Shelby blinked and rolled onto her other side.

And met Jack Cotter's big body halfway.

Chapter 5

He seemed surprised, as though he hadn't expected her to act on his suggestion so quickly. But he didn't move away. He stayed leaning on one elbow in the middle of the bed, looking into her half-opened eyes with an intensity that was impossible to ignore.

And impossible not to enjoy.

"Emi...?"

"Finally conked out about half an hour ago. I put her in her crib."

Shelby let her eyelids drift closed again, but she could still feel the dark heat of Jack Cotter's gaze. Part of her must still be asleep and dreaming, she thought. Why else would she be feeling with such certainty that she could see what Jack was thinking right now?

He wanted to kiss her. It was as clear as if he'd spoken.

He'd been leaning over her, watching her sleep, thinking about kissing her. The silent knowledge of it washed through Shelby, rippling all the way from head to toe.

"Jack?"

"Yeah?"

Shelby smiled, her eyes still closed. How was it possible for a man's voice to be so rough and so beautiful at the same time? The single word had sounded like battered velvet, like harsh granite polished smooth by the sea.

"Appreciate it." She knew she sounded sleepy, but she didn't care. Maybe she *was* dreaming this, she thought. It didn't seem to matter.

"What? All those renditions of 'The Ycllow Rose'?"

Her smile deepened. *Fine,* she thought. It didn't surprise her that Jack Cotter had shrugged off her thanks.

It *did* surprise her when she heard the bedsprings creaking underneath them, and realized he was starting to move away. She'd been feeling the warmth of his broad chest close to hers, and letting her body ease into the curves his weight made in the soft mattress. And she'd been enjoying it, enjoying the sense of waking up so near the strong masculine frame she'd been unable to keep from thinking about all evening.

And now he was backing away. Shelby opened her eyes and looked into his face, trying to figure out why he'd suddenly changed his mind about being next to her.

He stopped still the moment her gaze met his. His dark brown eyes were nearly black in the low light of the single lamp, and his face didn't look nearly as confident as she'd been picturing it.

He looked startled. Almost shaken.

"I should get going. I need to grab some sleep if I can."

"Where are you going?" She heard the note of protest in her own voice, and wondered where it had come from.

Jack arched one thumb over his shoulder. "I figured I'd stretch out in the truck cab," he said. "It's plenty big enough."

It wasn't, and they both knew it.

The only other option, though, seemed to be for him to stay in the cabin. And since all the available floor space had been taken up by Emi's crib, that meant staying in the bed with Shelby.

Even in her half-dreaming state, she wasn't sure about the wisdom of that. But still—

"That doesn't seem right," she murmured. "For you to put in all those hours with Emi, and then to have to leave—"

His eyes got a little darker, a little softer.

A little more sultry, more dangerous.

"I'm not sure staying here is such a good idea, Shelby." His voice was rougher now.

"No?" Shelby knew she was playing with fire. She knew she should accept his offer to sleep outside in the cramped truck cab, knew she should be grateful for his restraint.

But somehow, in her half-awakened condition, all she could think of was how quickly, how instinctively this man had seemed to understand things about her that very few people had ever grasped.

And how beautiful his eyes looked in the dim light.

And how good it felt when he rolled back onto his elbow to face her again. The heat of his body seemed to spread over her like sunlight after a year of dark days. Would his skin have that same warmth all over? she wondered. What would it be like to feel the whole hard length of him, to be held against that broad chest and to wrap her arms and legs up with his?

There was no way to keep these thoughts out. She was too sleepy, too grateful, too stirred by Jack Cotter's nearness. Her own voice was as husky as his as she added, "Why *shouldn't* you stay here, Jack?"

His reply was an inarticulate growl. He lifted his gaze to the room around them, but whatever he was searching for didn't seem to be out there.

And when he looked back down at Shelby, the last trace of color had disappeared from his eyes. Shelby could read both a menace and a promise in them in the same silent instant before he raised his hand to the back of her neck and pulled her toward him.

She went willingly, her breath already quickened by her awareness of him. She closed her eyes again as she felt his strong fingers sliding into her hair, felt his thumb tracing her hairline and his free hand curving around her other shoulder to pull her hair band free.

Most of her fine blond hair had already escaped the ponytail by now anyway. But Jack completed the process, tossing the elastic strap to the floor and combing her hair loose with his fingers. It felt wonderful to let him do it. It felt free and reckless and unfettered.

She hadn't felt that way in a long time.

"That's better." His voice was a growl at her ear. "That suits you better."

The idea that he'd been watching her this way, thinking how she would look with her hair untied, made Shelby's heart beat a little faster. She'd gotten so used to imagining herself alone, so used to not relying on anyone else for help. She'd even preferred it that way, or so she'd told herself. But now—

Now Jack Cotter was pulling her against him, and she was discovering that it felt even better than she'd imagined to fit the shape of her slender body against his harder, more masculine one. His hips next to hers were seductively lean, aggressively male. Being surrounded by the strength of his arms and shoulders made her feel sheltered, and alive and aroused.

She settled her hips more intimately against him, and heard him groan. The sensation of hard flesh pressing low down against her belly caught her by surprise at first, and she gasped in response as she recognized how deeply stirred Jack was.

She'd done that, she thought. She'd awakened him like this.

She'd gotten so used to thinking of herself as a mother, as a widow, as a kind of shadowy fugitive on the outskirts of life.

It was a shock to realize how long it had been since she'd thought of herself as a woman who might be desired—hotly, urgently desired—by a man.

When Jack's mouth came down to meet hers she was already eager for his kiss, hungry to know the taste of him. She ran her fingers through the dark tangle of his hair and felt the heat of his skin under her palm. The sensation was even more tantalizing than she'd imagined it. Her imagination had raced a long way in a very short time, but it hadn't conjured up the way Jack's low groan would sound in response to her touch.

His kiss was anything but gentle. And Shelby didn't mind. She let herself be captured by the sensuality of it, in the sweet slickness of his lips against hers, in the seductive way his tongue seemed bent on discovering what pleased her, what made her moan softly at the back of her throat.

She couldn't stop her mind from racing to the thought of how his tongue would feel against her breasts, her navel, against every soft and secret hollow of her body.

The idea of it made her shiver all over.

And that made Jack Cotter smile. She could feel his lips curving against hers, and his fingers pushing more insistently into her scalp as though the same erotic quiver had just run through his body, too.

"Tell me." He murmured the words against her mouth, so she could taste the low buzz of his voice. "Tell me what you're thinking right now."

She started to do it. She didn't care where this might lead. She only knew she couldn't stand in the way of such sweet pleasure, such intimate rediscovery of everything her body was capable of feeling.

She was smiling, too, as she followed Jack's lead and broke their kiss while he pulled her astride him, looking up at her with eyes that promised more pleasure than she'd ever dreamed of. She couldn't keep from falling more and more deeply into that seductive gaze of his, couldn't help wanting to follow wherever this unexpected, half-dreaming moment of passion was taking them. Until—

Until she put her weight down on her right palm and felt the room around her splinter into pain.

She yelped out loud with the suddenness of it.

And Emi, in the crib next to the bed, stirred in her sleep and gave an answering cry.

The shock of it was almost electric. Shelby's whole body felt jangled, short-circuited, as the sharp, stabbing pain in her wrist clashed with the desire that was still pulsing through her.

"Shelby? What happened?"

She was sitting up now, rolling away from Jack's big body, trying to pull her thoughts together. Emi was making more cranky little noises, and the sound of them, even more than the rough reminder of the agony in her wrist, dragged Shelby back into reality again in a big hurry.

It seemed to take Jack Cotter a while to catch up. When he finally did, he cursed softly, and got to his feet next to the bed.

"Shelby, I—" He stopped abruptly, and shoved his hands through his dark hair. Shelby let herself glance only briefly at him, but it was enough to see that his hands seemed to be shaking, as hers were. "Damn it, I'm sorry— I didn't think—"

And he still couldn't think, judging by the sharp movement of his palms in the air as he cut his words off a second time. Shelby knew how he felt. She was having a hard time getting her thoughts in order, too.

But Emi was helping.

How could she have let herself be so completely swept into passion and pleasure when her daughter was sleeping just a few feet away? And when there was still such danger hanging over both of them?

How could she have been so drawn to this man, of all people?

Jack Cotter belonged to a world that Shelby wanted nothing more to do with.

He'd come into her life at the worst possible moment, bringing the worst possible news.

And yet he'd fired her whole being with his touch. And she'd wanted him to do it.

The center of her body still quivered with an erotic ache that even the pain in her wrist wasn't powerful enough to chase away. If it had just been the two of them, she thought, she and Jack by themselves, even the sharp reminder of that hair-raising escape on the ranch hillside earlier today might not have been enough to stop what had started between them.

But Emi's whimpering *was* enough.

She couldn't let herself be distracted. Not now, not when there was so much at stake.

And not by a man whose whole world was hedged around with the kind of dangers that Shelby had worked so hard to escape from.

Quickly, she stepped toward the crib and tried to get her breathing under control to the point where she could speak.

"I think—" The words were husky and unclear at first, and she had to try a second time. "I think she's not really awake. If I get the light off and there isn't any more noise—"

He didn't have to have it spelled out for him. He raised both big hands and said, "I know. This was crazy, Shelby, I know. But—"

She shook her head. And it wasn't just Emi she was thinking about now. Whatever Jack Cotter had to say, she didn't want to hear it.

"Just go, Jack, all right?" Her voice was soft, but he seemed to hear the determination in it. "It would be better just to pretend this didn't happen."

Something flashed in his eyes at that, and she thought for a moment he was going to argue with her, or maybe that he was going to take a step toward her and prove—by another kiss, by a touch she still wasn't sure she had the willpower to resist—that something *had* happened, and he wasn't about to let her deny it.

But Emi's cries got a little sharper, and he seemed to change his mind. He glared at the crib, and then at Shelby, and nodded tightly.

"All right," he said. "I know."

Even after the cabin door had closed softly behind him and Emi had subsided back into sleep, it seemed like a very long time before Shelby's rapidly beating heart even started to slow down.

"Did you catch Jessie's cold? You sound terrible."

Jack waved off Annette Caniglio's comment as though he were standing next to her instead of being cooped up in a phone booth at the absolute edge of nowhere.

"Never mind," he said. "It's a long story." And it had seemed like a very long night. If he'd managed to salvage three hours of sleep out of the deal, he thought, he'd been lucky.

"I need to reach Jessie," he told his junior colleague now. "I've left messages, but—"

"Oh."

There'd been something odd about Annette's voice when he'd first gotten hold of her, but he'd attributed that to the fact that he'd obviously wakened her up when he'd called. The sound of her *Oh,* though, made him think something else was going on.

"I think they're still restricting her calls to family only," she was saying now, slowly. "But maybe if you talked to her doctor—"

"Her doctor? She's that sick?"

"She's not just sick, Jack. Shoot, I thought you knew— I thought that's why you were calling. But if you haven't heard—"

Jack closed his eyes and informed Annette that she had precisely three seconds to tell him what the hell was going on.

Shelby was giving the baby a bath when Jack got back to the cabin. Or rather, she was attempting to give the baby a bath. Emi was standing on the bath mat next to the tub while Shelby scrubbed her with a washcloth. This system, obviously a second-best replacement for their usual routine, didn't seem to be working very well for either of them.

Emi kept bouncing up and down, pointing to the shallow water in the tub and saying something that sounded like "rudda." Shelby looked hot and bothered, her blond hair pulled back into its ponytail but already starting to creep loose again, her fine-boned face drawn into a serious frown.

"I know, sweetie," she was saying. "We'll just have to do the best we can without it, that's all."

"She wants to go sailing?" *Rudder* was as close as Jack could come to interpreting Emi's repeated demands. He saw Shelby's gaze pivot to meet his, and felt a little jolt of disappointment as he realized his arrival hadn't done anything to improve her mood.

Rather the opposite, in fact. Her frown deepened as she told him, "She wants her rubber duck. Usually he takes baths with her."

"Is he in the bag? I could—"

"He's at home. At what *used* to be home. Along with all the rest of her favorite toys. She's annoyed with me this morning because she can't figure out where anything is."

She pushed a damp strand of pale gold hair away from her face and went back to sponging down her wriggling daughter.

Jack sidestepped the crib and the various items of baby gear in the main room of the cabin, and moved in to lean on the bathroom door. "I get the message, Shelby," he said. "It's not my fault you had to leave, you know."

"I'm still not convinced of that."

Jack felt frustration gripping him again, the way it had when Shelby had suggested yesterday that he'd somehow led Jerry Lawrence's men right to her door.

"Look, lady," he said sharply. "My boss—who happens to be a good friend of mine, as well—got run down on her way home yesterday afternoon, and is currently in the intensive care unit of a hospital in Houston. She's got a broken arm, a broken leg, and some internal injuries they *think* they've managed to patch up. They're worried about neurological damage as well—apparently it was a hell of a collision—but they won't know about that until she wakes up, which, with any luck, will be sometime today. To add insult to injury, somebody even snatched her purse while she was lying there waiting for the ambulance. Given all that, and given the probability that Jerry Lawrence had something to do with it, maybe you could lighten up a bit on your down-with-the-FBI attitude."

He saw Shelby's hazel eyes flare a little wider, and kicked himself for his own gut-deep reaction to the spirited intelligence he could see there. If she wasn't so smart, he thought—or so perceptive—or so beautiful—if she hadn't relaxed into his arms last night as though she'd wanted him just as badly as he'd wanted her...

Even now, even when the subject was life and death— Jessie's life and death, now, as well as Shelby's own—he felt himself responding to her as a woman, not just as a runaway witness with some very unpleasant people on her trail. He kept picturing her soft half smile when he'd wakened her, kept hearing the little sounds she'd made when he'd touched her, kissed her. He wanted to know more, wanted to push her past the edge of pleasure, wanted to hear her calling out his name with the kind of passion he sensed—no, *knew*—she was capable of.

He shouldn't be thinking about any of these things. But there didn't seem to be anything he could do about it.

"Your boss?" she was echoing. "You mean Jessie Myers?"

"That's exactly who I mean."

"Did they get the other driver?"

"According to the police, the skid marks indicated she swerved into the other lane on her own," he said. "Once they found out she was feeling sick and was on her way home to rest, they figured it was a simple case of Jessie having lost control of the car and crossing the median by accident."

"But you don't buy it."

Jack shook his head. "I've known Jessie a long time," he said. He could hear the worry coloring his voice. It was almost—but not quite—enough to block out the thought of how Shelby's mouth had felt under his last night, and how her fine blond hair, so like the baby's next to her, had cascaded across his palms like the first light rain after a long dry spell.

He must be losing his mind, letting a woman get into his bloodstream at a time like this.

At the very least, he was losing his edge, and he couldn't afford to let that happen.

"Jessie and I have been in a lot of high-pressure situations together," he went on grimly. "I know how she reacts under stress. If she was feeling that woozy, I *know* she would have pulled over somewhere. I'm as sure that Jerry

Lawrence is behind this 'accident' of hers as I'd be if I'd seen it happen."

Emi's fidgeting had become more determined now, and Shelby was having a hard time holding her still. Jack could see the cautious way she was holding her right hand out of the way, making all her movements awkward and tentative.

He wanted to offer to help, but there wasn't time. He wanted to get down on the bathroom floor and get all wet and messy and make Emily forget about missing her rubber duck. But he couldn't.

"Are you going to be able to manage for the day while I go into Houston?" he demanded.

"Of course."

Her prompt reply irritated him, even while he felt himself responding all over again to the stubborn spirit behind it. "Don't give me the Superwoman act, all right, Shelby?" he said. "Be realistic, for once. Are you *really* going to be okay?"

She reached behind her for a towel, and whisked it down off the rack with her left hand. Something in the way she wrapped Emi up in it made Jack think she was using it as protective armor as much as a device for getting the baby dry.

"You know, Jack," she said, "my husband was shot to death the same day I discovered I was pregnant. I got through widowhood and pregnancy and delivery and relocation all at once. And I've been raising Emily on my own for nearly a year now. If I can survive all that, I can survive a day without your help. Even with a sprained wrist."

She sounded so certain.

She *looked* certain. Her small chin was tilted in his direction, her eyes flashing green fire at him as she spoke.

Of course, this was a woman who'd once proclaimed her independence while standing on a church roof so steep she'd already been losing her footing.

But she'd learned a lot since then. As she'd just pointed out with such painful clarity, she'd learned things in the past couple of years that most women never had to learn.

"Just make sure you're here when I get back," he warned her, and saw her roll her eyes.

"How far am I going to get without the truck?" she demanded. "Just go, all right, Jack? Emi and I will be fine."

He was on the point of leaving when Emi finally caught sight of him. Until now she'd been distracted by the water in the tub, pointing one dimpled finger toward it as though she could conjure up her lost rubber duck by sheer force of will.

But now she noticed Jack standing in the doorway. And her face creased into one of those smiles he'd have done anything for.

"Dja," she said delightedly. "Dja."

Jack closed his eyes.

The memory of Shelby's astonishingly open sensuality wasn't the only thing haunting him this morning. He hadn't been able to forget the way Emi had warmed up to him last night, or how it had felt to settle her little body into the crook of his arm. It had been inexpressibly sweet to lift her out of the bed of pillows and into her crib once she'd finally fallen asleep. And unexpectedly moving to stand, watching her after that. Her nose was ridiculously small and round, her eyelids waxy and soft when she slept.

Her life was in danger, and she didn't even know it. She had such complete and innocent trust that the world would look after her, that the adults around her would make everything all right.

If Jack had ever had that kind of trust, he'd lost it a very long time ago.

If he'd had the luxury of time now, he'd have rolled up his sleeves and responded to Emi's smiling invitation by getting down onto the floor to play with her for the entire rest of the day.

If Jerry Lawrence hadn't gotten out of jail—if Jessie hadn't been injured—if Shelby hadn't been trying so hard to reestablish the distance between them—

There were a hell of a lot of "ifs" in the way. But if they hadn't been there, Jack knew he could very easily shove aside his own doubts, his own memories of too many losses and too little experience with love. He felt as if baby Emily were trying to tell him something every time she smiled up at him and pronounced her fractured version of his name. It was as though this blond child knew things Jack had long since forgotten, things it might not be too late to relearn.

If he could neutralize the threat that Jerry Lawrence posed to all of them, maybe he could take Emi up on her smiling invitation. It seemed like one more very good reason to get himself back to Houston and figure out what to do next.

The day was long, but fruitful. He met Annette at the office, and Garry joined them there, having hustled back from his family reunion as soon as he'd heard the news about Jessie's accident. In the Saturday stillness of the place, the three of them picked over the case files on Jerry Lawrence until they'd extracted every possible lead and distributed them among themselves, with a few left over for Mack MacGuire to investigate when he came in on Monday.

They'd called the hospital, and been buoyed by the news that Jessie was awake and out of immediate danger, although she still wasn't being allowed calls or visitors.

"The moment she *is* allowed visitors, I want a twenty-four-hour guard on her room," Jack growled to his younger colleagues, and they promised to arrange it.

He made a call to his brothers, too, apologizing for the continued delay. "I've gotten kind of caught up in something here," he told Wiley, and heard his older brother snort.

"Being trained investigators and all, we'd already figured that out," Wiley said. "Just make sure you get here for the big day, all right, little brother?"

It wouldn't have been fair to say that Jack was happy this case had come his way. He was worried as hell about Jessie, and dealing with Shelby Henderson and her baby hadn't exactly been a picnic so far.

But he was surprised, when he'd hung up after talking to Wiley, at what a relief it was to have gained a little distance from his brothers' weddings. The subject had been hanging over his head like a thundercloud, dark and threatening and uncomfortable. He wasn't sorry to be out from under it, even for a little while. The feeling of being walked out on by the people he cared for most in the world was one Jack hadn't really come to terms with yet.

He wasn't sorry to get rid of the asthmatic old red pickup truck, either. He stashed the vehicle in the FBI parking garage and requisitioned a company car to take its place. He would figure out later how to get the truck back to the ranch where it belonged, and how to collect his own car, as well. But for now he needed something with some speed. It was good to settle in behind the wheel of the turbocharged dark blue sedan. He requisitioned another gun, too, to replace the one he'd left in his own locked glove compartment back at the horse ranch. Then, he'd figured he was embarking on nothing more than the simple delivery of a message as a favor to his boss. Now, he knew better.

All in all, he felt more confident, more prepared, as he drove back out of Houston just ahead of the rush hour traffic. He stopped only once, at a toy store in a small town west of San Antonio. He'd gotten a fresh supply of cash in Houston, and rubber ducks, it turned out, didn't cost much anyway, even the kind that quacked.

"What else have you got that a one-year-old might like?" he asked the woman behind the counter.

They had lots of things, it turned out. Jack settled on a wooden train that clacked when you pulled it, a beanbag frog, and a set of stacking plastic rings in bright colors.

"A lot of parents find that a very stimulating toy," the woman assured him. "It teaches coordination and ordering strategies."

Jack didn't give a damn about ordering strategies. The rings just looked like something that would appeal to a baby's eye, that was all. He figured Emi's little fingers would be just about able to grasp them. And the clacking train reminded him of a toy he'd had himself a long time ago.

This was strictly a business purchase, he told himself as he paid for the toys. He was simply helping to amuse the child of a witness who hadn't had time to pack properly.

But he had to admit, as he started to drive west again, that he was looking forward to seeing the look on Emi's face when he plopped the blue-and-yellow frog down in her lap. The thought of it—the mental image of those dimples popping into view—made him smile.

His buoyant mood lasted all the way back to the cabin, even when he saw the door to the little building standing open. It was a warm day, and no doubt Shelby and Emi were just getting some air. They didn't seem to be doing anything foolish or obvious like standing around within sight of the road, so Jack didn't begrudge them the temporary escape from what was, after all, a very tiny space.

But when he looked around the property, he couldn't see them anywhere. And it wasn't Shelby he found inside the main room when he finally went into the cabin. It was the owner's wife, stripping the sheets off the bed with unruffled efficiency.

No, she assured him. There was no mistake. The cabin was empty, and the woman with the baby was gone.

Chapter 6

"So that's that."

Rae-Anne Blackburn plunked another draft beer down on the counter in front of Jack. "So you keep saying," she told him. "You know, Jack, one of the standard pieces of bartender wisdom is that a customer who keeps mumbling the same thing into his beer is a customer who needs to get something off his mind."

"Who's mumbling?" Jack grinned across the bar at his future sister-in-law. He liked Rae-Anne a lot—had liked her ever since she'd helped the FBI crack a case involving her former fiancée, who'd turned out to be more crooked than an angry sidewinder.

There was nothing crooked about Rae-Anne. She was a straight shooter, a red-haired, blue-eyed dynamo, the kind of woman who would look you right in the eye and let you know with a smile exactly what was on her mind.

Unlike some women. Jack looked down into his beer and recalled the precise tone of Shelby Henderson's answer when he'd told her to make sure she was at that damned cabin when he got back from Houston.

How far am I going to get without the truck? Her light, husky voice had held just the right note of surprise. And sincerity. And just a touch of indignation that he would question something so obvious.

And the whole time she must have been planning to run out on him just as soon as he'd disappeared over the horizon.

He'd been let down before, by people who meant a whole lot more to him than Shelby Henderson did.

Then why did this hurt so much? Why was he having such a hard time telling himself *It's over, and she's not your problem anymore?*

"Jack?"

Rae-Anne's voice brought him back to the present, to the cluttered, colorful barbecue joint on the outskirts of Austin. Across the street in the offices of Cotter Investigations, his brothers Wiley and Sam, and Sam's fiancée Kelley Landis, were wrapping up some last minute work. Wiley was in the process of transferring his interest in the agency to Sam and Kelley, and once that was done, the whole bunch of them were going to take the next couple of weeks off.

And Rae-Anne was busy too, making arrangements for the wedding reception that would be held at the restaurant next Saturday, and lining up staff to take her place and Wiley's while they were honeymooning.

But she still seemed to have plenty of attention left for Jack. And in spite of her teasing tone, there was a look of concern in her blue eyes that Jack found unexpectedly consoling.

He hadn't known he wanted to be consoled.

He hadn't known the simple disappearance of a witness could knock his feet out from under him like this.

And in spite of his repeated pronouncements to the contrary, he still couldn't convince himself to put Shelby Henderson out of his thoughts and move on.

"You want to tell me what this is really all about?" Rae-Anne wrung out a damp cloth and started to wipe down the counter behind the bar. "I know you said it had something to do with a witness with a baby—"

"A *former* witness. The case she was supposed to testify on went sour."

"Then she should be out of the picture, right?"

"Not really." Jack took a pull of his new beer and decided he might as well spell it all out for Rae-Anne. Maybe rehashing the facts he'd studied himself earlier today at his office in Houston would clarify his thoughts for him.

"Shelby Henderson was married to a guy named Emilio Sabinal, a cop in a little one-horse border town," he said. "Sabinal was acting as chief while the chief himself was up in El Paso having emergency surgery on his kidneys or some damn thing. Apparently the old chief was known to take a few bucks under the table from time to time, which was why Jerry Lawrence's boys came to talk to him."

"And this Jerry Lawrence runs a smuggling operation all along the border."

"Right. He doesn't specialize—he'll run drugs, stolen goods, cash, illegal aliens, whatever anybody needs to get across the line. His usual method is to bribe law enforcement officials—cops, customs officers, immigration people—but he picks a different border crossing every time, and a different official, too. He's slippery as hell, because we never know where to look for him next."

"He must have a good network for sniffing out who's open to bribes," Rae-Anne commented.

"He does. And he figured he'd sniffed out a likely candidate down in Lafayette, except—"

"The candidate's kidneys conked out. So Lawrence's men got the substitute chief instead."

"And Emilio Sabinal told them what they could do with their bribe money. Unfortunately, his answer got him killed."

Actually, it hadn't been quite that straightforward. But Jack didn't want to get into those details with Rae-Anne.

He didn't want to explain that Emilio Sabinal had asked for a day to think over the bribery offer, and had used the time to get in touch with federal authorities.

Unfortunately for Sabinal, he hadn't had the know-how or the connections to get his request straight into the hands of anyone with real clout. And by the time Jessie had gotten wind of it, and had put it together with her ongoing investigation into Jerry Lawrence's border-running operation, it had been too late. She'd immediately sent agents to Lafayette, but before they reached the place, Emilio Sabinal was dead.

And Shelby Henderson—Shelby Sabinal, as she'd been then—had been left alone with her unborn child and an abiding distrust of the entire world of law enforcement. He could still hear the hard edge to her voice yesterday afternoon. *The FBI couldn't do anything to save my husband's life. Why should I believe you'll do any better with mine or my daughter's?*

He'd seen suspicion coloring her view of him every time their eyes had met. Except for that one time, when he'd wakened her on the bed in the cabin, and seen that sleepy, trusting, welcoming smile. . . .

Jack glared at his unfinished beer. He didn't want to think about that smile, or the way his whole body had seemed to warm and melt the moment he'd touched her.

He didn't want to think about Shelby's husband, either. It was ridiculous to feel jealous of a dead man, especially one who'd met his end on the orders of a slimeball like Jerry Lawrence.

But Emilio Sabinal had known what it was like to feel Shelby's soft mouth open under his own. Emilio Sabinal had heard those sultry little sounds she made at the back of her throat when she was aroused, those piquant, half-smothered cries that spoke with agonizing clarity of the pleasure she was feeling. Emilio Sabinal had known the delights of her slender but exquisitely feminine body, had experienced all the openness Jack had sensed in that one sweet, disorienting moment when Shelby had smiled up at him and welcomed him into her arms.

Emilio Sabinal had planted the seed that had blossomed into that laughing, golden-haired, dark-eyed child.

And his death had put Shelby permanently on her guard against the world.

And against Jack Cotter.

"Maybe *you* can get some sense out of him."

Jack blinked. How the hell had he let himself drift so far away again? It must be simple lack of sleep, he thought. He'd never had this kind of problem focusing before.

He hadn't even noticed the three newcomers in the bar, or heard the screen door slam behind them. Rae-Anne's words were his first inkling that the Cotter Investigations crew had arrived. Wiley slapped Jack on the shoulder and slid onto a bar stool next to him, while Sam and Kelley leaned against the bar on his left, their arms twined around each other with a casual familiarity that Jack still found disconcerting.

The Cotter brothers stood alone. Always had.

But Wiley and Sam weren't alone any longer. And Jack still wasn't quite sure what that meant for himself and his world.

"He keeps telling me about this witness who gave him the slip, and then he gets this faraway look in his eyes and starts gazing into his beer mug," Rae-Anne was complaining. "I'm worried about you, Jack. In my professional opinion, you're acting like somebody who's just been dumped by his best girl."

That was enough to straighten Jack's spine and drive the thoughts of Shelby Henderson's soft, hungry kisses to the back of his mind. "My pride got hurt, that's all," he assured the quartet of interested faces. "I don't like being duped. Or lied to."

Or walked out on.

The thought was as potent and as troubling now as it had been when he'd stood staring in disbelief at the empty cabin at the other end of the hill country.

He'd trusted Shelby Henderson.

He'd felt himself opening up to her in ways he rarely did with anyone.

He'd let himself fall for her kid in a big way. He'd gone shopping for a rubber duck, for crying out loud. Jack Cotter, tough and savvy and experienced FBI investigator, had spent a good ten minutes determining which squeaky bit of yellow plastic would be most likely to coax those dimples out of baby Emily's cheeks.

And then Shelby had walked away without a word. Without leaving a note. Without a second thought.

He could feel the sting of it in his own voice as he brought his brothers up to speed on the case. "But now that I don't have to baby-sit Sabinal's widow and kid anymore, there's no need for me to stay involved," he added. "Annette and Mack worked with Jessie on this originally. And Garry's young, but he's eager. The three of them can get this under control without me."

"Sure they can." There was something funny about Wiley's quick agreement, but Jack couldn't put his finger on what it was.

"What did you come up with for leads while you were in Houston today?" Kelley Landis wanted to know.

Jack gave her a sharp look. Kelley's tone had been like Wiley's—carefully neutral, as though she were trying to placate him. Or humor him. In fact, all four of the faces around him—his brothers' familiar masculine features,

Rae-Anne's luminous blue eyes, Kelley's catlike elegance—had the same look.

He didn't understand it.

And he didn't like it. But he marshaled his thoughts anyway and gave them a quick rundown on the ideas he and his colleagues had developed earlier in the day.

"We had a witness to testify that the men who shot Shelby Henderson's husband were on Jerry Lawrence's payroll," he said. "That witness just got shot in Hays County. We think our best bet at the moment is to look into that. *Somebody* lured that guy out of hiding too soon, and if we can find out who it was, I'm betting we can tie it to Lawrence somehow. The file on the guy is buried in Records somewhere, but Annette's going to dig it up first thing on Monday."

"Anything else?" Wiley looked at his younger brother over the rim of his beer mug, and Jack wondered again what Wiley was thinking but not saying.

"Well, we're going to look into any recent deaths among law enforcement personnel all along the border," he said. "We figure it's worth checking up on any reprimands for possible bribery charges, too. If we can get Jerry back into custody—on any charge—we'll all be happier."

"Any leads on Jessie's accident?"

"Annette's working on that. We're going to look around for possible witnesses who haven't come forward yet."

"When you say 'we,' you really mean Annette and Garry and Mack, right?" Sam said slowly.

"Right. I'm going to be on vacation, helping you all get married. This isn't my case anymore." He paused. "It never really was."

They all nodded, then fell silent. From the rustic dining area there was the sound of laughter and conversation as the restaurant's patrons ate and drank and enjoyed themselves. But here in this quiet corner of the bar, nobody said anything for what felt to Jack like a suspiciously long time.

Finally Wiley spoke. "Hell of a shame about Jessie," he said.

Jack scowled. It *was* a shame about Jessie. And if the case was still hanging fire when he got back from his vacation, he'd be back at work at it first thing. But until then—

"Wonder where she is." Sam spoke slowly, with the gravelly drawl he used when he was trying to sound particularly nonchalant about something.

Happiness was definitely starting to erode Sam's once-tough mind, Jack thought. "She's in the intensive care ward in Houston," he said impatiently. "And just as soon as—"

"I meant the woman with the baby," Sam said. "This what's-her-name—Shelby Henderson."

Jack closed his eyes. It didn't matter where Shelby Henderson was, he told himself. Shelby Henderson had insisted she could take care of herself. And she'd fooled Jack more thoroughly than he'd been fooled in a very long time. Any woman capable of doing that was capable of surviving on her own.

Except that she wasn't on her own.

And Kelley was reminding him of that now.

"It can't be easy being on the run with a baby," she said. "How old is the little girl, Jack?"

"Not quite a year."

Wiley shook his head and whistled softly.

Jack wondered what they would say if he mentioned Shelby's sprained wrist.

"Do you suppose she has any money?" Rae-Anne wondered out loud.

"I don't know." Jack drained his second beer and clunked the glass down on the counter. "She didn't have a purse with her. And she certainly didn't put up any argument when I paid for the accommodations last night."

Heads shook slowly.

"At least she's safe from Jerry Lawrence, right?" Wiley sounded as though he was determined to look on the bright side. "With that corroborating witness dead—"

"Actually..." This was the part Jack hadn't been able to forget about, the part that had had him gripping the steering wheel hard all the way up here to Austin. "Lawrence is a vengeful son of a bitch. And thorough. Shelby Henderson is a loose end for him, and my guess is he'll probably try to do something about it."

His gut clenched in protest at the idea. The memory of those two shooters at the horse ranch had gotten clearer and more menacing with every mile he'd driven away from that cabin this afternoon.

If something happened to Shelby—

Or Emi—

"But she's disappeared, so what can I do?" He tried to clamp down on his own tension, but he could hear it creeping into his voice. "She doesn't want anything to do with us, or with the witness protection program. She's made that clear. And she didn't leave a trail, not that I could find, anyway."

"Well, that's final, then." Wiley finished his own beer.

"Sounds like it to me." Sam lifted his long arm from around Kelley's shoulders, and added, "Listen, we're beat. We'll see you all tomorrow." He paused, and something seemed to strike him. "You did talk to whoever worked the morning shift at the gas station coffee shop, right?" he said to Jack. "I mean, that's who would likely have seen Shelby Henderson meeting up with someone who might have given her a lift."

"The waitress who worked the morning shift had gone into San Antonio for the day. I couldn't talk to her."

"Oh. Well, there you go. At least you tried."

"It's a good thought," Wiley put in. "That's probably what happened. Unless there were buses coming through."

"Not on weekends. I checked." Jack clenched his teeth. He didn't want to talk about this. He didn't want to be reminded of his own helpless futility, standing on the side of the two-lane road wondering which long, empty horizon Shelby had headed for. He'd been nearly overrun by his own frustration, and by the need to take hold of Shelby's slim shoulders and shake her, hard, and then kiss her, just as hard. And then pull her into his arms and touch off those soft, impatient, hungry noises in her throat all over again.

Fortunately his brothers and their ladies seemed to be letting the subject drop at last. He shared a late dinner with Wiley and Rae-Anne, then bunked on Wiley's sofa for the night, trying not to listen to the easy, conversational noises of his brother and soon-to-be sister-in-law getting ready for bed in the next room.

Rae-Anne had run from Wiley, years ago, he knew. And Wiley had gone looking for her.

But that was different. They'd been in love, the two of them, although it had taken them a long time to work things out. Jack wasn't in love with Shelby Henderson, or anything close to it.

He was just concerned about her, that was all.

And worried as hell about her baby.

And unable, for some reason he couldn't fathom, to clear the memory of her feisty spirit and sweet mouth and warm, responsive body from his thoughts. Something buried deep in her hazel eyes, something lost and stubborn and challenging, wouldn't quite leave him alone, try though he might to chase it away.

The decision woke him out of a sound sleep.
I'm going to find them.
The words were as clear as though someone had spoken them at his ear.

Jack sat up on the sofa bed, disoriented for a moment until he recognized the shapes of the trees in Wiley's small backyard. His breathing was rapid, as though he'd just fought his way out of a nightmare.

But there'd been no nightmare. One moment he'd been in a deep, dreamless sleep, and the next he was wide-awake. And somewhere in the haze between sleeping and waking, he'd made up his mind.

He'd been been helpless to do anything the night his father and Sam had disappeared. He'd been hiding out in the tree house behind the Cotter family's small home, and he'd gone to sleep there, because his mother had been too distraught to come looking for him. He hadn't known until morning, when Wiley brought him the news, that his dad and Sam were gone.

Nobody had consulted him the day he and Wiley had been turned over to the youth services authorities three years later, either. There'd just been the social worker's car in the driveway one Monday morning, and his mother's unhappy face, blurred by alcohol and defeat, and Wiley's granite expression, refusing to betray what he was feeling.

Jack had had a hard time learning to bottle his own emotions up inside. Wiley fought with other kids just for the hell of it, it sometimes seemed, but Jack had fought in anger, flailing out in frustration at all the things he couldn't control in his life. And he'd fought a lot—so much, finally, that the authorities had decided it was best to put the two unruly Cotter boys into separate foster homes with a county or three in between them.

There hadn't been a damn thing he could do about it.

And there wasn't a thing he could do about his brothers getting married next Saturday, either.

But he *could* find Shelby Henderson and her baby.

And he *would* do it, too, if only to prove to her that Jack Cotter was no longer the kind of man who sat still for being walked out on.

He swung his legs over the edge of the sofa bed and got to his feet, grimacing at his watch. Five-thirty was early, but if he got started now, he'd be at the little roadside cabins all the sooner.

He tried to ignore the little clutch of eagerness low down in his belly as he headed into the kitchen for the orange juice he knew Wiley always kept in the refrigerator.

This spur-of-the-moment decision had nothing to do with the way the honeyed scent of Shelby's skin seemed to have woven itself permanently into his memory, he told himself. This was a matter of pride, nothing more. Professional pride, and a perfectly reasonable concern for a small child who'd gotten into the middle of a very ugly situation through absolutely no fault of her own.

It was annoying to feel the impatience starting to build inside him, and to recognize the unmistakable sizzle of desire somewhere in the middle of it.

It was even more annoying to see the note taped to the orange juice container.

"Good luck," it said in Wiley's bold, dark handwriting. "Just make sure you get yourself back to Austin in time for the wedding."

Jack stared at the note, and then snorted. "It would serve you right if I didn't, you smug son of a gun," he muttered.

But he refrained from adding any pointed comments to the bottom of Wiley's note. For one thing, it was too galling to have to admit that his big brother had somehow been one jump ahead of him all along.

And for another, he didn't want to spare the time. He had a woman and a baby to find, and suddenly he couldn't wait to get started.

"Bus doesn't get in 'til three-thirty. I'll be back before then."

The ruddy-faced, white-haired old character who'd sold Shelby her ticket slid a Closed sign in front of the clerk's window and flicked off the light in his little office. The narrow waiting room was still brightly lit—*too* brightly,

Shelby had found herself thinking, as she'd squinted up into the glare of the overhead lights high above her. Every-thing in the place cast harsh shadows, from the tired fan rattling with the effort of circulating the stale air, to the three drifters stretched out on the single bench in the mid-dle of the floor.

The trio had come in at about ten this morning, just about the time the station manager had arrived. They didn't seem to be going anywhere, and had watched Shelby buy-ing a one-way ticket to San Francisco with open curiosity, as though it had never occurred to them that people might hang around at a bus station for the purpose of actually catching a bus.

She'd staked out a chair by the door as her own, and she'd been doing her best to amuse Emily with the few available toys for the past several hours.

"I know it's a bit dull, honey," she'd murmured, when Emi had rejected both *Pat the Bunny* and the bus line's colorful brochure. "But we'll see all kinds of things once we get on the big bus."

"Dja." The word was pointed, and unexpectedly loud. And unexpectedly disturbing. Shelby frowned.

"Jack's gone, honey," she said firmly. "I know you liked him, but believe me, he was a dead end for us."

"Dja." Emi was watching her mother's face intently, clearly trying to put this together in a way that made sense to her.

And Shelby was trying to do the same thing. She wished she could get rid of the slight quaver in her voice as she told her baby daughter, "We're better off on our own, Em. Just the two of us. We can manage."

Emi looked unconvinced. She pulled at the top button of Shelby's faded denim shirt, her bottom lip gathered into a rosebud pout.

It was hard not to contrast her crestfallen expression now with the radiant smile she'd come up with for Jack Cotter. Shelby had never seen her baby so entranced by a stranger.

She couldn't remember ever feeling quite so entranced, herself.

Not even with Emilio.

She frowned, and picked up the little stuffed alligator Emi had just thrown onto the floor. She didn't want to be thinking these thoughts.

She didn't want to remember the way it had felt to dissolve into Jack Cotter's strength, to feel the hunger in him as if it were a passionate voice calling to something deep inside herself.

She didn't want his disruptive presence coming between her and the memories of the husband she'd lost.

Or disturbing the familiar, precious alliance she'd created with Emi over the past year.

Her life was fragile enough, uncertain enough, without letting a man like Jack Cotter into it.

And so she'd left him behind. It was as simple as that.

"That's a pretty little girl you got there."

She'd been so wrapped up in her thoughts that she hadn't noticed the way the three drifters were staring at her. It was the bigger of the men who'd spoken. His nasal drawl startled her, and she shifted Emi a little closer to her body.

"Thank you," she said, keeping her own voice as neutral as she could.

"You don't have a lot of luggage." The woman of the trio nodded at the padded bag. "You goin' on vacation or something?"

"We're visiting family."

"In San Francisco?"

So they *had* been listening in when she'd bought her ticket. Somehow that made Shelby uneasy. She pushed the padded bag farther under her chair with one foot, trying not to be too obvious about it. If they'd happened to notice that she'd paid for her fare with a hundred-dollar bill—

"Yes," she said. "In San Francisco."

The taller man got up off the bench and sauntered toward her corner of the room. Shelby held Emi a little tighter and wondered what would happen if she got up quickly and headed for the door.

In spite of his slow lope, the stranger got there ahead of her. He was blocking the only exit before she could think of a good way to get the strap of the bag over her shoulder and be on her way to somewhere else.

"What'd you think of our town so far?" The mockery in his tone was obvious now. "That Bide-a-Wile Inn's a pretty little place, ain't it?"

Actually, the only thing to recommend the Bide-a-Wile Inn—aside from its bargain rates—was the fact that it was close to a bus station. She hadn't liked anything else about the place. And she didn't like the fact that these three obviously knew where she'd been staying.

There were people who watched for travelers and targeted them, she knew. She glanced up at the wall across the room, but the clock face, dim under its clouded Plexiglas cover, showed that there was still almost an hour before she could hope for the bus to show up. Somehow she didn't think she could count on the station manager to return much before then. He'd had the look of a man on his way to do some serious communing with a bar stool.

She considered the lanky stranger who was leering down at her now, and answered him as calmly as she could. "Well," she said, "the guidebook said I wouldn't see bigger roaches anywhere in the state of Texas, and I'd guess they were right. I could have done without the one who wanted to arm wrestle me for my coffee this morning, though."

The man cackled and looked over at his friends. "Hear that?" he said. "That's good. You're smart, real smart."

The other two were chuckling, too, but it wasn't a friendly sound. "If she's so smart," the woman said, "how come she's carrying all that cash with her when she goes on a long trip? Doesn't she know about travelers' checks?"

You needed ID to use travelers' checks. And Shelby didn't have any official ID.

She didn't have any clear idea how she was going to get out of this situation, either. Emi was fussing on her lap, as though she sensed her mother's tension, but Shelby's calming words were absentminded, her thoughts taken up with the growing sense of threat in the room around her.

"I don't know what you're talking about. I used up what cash I had to buy my ticket," she said.

The man standing next to her seemed taller all of a sudden. He was peering down at her, prodding the bag under her chair with the toe of one cowboy boot.

"That so?" he said. "Sure didn't look that way from where I was standing."

The other two got to their feet and Shelby stood, too, clutching Emi against one shoulder and wishing her right wrist felt stronger. The sprain was healing, but she wasn't sure it would withstand the weight of the padded bag if she stooped to pick it up.

And she wasn't sure that was the wisest thing to do, anyway. The trio of raggedy-looking strangers appeared poised to cut her off the moment she made a move.

Which didn't seem to leave her very many options.

"Do you always pick on women with babies?" she demanded.

They all chortled. "We ain't fussy," the woman said. "Anybody with a wad of cash looks the same to us."

"I seem to recall that there *is* a police station in this town."

"Shoot, I wouldn't count on those old boys to be able to find a flea on a hound dog's backside. You happen to lose a little cash, they ain't gonna find it for you."

Even if the little town had the best police force in the state, Shelby didn't want to have to explain why she'd been traveling with nearly ten thousand dollars in cash, or who she was, or where she was headed. She liked the idea of appearing in official police records even less than she liked the thought of being robbed.

"How's about letting us see the inside of that bag, now?" The taller man was moving in on her, slowly but definitely.

There was no way to resist them, not with Emi in her arms. If the bag had contained a million dollars, she'd still have been willing to give it up to keep her daughter safe from these three.

Shelby was about to step aside when the tall man suddenly lunged for the bag and thrust his hand inside it. Unfortunately, the first thing he came up with was Emilio's wallet.

"Lookee here," he said in exaggerated delight.

"You can't have that." Shelby's voice was shaking.

"I already got it, little lady." He opened the wallet, displaying the few dollars it had contained the night Emilio had been shot.

The bills were permanently curved from being folded into the billfold. It was all just the way it had been when the Lafayette police had handed Emilio's personal effects over to her after he'd been taken to the morgue. The leather was worn smooth from years of riding in Emilio's hip pocket. His driver's license was still valid—Shelby took it out and looked at it from time to time, thinking how strange it was that it hadn't somehow expired when Emilio died.

She could almost smell the familiar, fading scent of the leather as the tall man rifled through Emilio's notes and credit cards. She'd saved this one small piece of her husband intact—something familiar, something that had been on his body the night he'd died. She'd packed it carefully into her emergency bag, unwilling to leave it behind. And now it was going to end up in a trash can somewhere, after this unsympathetic yahoo had pulled out the few dollars it contained.

She didn't stop to think about what she was doing. She lashed out with her foot and caught the mugger squarely between his legs. By the time he'd collapsed in a heap on the linoleum floor, Shelby had retrieved the wallet and tucked it between her body and Emi's.

She heard the other man's snarl of protest mixing with the gasps of the guy she'd disabled. *That was your one dramatic gesture, Shelby,* she told herself. *Now you'd better concentrate on getting out of here.*

She wasn't exactly sure how she was going to manage it. The smaller man was between her and the door, and the woman was circling around toward the padded bag. They both seemed galvanized by the attack on their buddy, and Shelby felt fear clutching at her as she registered the hostility in their eyes. The man, in particular, looked capable of far more than just robbery.

And then suddenly he was staggering forward, hands stretched uselessly out in front of him as he sprawled onto the hard floor next to his friend. Shelby could hear the impact of it jarring all the way through her own frame.

It took her a moment to realize that the door behind him had been flung open, and that someone had planted a foot in the small of the stranger's back.

"All right, fun's over." A familiar deep voice cut across the whine of the fan. "We can wrap this up any way you like it, but we *are* going to wrap it up."

Somehow—although Shelby couldn't imagine how he'd done it—Jack Cotter had managed to find her.

He was standing in the bus station doorway in a pair of blue jeans and a dark blue shirt, looking handsome and clean-shaven and grim as hell. He held the glass door open with his left hand, and Shelby could see the strength and the tension in his body as he braced himself there.

His right hand, though, looked steady, almost relaxed. The gun in it was leveled somewhere in the midst of the three people who'd tried to rob her, and judging by the look in Jack's eyes, he had no qualms about using it if he had to.

Chapter 7

"A gun, for heaven's sake."

Jack checked the odometer. They were thirty-two miles from the little town where he'd found Shelby and Emi at the bus station.

It had been thirty-one and a half miles since Shelby had spoken a word to him.

The first time had been while they were waiting out a red signal at the town's only traffic light. Emi had been squirming on her lap, and Jack had reached over to keep the baby from escaping.

The familiarity of it startled him. It wasn't just that the three of them were hitting the road together a second time, or the all-too-noticeable way Shelby was holding her injured wrist carefully out of harm's way.

It was the soft weight of Emi's little body under his palm, and the scent of Shelby's skin so close to him. Those things seemed to have gotten into his bloodstream, become a part of him in some way he didn't quite understand.

He was exhilarated already from having run off the three jackals at the bus station, and on top of that he was feeling a bolt of pure, unadulterated pleasure at being with Shelby and her baby again.

But her brisk "Thank you" had told him she wasn't feeling any of those things.

And her pointed comment thirty-one and a half miles later wasn't much friendlier.

"I suppose it was loaded," she said.

"Of course it was loaded." Jack glanced over at her. Emi had stopped wriggling and seemed to be dozing against her mother's shoulder, but Shelby was sitting rigidly straight against the upholstered seat.

Jack was a little surprised her glare hadn't melted the safety glass in the windshield.

"For all I knew, those three bozos could have been armed, too," he added.

"They weren't."

"I didn't know that until I'd frisked them."

He hadn't had to do much more than that. Jack's manner, along with his gun, had been more than enough to complete the job Shelby had started with her well-placed kick. The trio had quickly come to the conclusion that they'd picked on the wrong woman, and had cleared out of the station before Jack had even started to argue with Shelby about what they were going to do next.

She'd reluctantly admitted that maybe sticking with the idea of getting onto a long-distance bus wasn't so practical after all. Even if her wrist *had* been in working order, there were just too many risks in striking off without a coherent plan. She'd climbed into the car with Jack, but he could tell she hadn't been happy to do it.

And she didn't sound any happier now.

"I don't want Emi anywhere near people who carry loaded weapons," she said.

"Fine. I can understand that. And if you'd stayed at the cabin yesterday, instead of charging off on your own, Emi wouldn't have been in that situation in the first place."

"I would have managed."

"One of these days, Shelby, you're going to find yourself in a jam that that philosophy won't get you out of."

He found himself gripping the wheel hard. He didn't want to think about that happening. He wanted to help her, damn it. He wanted to make things easier for her, and for Emi.

And she wouldn't let him.

He didn't blame her for being leery of guns. Her husband had been shot dead practically in front of her eyes—he'd read the case files on it with grim fascination yesterday. But still—

"What did you do with my truck?" She was trying for the same clear, hard-edged tone she'd used with him when he'd first met her, Jack thought.

"I didn't realize it was yours. I thought the ranch—"

She waved the question away, then sat still again as Emi murmured in her sleep. "I just want to know where it is," she said. "I owe the people at the ranch a lot. I don't want to repay it by letting their truck rot at the side of the road like some unwanted—"

"It's safe in the FBI parking garage," Jack cut in over her words. "I'll see that it gets back to the ranch when—when this whole mess gets sorted out."

"When is that likely to be?"

"I don't know. My colleagues are working on one end of it right now. The rest of it—the part that concerns you and Emi—is pretty much up to you."

She gave a short, unamused laugh. "You mean it's up to me as long as I choose to do something that meets with your approval," she said.

"I'm not about to let you wander around loose until you've got a plan in your head," he told her. "If you call that meeting with my approval—"

"Why?" She half turned against the seat, ignoring Emi's soft whimper this time. Her hazel eyes were troubled, searching his for answers, or reassurance, or *something*. Jack didn't know exactly what she was looking for, or why he wanted so fiercely to be able to give it to her. But the connection between them was so strong he could feel his whole body humming with it, telling him he'd been right to come looking for her. "Why do you care what happens to me? Or Emi?"

He didn't have a clear answer. He didn't know what had wakened him before dawn this morning with an urgent certainty that he needed to find Shelby Henderson and her child. He didn't know what was behind the bolt of pure joy that had gone through him when he'd looked through that fly-specked glass door at the bus station and seen the pale gold halo of Shelby's hair and the pointed, stubborn outline of her chin.

He wasn't sure why it was so hard to keep his eyes on the road when she turned her gaze on him.

Or why it was that the two of them couldn't speak ten words to each other without arguing.

"I don't know," he said gruffly. Damn it, he could feel the snap and intelligence of those hazel eyes even when he wasn't looking at her.

"This isn't even your case, right?" Her voice had gotten a little huskier. "You're supposed to be helping your brothers get married, not running around in the middle of nowhere with Emi and me."

"Tell me something I don't already know." Jack spotted the exit he'd been watching for, and flicked on the turn signal. "If you hadn't somehow gotten Jessie concerned about you, and if Jessie wasn't such a good friend of mine—"

He didn't finish the thought. And it seemed to answer Shelby's question anyway. She turned away again, settling Emi's sleeping form back into the crook of her arm. Jack sat back a little, too, realizing for the first time how taut his body had become while she'd been watching him.

Why? What was it about this woman that affected him so powerfully?

Why *had* he come looking for her?

He tried to put the question out of his mind, but it was still there almost an hour later when he finally found what he'd been looking for—a hotel secluded enough to be safe and fancy enough to be comfortable. After a night on Wiley's sofa bed and one in the cab of a truck, Jack was ready for some luxury.

And Shelby didn't argue about it, miraculously. There were faint shadows under her eyes, and her pale blond hair had lost some of the luster that had caught Jack's eye when he'd first seen her in the stable yard. Emi was wearing a clean set of striped rompers, but Shelby herself was still in the same jeans and faded chambray shirt she'd had on two days ago, and it was beginning to look a little the worse for wear.

Just because she'd agreed to the idea of a comfortable motel for the night, though, didn't mean she was done wrangling with him.

"I thought credit cards could be traced," she said at the check-in counter, when he pulled out the company card he'd had the foresight to pick up at the office.

"This one can't." He spoke so the desk clerk couldn't hear him.

"And the car license number—"

"Same deal. Internal security keeps these numbers from getting into mainstream records. Nobody's going to find you here, Shelby."

She should have been reassured by that, he thought. She *did* seem pleased by the room—it was bright and airy and quiet, at the end of a long row at the back of the long, two-story hotel. And she'd nodded her silent approval when Jack had asked for an adjoining room. Clearly she wasn't eager for a repetition of the night they'd been cooped up so close together in that tiny cabin.

But as soon as the crib they'd ordered had been brought up, and she'd settled the sleeping Emi into it, Shelby was knocking on the door between the two rooms and demanding, "Don't you have the sense to recognize it when somebody doesn't want to be followed?"

Jack shrugged. "Guess not," he said.

"And how did you find me, anyway? I thought I'd covered my tracks."

"You did," he told her. "I waited for the waitress who'd served you breakfast yesterday to show up for her shift. She told me you'd fallen into conversation with a guy—a traveling salesman—who stays at the cabins from time to time."

He stepped back from the door and returned to opening the curtains in his room. The afternoon sun filtered through the oaks outside, making dappled patches of light on the pale blue carpet.

"She said the two of you seemed to have gotten quite friendly. So I figured it was worth tracking the guy, if I could."

Shelby stayed standing by the open door, arms crossed over her chest. Jack leaned against one of the armchairs near the window and tried to keep his thoughts on the story he was telling.

She looked so tired, he thought.

And so fragile.

And so determined not to show it.

He cleared his throat and went on. "The owner of the motel gave me the name of the van company the salesman travels for," he said. "It wasn't hard to call them up and pretend I was a car dealer on the guy's route who wanted to get in touch with him."

Her soft mouth tilted slightly, and Jack felt his whole body responding to it. It wasn't a real smile—there was something reluctant and cynical about it. But it was still enough to change her face, to remind Jack intimately and achingly of the way she'd smiled at him just before he'd pulled her into his arms the other night. If he could just make her smile like that again—if he could chase that wary look out of her eyes—

"Somehow I can't picture you as a car dealer," she was saying.

Jack grinned at her. He couldn't help it. "Hey, I cut a heck of a deal, sweetheart," he said. "Or at least I can *sound* like I do. It was enough to get the van company to track down your friendly salesman—"

"I told him—"

"Who told me he'd picked up this young woman who'd been on the run from her abusive boyfriend. Seems the woman had warned him that said boyfriend might happen to show up on her trail, in which case the salesman should be on the lookout for a guy about—oh, just about my height, with dark brown hair and eyes and a kind of smooth, charming way about him. That about accurate, Shelby?"

She nodded.

"I wish I'd known you found me charming," he said. "Somehow I'd gotten the opposite impression."

"I *don't* find you charming. I just—it seemed like other people might, that's all."

"Well, thanks. I'm overwhelmed. You did a good sell job to the van guy, by the way. He refused categorically to tell me where he'd let you off."

"Then how—"

"By putting in a lot of miles checking his route, that's how. I had to ask at four motels, two resort cabins, a dude ranch, and an awful lot of little restaurants before I picked up your trail."

And he'd done it just in the nick of time, too. He glanced through the open door into Shelby's room, and nodded at the padded bag that sat in the middle of the queen-size bed.

"That waitress told me you paid for your breakfast with a hundred-dollar bill," he said. "Just how much would you have lost if those three muggers had stolen that bag, anyway?"

She followed his gaze. "A lot," she admitted.

"Turned everything into cash, huh?" He'd been working this through on the drive out here. "You can't open a bank account without giving a social security number, and you didn't want to do that while you were in hiding. You need ID to use travelers' checks. So you converted your assets into cash and kept it ready to grab if you were threatened. What about Emilio's police pension? You must be getting that."

"It's going into a trust fund administered by a lawyer. It's for Emi, when—someday."

Someday.

The word should have sounded hopeful. But it didn't.

Shelby Henderson didn't trust the future, Jack realized. And the past wasn't a happy place for her, either.

It just didn't seem right to him.

"Shelby—" He pushed himself away from the chair. "Why don't you let us help you? You don't have to do this on your own. We can set it up so you can have a damn bank account if you want one—or a car, or a home, or anything you want, anything Emi needs. You shouldn't have to carry stacks of cash around with you—it's just asking to be made a target, like you were today."

"You don't understand." Her eyes seemed to be searching for escape routes, and not finding any. She held her ground in the open doorway, but Jack could sense her wanting to run, just as she'd run from him yesterday.

Why?

He took a step closer to her, and said, "I'm *trying* to understand. But you don't exactly make it easy."

Her hazel eyes veered back to his. She'd have been happier if he'd gone back to the window, he thought.

But he kept moving.

"What I want—what Emi needs—" The sentences didn't seem to be forming themselves the way she wanted. "You can't give us those things," she said finally, as though she was hoping it might be enough to convince him to let the subject drop.

He knew he should.

He knew she was right. He *couldn't* give her what she was looking for, couldn't fulfill any of the dreams she must have had in mind when she'd planned to start a family with the man she loved. None of that was Jack Cotter's style, and Shelby clearly realized it.

But—

He was nearly all the way to the open door now. He could see the way half a dozen pale golden strands of hair were pulling themselves free of her ponytail to join the ones that were already loose. The smile was long gone from Shelby's lips, but the soft rose pink curve of her mouth was driving him crazy just the same.

He couldn't help it. Reaching for her seemed as instinctive as breathing. He closed his palms around her upper arms and held her tight, feeling his heart beginning to thud against his chest wall as he lost himself in Shelby's half green, half brown gaze.

"I've never met a woman who knocks me off-balance the way you do." Somehow it was impossible to keep his thoughts to himself. "I don't know what the hell I'm doing here, Shelby. And I don't know what the hell we're going to do next. But so help me, I'm not going to let you disappear on me again until we've figured this out, so you might as well get used to the idea that we're stuck with each other until then."

"Jack—please—"

He waited, but she didn't finish the phrase. The longer he touched her like this, the harder his heart was pounding, and he cared less and less about all the words they'd been tossing at each other.

What did words matter when his blood was singing like this?

What good were words, when the questions Jack wanted to answer had nothing to do with logic, or professionalism, or common sense, and everything to do with the way he felt when the perfume of Shelby Henderson's skin twined around him so sinuously, so seductively?

Jack—please— The husky note of her voice was still echoing in his ears, connecting, in some supremely magical way, with parts of himself that she seemed to be able to stir without even trying.

"Please what?" To his surprise, the question came out as a husky whisper. "Please what, Shelby?"

He was already pulling her closer to him as he realized she might not know the answer.

Maybe she didn't understand what was happening between them any more than Jack did himself.

And the instant his lips touched hers, it didn't matter anyway.

For a long moment he was simply overwhelmed by the sweetness of her, by the warm, honeyed recesses of her mouth against his own. He closed his eyes and let himself fall into that embracing darkness as though everything he'd ever lost and longed for was contained in the promise of it.

Shelby leaned back against the open door as he wrapped his arms around her. He wondered for one brief, protesting moment if she was going to resist him, push him away, tell him he was all wrong about this, wrong about any idea he might have that there was anything sensual or significant happening here.

She stayed motionless at the first touch of his lips. He almost had the sense that she was willing herself not to respond.

But then she did.

He could feel it like a slow wave building from somewhere inside the shared tension of their embrace. It was just a whisper at first, a faint sound like a breath of wind at the back of nowhere. Jack sensed something changing in Shelby's stance at the same instant as he tasted her soft, eager sigh.

She was as hungry for this as he was.

The thought bolted straight through him and came to rest low down in his loins, where the same blind urges that had wakened him out of a sound sleep early this morning were pulsing insistently now.

And the sudden possibilities that came with it made Jack's knees so weak he wasn't quite sure he could trust them to hold him up.

This shouldn't be happening.

Shelby tried to cling to the thought, but it kept slipping away from her. It *was* happening—whatever it was that kept striking sparks between her and Jack Cotter. And it was escalating with every subtle shift in the way he held her, with every probing, enticing movement of his mouth against hers.

Whatever was going on, it was picking up steam like a midnight express train heading across the longest, straightest stretch of Texas territory there was.

And Shelby felt herself being swept along with it.

She heard one of Jack's broad palms thudding against the wooden door next to her head, and realized the new intensity of their embrace had knocked them both off-balance. She wrapped her uninjured left arm around his waist and felt the hard, springy strength of his body under her hand.

A faint, small voice at the back of her mind was trying to tell her that it was a bad idea to let this happen. But the warning note was being drowned out by the sudden rush of sensation hurtling through her body.

Jack's dark blue polo shirt wasn't tucked into his jeans. The sight of it—loose edges draped over the masculine slant of his hips—had been catching her eye ever since she'd gotten into his car this afternoon. What would his skin feel like, she'd wondered, if she was to slide her fingers over it, exploring the way his chest broadened over his rib cage, tracing the hard outlines of the muscles she'd seen whenever he moved?

She tried to resist the temptation to find out, but it was a losing battle. She'd never met a man who stirred such wanton imaginings in her mind and such fierce longings in her body—not Emilio, not anyone.

She flattened her left palm against the small of his back and heard him groan softly against her mouth. The idea that he wanted her to touch him was almost as enticing as the feel of his warm, tanned skin under her fingertips.

She followed the smooth curve of his spine upward, then fanned her hand open against his shoulder blade. The sharp throbbing in her sprained right wrist started to recede as she closed her eyes and imagined the wide strength of Jack's shoulders and the way her own slender fingers must look against that hard expanse of muscle and sinew.

She wanted to be able to touch him with both hands, to trace the whole tantalizing outline of his body. Cautiously she pushed the knuckles of her right hand under the edge of his shirt and let them graze the solidly muscled ridges of his stomach. Her wrist still hurt, but pleasure was beginning to mask the pain of it.

She felt his belly tighten at her gentle exploration. When he shifted his stance to lock the two of them more securely together, it was impossible not to imagine how his angular hips must look when he was naked, how his flat stomach would slope down to the dark juncture of his thighs. Shelby caught her breath at the image of it against her closed eyelids, and heard Jack's sudden inhalation echoing hers.

"Would you—do that again?"

"That" was the soft caress of her knuckles over the inverted V at the center of his rib cage, followed by the light movement of her open palm over his chest. She could feel taut muscle and dark, curling hair—it must be dark, like everything else about him—and the tantalizing hardness of his tightly beaded nipple.

Shelby leaned back into the solid circle of his arms and drew her hands together at the waistband of his jeans. She didn't understand the hunger that seemed to consume both of them whenever they were close together, but there was no denying the power of it. She could see it in Jack's half-closed eyes, and in the way his whole expression had changed. He looked younger when he wasn't holding his jaw in that tight, tenacious line. He looked so much more open this way, so vulnerable.

Just like Shelby felt.

And so aroused.

Just like Shelby.

There was something inexpressibly sexy in the way he responded to her caress. Shelby swept both hands in a slow oval over his chest again, and felt his whole body shudder as she did it. She sensed him holding himself still, savoring the lightness of her fingertips against his skin.

His desire for her was tantalizingly evident—she could feel it where her hips met his, and see it in the way his lips parted slightly when she drew her hands down again toward his belly. Yet he was deliberately waiting for her to take the lead, banking the passion she sensed in him. The quivering low down in his body told her exactly what her touch was doing to him, but after the initial wildness of his kiss, he was letting her set the pace, giving her control over where they went next with this.

It occurred to Shelby—suddenly, dizzily—that making love with Jack Cotter might be the kind of experience that could knock her life completely off course.

And at the moment that didn't seem like such a bad thing.

She'd felt so fearful, so bruised, for the past two years. It was immensely freeing now to give in to the sensation of Jack's strong body against hers, to push his dark blue shirt upward and feel him unclasp his grip long enough to pull the shirt over his head and leave him standing half-naked in front of her, dark eyes blazing, the unclothed magnificence of his chest rising and falling with quick, shallow breaths that matched her own.

It was wonderful not to care what might happen beyond the four sheltered walls of this sunlit room. Shelby raised her hands to Jack's chest again, expecting him to pull her back into his arms. Instead, he began working on the knot at the waist of her chambray shirt, his big fingers stubborn and awkward around the tight twist of blue fabric.

"Were you planning to stay in this shirt for the rest of your days?"

Shelby smiled in spite of the gruff frustration in his voice. "I guess I was a little—wrought up when I fastened the knot this morning," she said.

He snorted. "And here I've been worried about your wrist," he said. "Any woman who can tie a half hitch this tight is a woman I'm not going to argue with."

It felt good to know he'd been worried about her.

And even better to hear the rough, gently mocking sound of his voice.

She'd missed this, Shelby thought. She'd missed having a companion, partner. And in some way that didn't make complete sense to her, yet Jack Cotter seemed to be offering her that—an equal partnership, the kind of give-and-take that only happened between two people who respected and trusted and desired each other.

She hadn't had time to sort out what that meant when he made a move that took her completely by surprise. With a low growl, he gave up his battle with the knot and slid his arms around her again, one at her waist, one behind her thighs. Before she could speak, he lifted her off her feet and carried her toward the queen-size bed.

It seemed like heaven to let her head settle back among the pillows, and to feel Jack Cotter's long legs tangled up with hers as he surrounded her and turned his frowning attention back to her shirt. His dark hair—so disheveled now, compared with the slick, buttoned-down look he usually cultivated—was like heavy satin between her fingers when she ran her hands through it.

She circled the back of his neck and felt him lean his head toward her caressing palm, as though her touch held some magnetic pull for him. When she dropped her hands lightly onto his wide, tanned shoulders, the shifting of his hard muscles under her fingertips made her quiver inside.

By the time he'd wrestled the knot into submission, Shelby's whole body was pulsing with a need that seemed to radiate out from the very core of her. She didn't realize her fingers were trembling until she raised them to the buttons of her shirt. She met Jack's hands halfway, and felt herself smiling as they tussled briefly over the final button.

Jack won, and Shelby's smile widened as she realized how natural it felt to test her strength and her will against Jack Cotter's. They'd done it since the moment they'd met, and even in the throes of passion they seemed instinctively to challenge each other in ways that were maddening and arousing all at the same time.

He was pushing her opened blouse aside now, and Shelby let out a long sigh of delight as he gently kissed the smooth skin just above her navel. She could feel his big hands at the sides of her ribs, cradling her, then moving upward to encircle the softness of her breasts.

"Shelby..." He spoke with his mouth against her belly. The deep sound of his voice seemed to resonate right through her. "I've been dreaming about doing this. And this—"

He pulled himself up over her, and Shelby gave a little cry as their legs wound even more intimately around each other. The weight of his big body pressing her down into the soft mattress seemed to flood her mind with half-forgotten yearnings and half-imagined possibilities.

The heat of his breath through the thin fabric of her bra chased everything out of her consciousness except the sweet pleasure of this moment. His chest was warm and strong against her body, and the way his lips closed so gently and suggestively around her tight nipple made her tremble all the way down to her toes.

Clothing suddenly seemed an intrusion, a barrier. Shelby kicked her sneakers off and heard them clunk onto the floor at the foot of the bed. She could feel Jack's mouth curve into a smile at the sound, and for some reason the thought of how he looked right now—of his sun-darkened skin and that sexy grin slanting against the whiteness of her breast—pushed her past whatever doubts were still lingering in the back of her mind.

She wanted what Jack Cotter could give her, and suddenly nothing else mattered.

Chapter 8

She rolled to one side, pushing herself to a sitting position. Jack came with her, lifting his head just long enough to capture her lips for a long, searching kiss. Shelby felt her head spinning with the hunger in it. It was all she could do to hang on to the thought that had prompted her to sit up in the first place.

She reached behind her back and quickly unsnapped her bra before shrugging out of it. Jack caught the scrap of fabric and tossed it onto the floor with his shirt.

"Just because I had a little trouble with that knot doesn't mean I couldn't have handled a bra snap, you know," he growled against her mouth.

Shelby smiled. "You've got snaps of your own to worry about," she told him, and tapped his belt buckle with her left forefinger.

She saw his gaze darken as he lifted his head from hers. She'd been right, she realized—it was her own hunger, her desires, that seemed to arouse Jack most. Her teasing suggestion that he shed his jeans acted on him like a dose of accelerant on an already blazing fire.

She'd never experienced this kind of passion, this kind of excitement. She'd never felt so challenged and so cherished at the same time.

Jack started to undo his belt buckle, but then he paused. There was something almost reverent in the slow way he shook his head as he looked at Shelby.

"You're so beautiful," he murmured. "You should look this way all the time. You should *smile* just like that all the time."

She hadn't realized she was still smiling. But as Jack reached out and pulled the band away from her hair, combing it free with his fingers, she suddenly realized what he meant. Mixed with the yearning that was still pulsing through her, she could feel a slow crest of satisfaction building, smoothing over all the rough edges, reminding her just how sweet life could be.

Jack was framing her face with his hands, looking deeply into her eyes. A slight breeze stirred the curtains to her right, and out of the corner of her eye Shelby saw the sunlit patterns shifting on the light blue carpet. Pleasure and desire and wonder were shifting the same way inside her, she thought, as though she'd found herself in some kind of magic kaleidoscope the instant Jack Cotter had captured her in his arms.

She closed her eyes as he kissed her forehead, then her cheekbones, then the point of her chin. She'd never known the soft stretch of skin beneath her jawline was so sensitive until he caressed it, too, with his mouth. She felt her already taut nipples tighten even more as he lowered his lips, dropping featherlight kisses along her collarbone and then down to the hollow between her breasts.

He seemed determined to seek out and savor every corner of her, and Shelby quivered deep inside when she thought about the thoroughness she knew he was capable of. She arched her spine as he stretched out one broad palm against it to hold her up, and gasped when his lips surrounded the hard bead of first one nipple, then the other.

He didn't stop there, but kept going, kissing her rib cage and belly so provocatively that Shelby didn't even realize for a moment he was lowering her back onto the pillows at the same time, or that his hands—those slow, patient, attentive hands—were reaching for the waistband of her jeans.

The sound of the snap coming free was like a pebble thrown into a pool heated by the sun. Shelby could feel ripples from the sound traveling all the way through her. The soft growl of her zipper sliding downward only quickened the circle of liquid heat that began in the core of her body and spread outward from there.

"Oh . . . Jack . . ."

Suddenly she couldn't wait to feel his lips and hands exploring the most secret parts of her. It had been such a long time since she'd felt so utterly alive, so completely aware of her own body. Or maybe she'd *never* felt exactly this way, and that was why the world seemed to be tilting around her, settling itself into new and exhilarating patterns.

She murmured Jack's name again as he dug his fingers gently under her waistband and pushed her jeans and panties onto the floor with one long, swift motion. The moisture he discovered at the meeting place of her thighs seemed to astonish and delight him. She arched upward toward him as he slid two long fingers inside her, and felt herself contracting around him, longing for more, desperate for his touch.

She hadn't known she was so eager. She hadn't realized how much she'd been longing for the exhilarating free-fall of physical release, or how impatient she was for all the fulfillment she was sure Jack Cotter could bring her.

Her own hunger caught up with her and swept her along into a surprised cry of delight as he probed deeper into her.

The world seemed to melt into soft, velvety darkness as Jack added the sweet caress of his mouth to the pleasure he was already creating, first with his warm breath, then with the devastatingly slow and sure movements of his lips and tongue.

It was impossible to hold back. Shelby was vaguely aware of her own sharp cries spiraling higher as she lost herself in Jack's touch and her own desires. But there was no way to control what was happening to her, no way to pull away from the chasm that was opening up at her feet.

She plunged into it willingly, trusting Jack to keep her from breaking into fragments when the world started to shake loose around her. She felt everything inside her clenching into a compelling embrace, then trembling as though all her muscles had reached their physical limit and were beginning to dissolve.

It was a release unlike anything she'd ever experienced—sudden, shattering, all-consuming. Her own voice was somewhere on the edge of it, calling out on a note that seemed to be dredged from the very roots of her being, so astonished and overwhelmed that there was almost an edge of protest in the sound. It was as if the universe were turning itself inside out, sweeping her along with it and half drowning her in the sheer joy and terror and intensity of being alive.

Her own wordless cry seemed to echo on and on after the tremors in her body had begun to subside. Shelby felt too drained, too satisfied, to follow the noise at first. She wanted to linger here forever, with Jack's handsome profile half-turned toward her thigh and his warm breath still making her shudder deep inside.

But something was pulling her back into everyday reality, starting to counter all the erotic sensations washing through her. Shelby frowned, and fought to open her eyes.

The light seemed dim after the fireball that had just exploded inside her. And the noise coming from the crib in the next room sounded reedy and far away. But it was becoming more familiar and more urgent with every passing second.

She wasn't orbiting the heavens somewhere, propelled by the sinfully sweet pleasure of Jack Cotter's touch. She was in a Texas motel room with more unanswered questions hanging over her than ever. And only a dozen feet away, her baby daughter was wide-awake and wailing.

Emi only woke up this way when something had startled her—a storm outside, or a tooth coming in, or whatever bad dreams babies sometimes had.

Or, in this case, her mother's long cry of ecstasy from the next room.

Shelby bit back a quiet curse as she reached for her jeans and shirt. She could see Jack rolling over to follow her movements, but she refused to look at him.

"Shelby—"

She could hear him trying to marshal his thoughts, the same way she was. She hadn't been the only one lost in the mists of passion, she thought.

But she seemed to be the only one with the sense to try to escape again now.

"Shelby, wait. Don't run away like this."

"I'm not running." She had her shirt around her now, and she was trying to step into her jeans. It would have been easier if the floor hadn't kept tilting under her feet. "Emi's crying, in case you hadn't—"

"She can cry for a couple of minutes without doing permanent damage. But you and I—"

Fear caught at her almost as suddenly as that sweet starburst had a few minutes earlier. "There is no 'you and I,'" she said quickly. "Please don't imagine that there is. This shouldn't have happened."

"Shouldn't have—"

He cut his own words short. Shelby could hear the disbelief reverberating in his voice as she forced herself to draw in a slow breath. When her fingers finally stopped shaking she zipped up her jeans, snapping the waistband shut with what she hoped was a very definite sound.

It wasn't just Emi's cry that had jolted her out of Jack's embrace.

And it wasn't just the aftermath of pleasure that was making her knees so unsteady as she crossed the carpeted floor into the other room.

It was fear—fear of everything Jack's touch had conjured up inside her, everything his slow caresses seemed to promise her.

If she let herself need this man—

If she let herself want him—

She shook her head and leaned over the crib, where Emi was clinging to the bars and turning nearly purple with the effort of crying so hard.

"Hush, sweetheart." She lifted the squalling baby out of the crib, trying to ignore the twinge of pain from her right wrist as she supported Emi's body. "You're all right. You're all right now."

She was aware of Jack moving off the bed in the other room, coming into the doorway between their rooms, but she kept her attention focused on Emi, smoothing her daughter's soft blond hair away from her damp forehead, kissing the velvet-soft skin at the baby's temples.

"I know," she murmured. "You woke up and you didn't know where you were. But you're okay now. Mom's here. You're okay."

Usually the familiar litany of phrases comforted Shelby, too, as well as Emily. But even when the baby's panicky sobs gradually quieted, turning into hiccups and then into occasional whimpers, Shelby's own heart was still racing. She couldn't make herself forget Jack Cotter's big, dark presence in the open doorway, or the trembling in her own body as the aftershocks of pleasure rolled through her.

"So you don't call this running away, huh?" His voice was deep and rough.

Shelby didn't want to meet his eyes. Every time she did, she found herself responding to him in ways that she didn't intend. There was something in his deep brown gaze that spoke too eloquently to her, that touched places she couldn't afford to pay attention to if she was going to keep her head clear about all of this.

"I call it being practical," she said, laying Emi on her back on the bed. A diaper change would probably complete the transformation back into Emi's usual sunny self, she thought. "That's my life right now, Jack. It's what any parent's life is—figuring out the best thing to do, and then doing it. Maybe it's not very romantic, but it's my reality at the moment."

And dirty diapers were one of the most effective reality checks Shelby knew of. But somehow even that mundane task wasn't enough to dispel the memory of Jack's handsome, darkly tanned profile against the white skin of her thighs.

She tried to resist the temptation, but she couldn't quite manage it. As she reached for the talcum powder, she looked up at him.

He was still arrestingly half-naked, and she had the distinct impression—although she didn't dare let her eyes linger too long to make sure of it—that he was still dealing with the same desires that were surging through her own body despite her best efforts to subdue them. The sexy tilt of Jack's hips as he leaned on the doorframe was enough to make Shelby's heart beat faster again, and the idea that he still wanted her—that his own hunger hadn't found release as hers had—

She shook her head and made herself focus on the task at hand.

"This is all wrong, Jack," she said. Her voice didn't sound quite as decisive as she'd hoped, but at least the words were blunt enough.

They didn't seem to convince him, though. "I was admittedly a little swept up in the moment myself just now," he began, and then paused.

Shelby felt herself blushing, and wished she could get past her sudden breathlessness at the memory of the way Jack had made all her senses reel with the hot touch of his mouth and his hands.

His eyes darkened as he was speaking, and she wondered if he was reliving those same dizzying moments, and if that explained the rough, ravenous edge she could hear in his voice.

"But I could have sworn you were enjoying yourself, too," he went on. "Why the sudden change of heart?"

A change of heart... The description was far too accurate. Jack Cotter *had* changed something in her heart, something she didn't understand and didn't want, but that seemed to be calling all kinds of things back into life at the very moment when she was least equipped to deal with them.

"We're just wrong for each other," she said, powdering Emi briskly and reaching for a fresh diaper from the bag. "Can't you see that?"

All Jack could see was the way Shelby's fair skin was still touched with pink, and the tantalizing gap where she hadn't buttoned the front of her shirt all the way.

And he could see baby Emi's smile, too, when she rolled her head back on the bed and caught sight of him. She waved her dimpled little arms in the air and crowed with undisguised delight.

"Dja," she said. "Dja voo. Dja voo!"

"Emi seems to think we're suited just fine," Jack said.

Shelby was refusing to be drawn. "Babies' tastes are a little unrefined at this age," she told him. "And I'd just as soon leave Emi out of this, if you don't mind."

Jack recrossed his arms over his chest and tried not to think about how it would feel to step up behind her, to slide his hands under the edge of that faded chambray shirt and settle his palms around the soft weight of Shelby's breasts again.

Think, Cotter, he told himself. *Fantasizing isn't going to accomplish anything.*

"Seems to me like you're trying to have it both ways, lady," he told her. "First you say you have to be practical because you have Emi to consider, and then you tell me she's not a part of the discussion."

Shelby didn't answer, although he could tell she was turning his words over in her mind, trying to find a hole in his logic.

"You know what I think?" His own frustration made him blunt. "I think you just don't want to share Emi with anyone else. You're used to having her to yourself. You don't like anybody else calling the shots."

Her hazel eyes flashed so suddenly that he knew he'd hit a sore spot. "I thought that was *your* stock-in-trade," she told him. "You're the one trying to make all the decisions around here."

"What I'm trying to do—" Jack paused.

What exactly *was* he trying to do? Why had it been so utterly impossible to resist the soft sweetness of Shelby's mouth, impossible not to follow the impulses that had pulled him close to her? And why, in spite of her determined resistance, was he still aching with the need to hold her again?

"I'm trying to understand what the hell is going on between us," he said finally, gruffly. "I'm supposed to be good at figuring things out—that's what I get paid to do. But I'm really not getting anywhere with this one."

There was a very long silence in the room.

Even Emi seemed to sense the tension between her mother and Jack. She lay silently with her blond head swiveling on the flowered bedspread, turning her upside-down stare first one way, then the other.

"All I know—"

Shelby's voice was lighter and huskier than usual when she finally started to speak. Jack wondered why that soft, uncertain note touched him so deeply.

And why her words had petered out on her.

She shook her head and tried again. "The only thing I can figure out about this is that it shouldn't be happening," she said. He started to argue, but she jumped in ahead of his words. "I'm not denying that what just happened felt good. It felt—better than it had any right to feel."

Well, that was something, anyway. At least he hadn't completely misread her reactions.

But—

"I just don't want any part of the world you live in," she said. "And I don't want Emi having any part of it, either. My God—you carry a gun around with you, you walk into situations any sensible person would stay miles away from, you—" She cut herself off this time. "It scares me, Jack. I've been there once, and I don't want to go back. Can't you see that?" He could, only too clearly.

But there was something she *wasn't* saying, too.

She'd lost her husband to a criminal's bullet. Jack didn't blame her for hating the idea of getting involved a second time with a man whose work took him into the grim world of crime every day of his life.

But she'd loved Emilio Sabinal. Loved him enough to have his child. And then she'd lost him, without any warning, in the grimmest possible way. Jack had had a hard time forcing himself to look at the photographs in the case file at his office yesterday, because his mind's eye had insisted on presenting him with the image of Shelby cradling her husband's shattered body in her arms, holding his lifeless form against her belly, where their baby was just starting to grow.

He didn't need to have that part of it explained to him.

What he *didn't* understand was why she was so reluctant about Jack.

If she was so worried about what might happen to Jack in the course of his job—didn't that mean she had to have some kind of feeling for him in the first place?

That was the part she wasn't saying, and it was driving Jack nuts.

He was used to laying his cards on the table anytime it suited him. If this had been a routine assignment—if Shelby Henderson had been just another witness in need of help— he'd have put his thoughts into words by now. *You can't be scared of losing me unless you care about me to begin with.* He could almost hear his own voice tossing the challenge across the charged space between them.

But he was scared, too, damn it. He was out of his depth here, and he knew it.

The connection he shared with his brothers was something the three of them never discussed. It was there, and it was important. But it was unspoken, because Sam and Wiley, like Jack himself, had learned early in their lives to be cautious about opening themselves up to other people.

This was something different.

He didn't know where he stood with Shelby Henderson. And he wasn't entirely sure he wanted to find out.

"Ba-ba," Emi said suddenly, reaching one dimpled hand over her head toward Jack. "Dja. Ba-ba!"

"Is that so?" He held a forefinger out to her, and was amazed at the strength of her grip when she seized it and waved her arms up and down. "I'm glad to hear you expanding your vocabulary, sweet pea, but I can't say I'm exactly sure what you mean."

"It might be bath related." Shelby was eyeing her daughter critically. "She hasn't had a proper bath for ages. Usually we have one every couple of nights."

Emi let out a high-pitched squeal, which Jack assumed meant she approved of the bath idea. Before he could offer to help, though, Shelby had scooped the baby up and was disappearing into the bathroom with her.

Any port in a storm, Jack thought. He wondered what Shelby would have used as an excuse to avoid him if the bath hadn't presented itself.

He went back into his own room and pulled his shirt over his head. He could hear running water as he dialed room service and ordered some supper for himself and Shelby. Then he tried to focus his attention on the notes he'd taken in Houston yesterday. But his own tight, dark handwriting seemed indistinct and hard to read, and he kept catching himself listening to the sounds of baby laughter and splashing water from the next room.

At one point the laughter turned to protest, and then to a wail, which started and ended abruptly. A few minutes later Jack heard the bathroom door squeak as it opened.

"Jack?"

He was on his feet before he realized just how eagerly he'd been hoping to hear her voice.

"Yeah?"

"Can you spare a hand for a couple of minutes?"

It was a ridiculous question. Here he was, sticking with Shelby Henderson like a burr, refusing to leave her on her own despite all her attempts to convince him that he should, and she was politely asking whether he could give her a hand for a couple of minutes. Jack shook his head, grabbed the rubber duck he'd bought from the bag at the foot of his bed, and headed into the other room.

The problem seemed to be shampoo. "I can't hold her up and wash her hair with only one good hand," Shelby said as Jack knelt on the bath mat beside her. "And she hates getting shampoo in her eyes."

"I don't blame her. I hate it myself." He flattened one palm against Emi's back and waited while Shelby squirted shampoo into her left palm. "God, she's so slippery," he added. "Aren't you afraid she'll slide under the water?"

He saw her smile faintly. "Welcome to parenthood, Jack," she said, and reached forward to massage the shampoo into Emi's fine blond hair.

How did you wash something that was barely there to begin with? Jack wondered, as he helped Shelby rinse the suds out with a washcloth. How did you keep hold of a squirming little creature who didn't know that the water she was splashing in so contentedly could kill her if she landed in it the wrong way? How did you explain that soap wasn't a toy, and it wasn't food, either?

Jack was used to coping with bullets, and bombs and knives—all the standard types of danger. He'd never considered how hazardous a simple evening bath could be.

He thought about the criminals he'd had to face down at one time or another. Most of them had been susceptible to distraction, if you timed your move just right. He waited until Emi's hair was clean and she was trying to get to her feet in the tub, and then he pulled out the rubber duck.

"Bribing a baby?" Shelby's comment was almost drowned out by Emi's loud peal of laughter. "Taking your cue from Jerry Lawrence, are you, Jack?"

"I prefer to think of it as cementing a done deal." Jack pushed the rubber duck under the water and let it bob to the surface again, to Emi's obvious delight.

"Diggin!" she said firmly.

"That means 'do it again about a thousand times,'" Shelby translated.

"Yeah, I kind of figured that."

It felt good to make Emi laugh, and to see Shelby finally start to smile, too. It was amazing how little it took to amuse an eleven-month-old baby, and how versatile a toy a rubber duck could be. The duck could quack, it could sing—Emi didn't seem to notice that its singing bore a distinct resemblance to Jack's own rendition of "The Yellow Rose of Texas"—it could hide under the bedspread once bath time was over, it could fly through the air with the greatest of ease and severely startle the hotel attendant who'd brought their dinner.

"Sorry about that," Jack said, as he added a couple of bucks to the guy's tip. "You know how it is during migrating season."

"Yeah, sure." The young man rubbed the spot where the duck had bounced off his head and gave Jack a funny look.

It was good to know with certainty that they were safe, that Jerry Lawrence couldn't trace them to this out-of-the-way hotel.

It was good that he and Shelby seemed to have arrived at some kind of truce, that she even let him kiss Emi goodnight before she settled the baby into her crib for the night.

It was good, but it wasn't good enough.

Jack waited until Shelby had dimmed all the lights in her own room, and then he stepped through the connecting door and said, "We need to talk."

Chapter 9

"I agree."

She stepped through the door after him, leaving it half-open behind her. She sounded brisk again, as if she'd decided that keeping her distance was the best way to deal with the attraction that still hummed between the two of them.

She didn't *look* brisk. Most of her blond hair had pulled free of its elastic while she'd been leaning over the tub bathing Emi, and she'd finally given up on the ponytail altogether, letting the silky strands fall loose over her shoulders. Her skin was still rosy and glowing from the moisture in the bath, and there was a buried gleam in her hazel eyes that kept snagging Jack's own gaze.

She looked as though she were still as deeply stirred as he was. But on the outside, at least, she was trying to come off as pure business.

"Where exactly does your investigation stand now?" she was asking, as she seated herself in one of the two upholstered chairs in Jack's room.

He lowered himself onto the edge of the bed, wishing he could forget how it had felt to settle onto the mattress with Shelby clasped tightly in his arms a few hours earlier. "We set a couple of different things in motion yesterday," he told her.

"Such as?"

Jack's concentration, when he was in the midst of an investigation, was near-legendary among his colleagues. His brothers, too, joked about it from time to time. *You'll be looking for clues at your own funeral, big brother,* Sam had told him more than once.

He wasn't looking for clues tonight. He was watching Shelby Henderson's slender fingers lacing themselves together in her lap, and wishing he could feel those same gentle hands tracing the outlines of his body again.

He frowned, and tried to stick to the facts. "We figure the best way to wrap this up is to get Jerry Lawrence behind bars in a hurry, on a charge that'll stick this time," he said. "We've got a couple of different ideas about how to do that."

"What are they?"

She wasn't going to let him off with generalities. Well, Jack could understand that. He didn't believe in easy answers, either.

"The witness who got shot—the guy who was supposed to testify that the men you saw in Lafayette were on Jerry Lawrence's payroll—had a wife who might have seen something we can use as evidence," he said.

"You think she'll be in the mood to talk to you?" Her voice was light but challenging.

Jack shrugged. "Won't know 'til we try," he said. "Some people are hungry for revenge. Some aren't." He saw the gleam in her eyes intensify at that, but he went on before she could speak. "So far we don't have specifics about exactly where this woman is—Jessie filed most of the information on it—but we're working on it. And we're looking into Jessie's accident, too. We figure there's got to be a connection with Jerry Lawrence, and if there is, an eyewitness might be able to give us something—a license number, a physical description of a driver—that we can use. The police have accepted it as a simple accident, but if we keep looking—who knows? We might turn up something."

"Even if you do, you'll still have to link it to Lawrence somehow."

"I know. I didn't say this was going to be simple, Shelby. Lawrence still has an efficient operation set up, even though he's been out of the picture personally for the past while. Or at least we've been assuming he was out of the picture. On the off chance that we're wrong, we're going to get my buddy Mack MacGuire to look into any cases he can find of possible bribery cases in towns along the border. If Lawrence has been active on a smaller scale without us being aware of it, we might be able to nail him on bribery charges."

She considered that information. "What are the chances of these things working?" she wanted to know.

"Of the three, I'm putting my money on the witness's wife. The other two are outside shots, but once in a while those turn up pay dirt."

She nodded, as though his words confirmed what she already knew about police work. She was a policeman's widow, after all. She knew—all too well—that there were very few guarantees in the world of law enforcement.

For some reason Jack didn't want to think about that. He knew it was irrational. After all, he had no claim on Shelby Henderson, and she'd made it very clear that as far as she was concerned, he was the wrong man for her and Emi.

But he still hated the idea of Shelby being in love with another man, a man who'd no doubt been steady and predictable and domestic and all those things Jack so conspicuously was not. Thinking about Shelby's recent past made him uncomfortable as hell, so he turned his thoughts to her future, instead.

"Assuming we *can* get Jerry Lawrence back behind bars, will you listen to reason and let us find you a safe place to stay?" It felt like the hundredth time he'd asked her the question.

And her answer hadn't softened one bit. "I'll listen to reason," she said. "But I won't let the FBI—or anyone—dictate what I'll do with my life, or with Emi's life."

Jack leaned back on his hands, crossing one leg over the other, trying to rein in his frustration. "Some people would say you were ignoring Emi's best interests here," he pointed out. "What kind of a life is she going to have if you're forever in hiding?"

"She'll have her own life—not some storybook identity concocted by the witness protection program." Shelby was sitting up straighter now, Jack noticed. She looked like a rider on a horse that was starting to show signs of rebellion.

"Would that be so bad?"

"Yes." Her answer shot back without hesitation.

"Would you mind telling me why?"

For an instant he thought she was going to tell him that she *did* mind, that she had no intention of sharing her thoughts on the subject with him. She got to her feet and paced as far as the windows as if looking for escape. But when she reached the darkened panes, she turned and answered him.

"I know what it feels like not to know who you really are," she said. "I won't do that to my daughter."

"Wait a minute." Jack stood up, too, shoving his hands into the pockets of his jeans as he moved to lean on the doorframe. "What are you talking about? You said you were a minister's daughter from Almagorda, Texas. Hell, your file said so, too. I looked it up. How can you—"

For some reason she looked angry about having to say the words. "I was *adopted* by a minister and his wife," she said tightly. "They found me on the church steps in a plastic laundry basket."

"Good Lord."

It was the last thing Jack had expected. He'd been picturing Shelby Henderson as a product of the most settled life possible—a minister's daughter, for Pete's sake, in a small Texas town. But what she was telling him—and the defiant look in her eyes underscored it—was that the reality was something very different.

He sat down in the chair opposite the one she'd just vacated, and leaned his elbows on his knees, hands clasped in front of him. "Who were your real parents?" he asked.

He saw her hesitate again. He'd made his manner as matter-of-fact as he could, calling on all his experience of questioning reluctant witnesses. People would talk about the most unspeakable things, he'd found, if you didn't make a big deal out of it.

But Shelby Henderson was more stubborn than most people. More determined to keep her own counsel. More—well, hell, Jack thought. She wasn't like anyone else he'd ever met. The taut exterior she worked so hard at covered the most astonishingly vivid depths, the most amazing openness and passion.

And what she was telling him now seemed to go a long way toward explaining why she'd pulled that taut exterior around herself in the first place. Jack did his best to put a lid on his impatience, and waited for her answer.

It was brisk, when it finally came, but he knew by now that the crisper she sounded, the more she was trying to cover up. "I have no idea who my real parents were," she said. "Almagorda is just off the highway that leads to and from Louisiana. It would only have taken ten minutes for somebody to stop, leave me at the church, and get back on the road."

Just like dropping off the laundry. No big deal. That was what her tone was trying to tell him, but Jack didn't buy it.

"So the minister and his wife took you in."

"Apparently it struck them as the Christian thing to do."

"Do you think they really wanted you?" It wasn't the gentlest of questions, but Shelby didn't blink at it.

"Yes and no," she said. "They were conscientious parents. I owe them a lot. But—"

She hesitated, and for the first time Jack saw a tiny crack opening up in that impervious facade.

She was thinking of Emi, he thought suddenly. She was thinking of everything she wanted to give to her daughter, all the things she hadn't had herself. He wasn't sure why he knew it, but he would have bet money that that was what was running through her head.

"They were elderly," she said at last. "They'd raised their own kids already. They were looking forward to retirement. I was—a duty to them, more than anything else."

Jack felt something inside him flare without any warning at all.

From the moment he'd set eyes on Shelby Henderson, he'd had the feeling the two of them shared something important, something hidden and instinctive, something most people didn't even know the name of. Although their plans and their life-styles and nearly everything else about them had clashed from the very beginning, something had been drawing them together at the same time.

And suddenly he began to understand what it was.

He got to his feet as well, because he felt too restless to stay seated in the chair.

"It's rough, isn't it?" His voice was also rough, as though these words had waited a long time to make themselves heard. "Being somebody's Good Deed, I mean."

"Yes. It is." Her agreement was quick. "I suppose you know all about that."

"You bet I do." Jack pushed his hands through his hair, and shook his head. "Foster parents—at least the kind I ended up with—tend to be quick to point out that they're doing you a favor, so you have no real right to complain."

"Or to try to change the program."

Jack snorted. "I know," he said. "Hell, I had one set of temporary parents decide that my brother and I would grow up quicker if we weren't together all the time. First thing I knew, Wiley'd gotten shipped off to another home at the far end of the state."

"That's terrible!" Her eyes blazed with sudden indignation.

Jack fought back his own instinctive response to the flash of feeling in Shelby's face. He wanted to step closer to her, to reach for her, to pull her into his arms. But he knew—with that same quick, bone-deep certainty—that she would resist his embrace right now. They were touching on things that were too tender, things she didn't normally let up into the light of day.

And he wanted the moment to continue. He wanted to know everything there was to know about Shelby Henderson.

"It hurt like a son of a bitch at the time," he said. "Hell, Wiley was all I had in the world in the way of family. But being on my own taught me a useful lesson or two."

Shelby was shaking her head, but it wasn't her usual gesture of defiance. There was something sad in the way her eyes met his, and then glanced away.

"I know," she said. "You grow up quick, and you grow up resilient. It's just—I don't want Emi growing up that way, that's all."

"God, no." Jack shook his own head. He thought about Emi's sunny, trusting nature—about the way she greeted the world with such abandon, such glee. He couldn't imagine those wide baby smiles gradually shutting down into the tight, cautious responses of a child who'd discovered too early that the world could be a cruel and deceptive place. "But I still don't see—"

Shelby swung her eyes back to his and held them this time. She looked as though she'd been forced into a place where she didn't want to be, he thought. As though she were telling him things she hadn't wanted to say.

But she said them anyway, steadily, not taking her eyes from his. He could feel the intensity in her gaze, and the ache of vulnerability at the very back of it.

"I was six when I discovered I wasn't who I'd thought I was," she told him. "I'd had an argument with a girl I was playing with, and she tossed the information at me that my parents weren't really my parents, and that I'd been found by the side of the road like somebody's cast-off shoes."

Jack shoved his hands into his pockets and made himself stay silent.

"Do you remember what it feels like to be six, Jack?" From the fierce edge to her voice, she remembered it all too well. That was what made her such a good mother, he thought.

Somehow—almost magically, it seemed to Jack—she seemed able to see and feel things from her daughter's point of view.

"At six, you're just starting to figure out where you fit in relation to the rest of the world," she went on. "I thought I had my world picture pretty much in place. And then I found out it was based on nothing—that nobody knew who I really was, or where I really came from."

At least Jack had had that, he thought. He'd had his own life. His own brothers. For better or worse, he was a Cotter, and he'd always been certain of that.

Shelby hadn't been certain of anything at all.

"It colored my whole world from that moment on," she said. "My parents didn't understand it—hadn't they given me everything I needed? They couldn't seem to see that they couldn't give me what I needed most of all. I needed *myself*."

And she'd had to create that for herself. Jack had a sudden mental picture of Shelby at thirteen, mutinously climbing out onto the church roof to make a gesture of freedom, a declaration of independence, announcing to the world that she didn't want to go with her adoptive parents to a place where she didn't belong.

She'd fought hard for that freedom, that certainty of who she was.

And she didn't want Emi to have to fight for it, too.

"I won't take my daughter's identity away from her the same way." Her determined words confirmed it as she stepped around Jack and closer to the open doorway between their rooms. "I won't tell her lies about who she really is, or where she really came from."

"Even to save her life?"

She lifted her chin toward him. "There are other ways of keeping her safe," she said. "I want her to know about Emilio, and about the place where she was born. I don't want her to discover when she's six—or nine or nineteen— that her past is a fraud. And I don't want her to live her whole life believing in a lie, either. I won't compromise on that, Jack. You can't ask me to do it."

He tried to come up with a good argument.

And failed.

He knew how hard it was to forge a life on your own—to grow up knowing there was no one you could trust but yourself.

He didn't wish that on Emi—sweet, sunny Emi.

And he didn't know what to say to Shelby, either, as she stepped back into her own room. She'd stirred too many things in him, left him grasping at too many questions he'd never really answered for himself.

Once you'd lost that innocence, that trust, how in the world did you get it back again?

Shelby had done it, somehow. She'd found the inner strength to create a family of her own, and to carry on raising her child after her husband's sudden death.

Jack's own brothers had done the same thing. Hell, they'd grown up as cynical and hard-edged as Jack was himself.

But they were about to ally themselves to the women they loved, declaring to the whole world that two of the Cotter brothers, at least, had found a way to trust that happy endings might actually come true once in a while.

For the first time Jack realized that there was a very good reason why he hadn't been feeling pleased about his brothers getting married.

It was jealousy, pure and simple.

They'd found a way to make it work. They'd discovered something Jack didn't even know how to begin searching for.

In some sense it seemed as though he and Shelby had become allies in the past hour—as though by exposing those deeply hidden, deeply suspicious parts of their natures, they'd begun to find their way toward some kind of bond, some shared strength.

And in another way, Jack felt more alone than he'd ever been in his life as Shelby gave him a cursory good-night and disappeared into her own room.

He didn't know what time it was when her soft cry awakened him.

He'd been sleeping restlessly, unable to find a place that seemed comfortable on the big mattress. Eventually he must have dropped into an uneasy slumber, because Shelby's voice pulled him out of a shadowy dream filled with people he couldn't quite identify and places he'd never been before.

"*No...*"

It was just a single word, ending in a shuddering gasp. But Jack was out from under the covers instantly, clicking on the bedside lamp, shrugging off sleep, ignoring the jeans he'd draped over the chair next to the bed and heading straight for the connecting door.

His first, confused thoughts were about Jerry Lawrence. Damn it, he'd been *sure* they were safe from Lawrence here, hidden from everyone except Jack's colleagues in the FBI. If they'd been tracked—if someone had gotten into Shelby's room—

No one had. The room was very dimly lit by the nightlight Shelby had plugged in next to Emi's bed. Jack could see Emi's little sleeping form stretched out in the crib, covered by a soft pink blanket. No one had invaded their sanctuary—at least, no one real.

Judging by the way Shelby was turning her head on the pillow and thrashing against the sheets, she was fighting off an invasion from inside, from her own sleeping mind. She was dreaming, Jack realized, and paused briefly in the doorway to give his heart a chance to stop slamming against his ribs quite so hard.

"Shelby..."

He murmured her name as he stepped forward again and settled himself gently on the edge of her bed. Her hair was loose and tangled, half covering her face, and Jack couldn't keep himself from reaching out to brush it softly back from her cheek as he said her name again.

"Shelby, it's okay. You're just having a bad dream."

It struck him that his low words were an echo of the way Shelby had calmed Emi down earlier in the evening, when the baby had awakened crying.

As far as Jack could see, the similarities stopped there.

The hunger that was rolling through his body now had very little to do with comfort, and a great deal to do with the way Shelby's silky golden skin felt under his fingers.

He'd come into her room half expecting danger.

But it was desire that was waiting for him instead.

He watched her smooth forehead furrow as she wrestled with whatever demons had intruded into her sleep. And then her eyes opened, suddenly, and he could see the same confusion and protest on her face that he'd heard in her voice just a minute ago.

Jack couldn't help it. He leaned down on one elbow and slid the other arm around her, breathing in the sweet scent of her skin as she pushed herself free of the covers.

"Shh, sweetheart," he said. "You were dreaming."

"Jack?"

There was no mistaking the astonishment in her voice. She sounded as if he were the last person in the world she'd expected to see when she opened her eyes.

"Yeah, it's Jack." He tried to convince himself not to thread his fingers through her hair again, and then gave up. It simply felt too good, too right, when those golden strands cascaded over his palms like this.

"It *is* you." She still sounded amazed. She put a hand up to his bare chest, resting her fingertips on the beating pulse point at the base of his neck. Jack felt his loins tighten as a surge of desire swept through him. "You're all right."

"Why wouldn't I be all right?"

The question was out before he'd thought it through. When he realized what the answer must be, the longing that had taken over his body was suffused with something new—something halfway between wonder and gratitude. He could feel it singing in his blood, demanding and triumphant and amazed.

She'd been dreaming about *him*.

Dreaming that something had happened to him.

And the astonishment in her voice—the relief that was so clear in her sleepy, husky tones—was because he was all right.

It was impossible not to ease himself down beside her, impossible not to pull her against him and to revel in the soft warmth of her body against his. He didn't ask her to tell him what she'd dreamt that had made her cry out on that note of fear and protest. He didn't want anything to interrupt this moment of exquisite intimacy, this fragile, potent connection that had somehow grown in the midst of all the darkness and uncertainty around them.

Jack didn't want to talk at all. Or to think.

He wanted to make love to Shelby Henderson.

And her soft sigh as she drew him closer to her told him that she wanted exactly the same thing.

Chapter 10

The shrouded edges of the dream were still swirling around her, but the heat of Jack's upper body and the reassuring strength of his presence was starting to banish the terror that had been crowding at Shelby when she'd wakened.

Jack's here. He's all right.

She repeated the words to herself as she nestled into his embrace. He *was* here, not lying on a street corner with a killer's bullets in his body, the way she'd been dreaming. She was holding a living, breathing man in her arms, not a dying one, as she'd held Emilio, as she'd dreamed—so vividly her heart was still pounding with the horror of it—just a few moments ago.

Jack was more than just here. He was cradling her with infinite care, with suggestive intimacy, as though his own dreams had been more of the erotic variety, and he was sliding back into them now, pulling Shelby with him.

She couldn't think of a single reason in the world not to go with him.

She knew there *were* reasons—that she'd been trying to keep her distance from Jack Cotter because he posed a serious threat to her hard-won independence, and to the security she needed if she was going to keep her heart intact.

But those reasons belonged to the daylight, to the cold scrutiny of common sense. They had no place here, in the depths of the night, when the simple facts of his nearness and his desire were enough to sweep aside all the questions Shelby had been grappling with for what suddenly felt like forever.

Right now, all she wanted was the shared strength that was hers for the asking.

All she wanted was this single moment of heat, of sensation, of respite from the dangers around her.

The tremors of nightmare-induced fear were gone now, replaced by the quivering of awareness in all her limbs as Jack's legs twined with hers under the sheets, and his arms gathered her even more closely against him.

His skin was warm and rough against hers. She was still wearing her blue chambray shirt—somehow she hadn't wanted to go to sleep naked—but there was nothing underneath it, and Jack's boxer shorts were a scant barrier between her body and his.

She couldn't hold back her moan when he shifted his position, easing one strong thigh deliberately between her legs. She couldn't hold herself back—couldn't stop herself from wrapping both legs around the muscled length of him, feeling his strength and sexuality seeping into her like a warm rain after a very long drought.

She was aware of Emi's sleepy voice in the crib by the door, murmuring something in response to her mother's low groan. Jack lifted his head to look over at the crib.

"Maybe we should relocate," he said huskily.

Earlier, Shelby had jumped at the excuse of tending Emi to escape Jack's all-too-suggestive embrace. Now she couldn't imagine denying the feelings that were coursing through her. How was it possible that so much had changed in such a short time?

She had no intention of pausing to answer the question. And maybe there was no logical answer to it, anyway. What she and Jack seemed to do to each other had nothing to do with logic.

"Maybe we should." She pushed her disheveled hair back behind one ear. "Do you think—"

"No. I don't."

His words were blunt, his voice abrupt, but Shelby didn't sense bitterness or anger in it. He was impatient, she thought, that was all. Just like she was herself.

His words underlined it. "I'm not thinking, Shelby," he told her. "Not just for the immediate future, anyway."

And with that pronouncement he swung his big body off the bed. Her sense of loss as he moved away from her lasted only a moment, until he leaned down and lifted her off the bed.

Shelby laughed. She couldn't help it. "Do you make a habit of sweeping women off their feet?" she asked him.

"Only when there's extreme danger involved." His voice was sensuously rich at her ear.

"What kind of danger are we talking about here?"

He gave a quick nod in the direction of Emi's crib. "Possible corruption of a minor," he said, and added, "One of the hazards of parenting, I guess."

"I guess." Shelby glanced at the crib, too, then looked back into Jack's eyes. Emi was safe, and warm and contented. And just at the moment, Shelby's mind was tantalized by other, more adult possibilities.

"It's—not a hazard I've had to deal with before now," she admitted, as Jack stepped into the other room and pushed the door half-shut with one bare foot.

Something sizzled in his dark eyes at her words, and she wondered if it was the same thing that was making her so breathless, almost light-headed.

There was a whole range of feelings and desires that she'd assumed had been obliterated by the loss and worry and responsibility she'd dealt with since Emilio's death. But earlier today, when Jack Cotter had caressed her into such overwhelming fulfillment, she'd realized they weren't gone after all. They'd been driven far underground, but they were still there.

And Jack seemed to know that as well as Shelby did.

It was a heady thought.

It made his kiss seem ripe with suggestiveness, when he'd lowered her onto his bed and eased himself down next to her.

It made Shelby's hands bold in ways that amazed her just as much as they seemed to astonish Jack.

She slid her fingers under the elastic waist of his boxers and heard him gasp against her mouth. The twinge of pain from her wrist was more than balanced by the way it felt to run her fingers over the seductively smooth place at the crease of his thigh. The sexy fold in his blue jeans at exactly that spot had been driving her crazy ever since he'd appeared in the bus station door.

The picture of him standing there, gun leveled, face grim, threatened to intrude into her pleasure for a brief moment. But Shelby chased it away again. Guns and bullets belonged to the nightmare Jack had just helped her escape from. They didn't belong here, not in the same room with the sweet sensation of Jack's hands curving up over her breasts under her half-unbuttoned shirt, or his tongue sliding alongside hers with such slow, erotic intent.

Her fingertips danced over the dark nest of hair at the meeting place of his thighs, and she felt his low groan buzzing all the way through her. How could she have resisted an attraction this powerful, this pleasurable? she wondered. She'd never felt anything like this rush of desire, this sense of stepping into a whirlwind without caring whether it tore her to pieces—hoping, in fact, that it might do exactly that. She could almost feel the force of her desire and Jack's tugging at her like a gale-force wind.

She slid his boxer shorts lower over his hips and circled the hard strength of his arousal with her hand. His groan this time was almost a protest.

It only made Shelby more daring. She stroked him with instinctive skill, enticing him almost to the point of release and then shifting her caresses to the slight indent at his hips, the warmed hollow at the small of his back, the long, muscular stretch of his thighs.

"Sweetheart..." His voice was even huskier now, ravaged by desire. "If you're trying to spin this out, you're going about it all wrong."

Shelby wasn't *trying* to do anything at all. She was letting the moment take her where it wanted to, as she hadn't done for a very long time.

It took her further, prompting her to toss her shirt onto the floor next to Jack's shorts, urging her to slide herself over him as he rolled onto his back. She felt the hardness of him pulsing at the juncture of her legs, and she wrapped herself around him as though she wanted to take all of his strength, all of his potency, into the core of her being.

She'd never felt so aroused and yet so much in command. She was aware of such tiny details—the dark shading of stubble along Jack's jawline—the masculine curve of his eyelashes when he closed his eyes at the sensation of her legs surrounding him—the way the light from the single lamp at the side of the bed fused their shadows into a single body on the flowered bedspread.

She leaned her weight on her right elbow and smoothed Jack's hair back from his face. His skin, when she kissed his forehead, then his cheekbone, tasted slightly salty, slightly sweet. His hands on her back, her thighs, her waist, were slow and sure, taking such obvious delight in the smooth curves of her body that she ached with it.

Suddenly Jack's patience seemed to reach a breaking point. His fingers became inquisitive, seeking out the secret responsive places he'd discovered earlier this evening, stroking her into a frenzy of delight until her sense of command was long gone and her voice sounded as ragged as his, and as pleading.

"Jack—this is driving me crazy..."

"Good." There was a rich satisfaction under the roughness of his words. "That'll teach you to wrap yourself around a man like that. If you had any idea how it feels—"

She had a pretty good idea. Jack slid one strong hand to the back of her neck and lowered her head to his for a long, demanding kiss, as though the language of touch and warmth and liquid was the only way, after all, to express what they needed to say to each other. She leaned into the kiss eagerly, tasting the explicit invitation in it, positioning herself above him at the same moment.

The feeling of him entering her body was like a return to life itself—like an awakening after an endless sleep. Shelby drew away from his kiss and spread both her hands on Jack's broad chest, arching her spine as she absorbed the whole length of him into her. Everything in her body realigned itself to the sensation of it, to the realization that something hollow and aching in her world, in her heart, had been suddenly and gloriously filled.

"Shelby—smile for me like that again."

She hadn't even known she was smiling. Her eyes were closed, her whole being focused on what she was feeling inside. Whatever her face looked like on the outside, it seemed to satisfy Jack. She could feel him reaching up to follow the curve of her cheekbone with one hand—could feel the wonder in the trembling touch of his fingers, the near reverence that matched the sound of his voice just a moment ago.

She started to move, slowly, erotically, and heard Jack groan as the unhurried motions of her hips pulled him deeper into her.

"Shelby, oh, sweetheart..."

She closed her eyes tighter. It was strange, she thought. Jack's voice—the rough, aching sound of her name as he called to her—seemed somehow familiar, almost as though she'd heard it in a dream a long time ago. She felt herself reaching toward that sound, her eyes still closed, her body moving to an instinctive rhythm that was beginning to build and assert itself.

Something was guiding her, some hidden, unsuspected wisdom that seemed to come from deep in her own body. *Slowly,* it said, and so she moved with excruciating slowness, drawing every possible instant of pleasure from Jack's closeness, from the way he moved in unison with her, from the slick sensation of their two bodies joining together, creating the kind of magic that had been beckoning to both of them since the first charged moment when they'd met.

"I don't know... how much longer..."

She could feel Jack fighting to maintain their slow pace, and losing. Her smile—she *was* smiling, she realized—grew broader. The bliss Jack had unlocked in her body had spread right through her now. And the moment felt so right—more right than anything she'd ever imagined. Every muscle she possessed was trembling with anticipation, with pleasure, with certainty that this had been meant to be.

She'd never felt a climax anything like this. Instead of the sudden starburst Jack had set off inside her before, she felt herself moving almost serenely toward a broad horizon that was growing brighter and brighter the closer she got to it. There was no sense of haste, no desperation. She seemed to have all the time in the world to savor the glow behind her eyelids, the way Jack's body was constricting and growing taut with release, the slow tremors from deep within that heralded the cresting of the wave inside her.

Her whole inner landscape had turned as bright as the sun itself before Shelby realized that this languid sense of serenity was deceptive. She'd been letting herself fall forward into the brightness of the light, certain she was sailing into a calm harbor, but now, without warning, everything started to shudder apart inside her.

She heard herself calling Jack's name—felt his arms circling her, holding her close to his still-heaving chest—and suddenly, achingly, utterly, everything came to pieces. Not just her nerves and sinews, but her thoughts as well, everything she was, everything she'd ever wanted or hoped for. When it was over, Shelby was left gasping for breath, clinging to Jack as though her life depended on it, almost weeping with the power of what she'd just experienced.

It was a long time before she was even aware that he was stroking her hair lightly, circling one gentle hand across her back.

It was even longer before she could bring herself to move. Somehow she wanted to stay here forever, where life seemed clear and tantalizing, and release brought such sweet, sweet pleasure with it.

But she was starting to feel cold. Jack seemed to realize it—he was already rolling to one side, lifting the covers as she moved slightly away from him.

Neither of them spoke. What was there to say, Shelby wondered, that their lovemaking hadn't already expressed more completely, more vitally than words ever could? What was there to add to the incredible sense of well-being that was washing over her as she settled back into the bed with the covers over her and Jack's strong, warm body curled around hers?

She thought she saw the faint light of very early morning under the bedroom curtains when Jack reached out one long arm to switch off the light.

She couldn't remember the last time she'd greeted a new day with such an overwhelming feeling of peace.

* * *

Click.

Somewhere at the back of his mind Jack knew what the faint sound meant, but he was too sleepy—and too contented—to figure it out.

Through a two-inch crack in the curtain, morning sunlight was streaming into his room. It mingled in his vision with the golden glow of Shelby's blond hair on the pillow next to him, and all of it—the warm haze of the light, and the honey-sweet scent of Shelby's skin, and the feeling of his naked body wrapped around hers—was gathering itself up into the slow burn of desire, stirring Jack's senses back into arousal before he was even awake.

And then he heard the second sound.

It came twice, and it was quick and harsh, like a tight, mechanical sigh.

And it was coming from the room next door.

Jack tried to fight off the sleep that was clinging to him, and the longings that were humming irresistibly through his bloodstream.

Something was wrong.

And he needed to figure out what it was.

"Jack...?"

Shelby's voice, hazy with sleep and satisfaction, didn't make it any easier to push himself away from her. More than he'd ever wanted anything else, Jack wanted to slide back down under the warm covers again. He'd never experienced anything close to the explosive passion of what had happened between them last night, and his body was telling him in no uncertain terms that he'd be crazy not to respond to the soft invitation in her voice this morning.

But something had snagged his attention, and he wanted to know what it was.

"Just a moment, sweetheart." He paused just long enough to drop a kiss on the hidden spot at the base of her ear, and then he pushed the covers aside and reached for his jeans. "You did put the chain on your door last night, didn't you?"

"Of course. And I bolted it. What—"

She didn't bother to finish her own question. Jack could see awareness flooding into her delicate, fine-boned features. He cursed himself for having stirred her out of her sleep and not into passion, as he'd wanted to do, but into fear again.

Still, fear wasn't something they could afford to ignore at this stage. And the next sound from the room where Emi was sleeping told Jack he'd been dead wrong to shove it out of his thoughts for as long as he had.

It was a grating noise, hard and clear. And while Jack wasn't a hundred percent certain what it meant, he knew it wasn't good news.

He was into his jeans by now, zipping them up in more of a hurry than his body would have liked. His gun was on the table next to the window. After the silken warmth of Shelby's skin under his hands, the weapon felt cold and foreign in his palm.

Shelby was out of bed now, too. From the corner of his eye he could see her pushing her pale gold hair back and reaching for the blue chambray shirt that lay in a crumpled heap next to the bed.

By the time she'd put it on, Jack was in the other room.

And he was too late.

The grating sound he'd heard had been an oversize set of cutters, almost as heavy-duty as the ones used to cut people out of wrecked cars. It had made short work of the security chain on Shelby's door. And the locks—Jack kicked himself as he belatedly identified the sound of a silenced gun—had already been shot off.

Please, God, he thought, *let them be after me, not Shelby, not—*

His worst fears were realized before he'd even had time to frame the thought. There were two men in the open doorway, silhouetted against the bright light from the hall. One of them held a .44 Magnum. The other had already reached into Emi's crib and was lifting her out.

He heard Shelby's soft gasp of protest from behind him.

"No—Emi—"

The baby was waking up. Jack could hear her first cranky little noises as the stranger plucked her out of her bed, or maybe it was her mother's cry she was responding to.

The one mercy, Jack thought, was that Emi didn't know what that cold circle of metal at her forehead meant.

Shelby started to launch herself toward the two strangers, but Jack put out an arm to stop her, barring her way.

"No," he said hoarsely. His heart was slamming urgently against the wall of his chest, making it hard to breathe.

"Wise move." The man with the gun was giving him a mocking smile. "One step, either of you, and she's finished."

They hadn't bothered to mask their faces. Why should they, when both Jack and Shelby had already seen the pair of them at the horse ranch a few days ago?

They'd been a jump ahead of these two men the first time. Now it was the strangers—Jerry Lawrence's hired killers—who had the upper hand.

Emi was squirming in the grip of the man who held her, but the second man didn't seem to mind. He stood close behind his buddy, shoving the muzzle of that damned gun up against Emi's soft baby skin.

It wouldn't matter where the bullet went, Jack thought with sick certainty. Emi was so little. The .44 was a big gun, more than big enough to—

He couldn't bear to think what it would do. His throat suddenly felt so thick he could hardly swallow. Emi's fractured cries were cutting into him like barbed wire.

They were affecting Shelby the same way, but at least she had the sense to stay where she was. Jack clamped down on the fear and protest and fury that were boiling up in him, and tried to get his mind to work.

Damn it, he'd handled kidnappings before. And hostage situations. There were rules for this kind of thing, ways to minimize the danger.

If only he could remember what they were—

If they wanted her dead, she'd be dead by now. The single thought spun into his mind.

The two men didn't want to kill the baby. They wanted her alive, as leverage for something Jerry Lawrence would probably get around to spelling out before long.

And the important thing was to make sure Emi *stayed* alive long enough for that to happen.

"Jack—we have to do something—"

Shelby was gripping his arm with convulsive strength. She'd held him this tightly last night, too, when their two bodies had catapulted together over the edge of a passion more intense than anything Jack had ever felt before. It was impossible, even now, even with Emi in such deadly danger, to clear those thoughts completely out of his mind.

This case had begun so simply, as a quick favor to his boss.

And somehow, without Jack realizing it, things had spiraled out of his control to the point where nothing was simple, where Shelby's touch and Emi's wails stirred such powerful emotions in him that it was all he could do to hold himself together.

"How about putting the gun down?" The man who held Emi gave a curt nod at the table behind Jack and Shelby.

Slowly, Jack put the weapon down. "Might save us all some time and effort if you tell us right now what you want to trade the baby for," he said.

The taller man, the one with the .44, gave a short bark of laughter. "You think Jerry tells—"

"Shut up." The other man glared his buddy into silence. "And you two, get into the other room. Now."

Emi's cries were heartbreaking. She might not realize exactly what was going on, Jack thought, but she knew perfectly well that things weren't right. She wanted comfort, and reassurance. She wanted her mother.

And Jack had to pull Shelby with him into the other bedroom, clamping an arm around her tightly resisting shoulders, ignoring her protests.

"Jack—I can't leave her—not with them—"

"We have to, sweetheart. We'll get her back, I promise."

The words nearly stuck in his throat. What right did he have to promise anything, when he hadn't been able to keep Emi safe in the first place? He'd been relying on his wits, and his experience, and his colleagues, and they'd all let him down, disastrously.

"Close the door behind you." The shorter man's voice cut through his churning thoughts.

It was all happening too fast. Jack clamped his back teeth together and told himself he couldn't afford to be sidetracked by the anguish in Shelby's voice as she called her daughter's name, or by the rising note of Emi's sobs. He needed to figure out—fast—what he was going to do next.

In all his years as an FBI agent he'd never been stuck in a situation this volatile without a contingency plan in the back of his brain. And now he had nothing—no gun, no backup, barely enough presence of mind to see that the worst possible thing he could do right now would be to lunge through the still-open door and try to take Emi back from the two men who'd grabbed her.

The only thing that would accomplish was to get himself killed. And although he was kicking himself as hard as he knew how, it wouldn't help Shelby or Emi if Jack got taken out of the picture at this point.

So he followed the kidnapper's orders and pulled the connecting door closed after he and Shelby had stepped through it. It took only a few seconds before the lock slid into place on the other side.

"Don't do anything stupid like trying to follow us." It was the one with the gun who was speaking from the other side of the door, Jack thought. He could hear Emi's cries receding in the background, as if the other man was already on his way out into the hall. "You'll find your car's got a couple of flat tires anyway. You just sit tight, and Jerry'll be in touch."

Jack was already reaching for his shirt and shoes as the door to the other room clicked shut. His gun was locked inside, inaccessible for the moment, but that didn't mean he was going to sit here chewing his nails while Emi's abductors made a clean getaway.

"Jack—if they see you following—"

He pulled his laces tight and wished his fingers weren't shaking so hard as he tied them. He was at the door before he answered Shelby's words.

"They won't see me," he told her.

Emi's cries were getting fainter. They'd taken the stairwell, he thought. It was what he'd expected—two burly men carrying a screaming baby would want to make as unobtrusive a getaway as possible.

It probably meant they had a vehicle already waiting outside the emergency exit on the ground floor. Thanking his lucky stars that he'd remembered *some* of the basics—he'd at least had the sense to check out the floor plan of the hotel when they'd arrived yesterday—Jack pushed the door open and sprinted out into the hall.

If he hurried—

If he could keep his head down—

A license number wouldn't tell him much, but at least it would be *something*—one small clue in the midst of too many questions.

He'd made it to the elevators before he realized Shelby was following him.

"Damn it, Shelby—"

She'd pulled his boxer shorts on under her long chambray shirt, and she was running barefoot along the carpeted hallway, making almost no noise. At first glance she looked pale and determined and focused, but when she caught up to him, he could see that her hazel eyes were wide with fear.

"Come on." The middle elevator dinged, and Shelby ducked inside a step ahead of Jack as the doors slid open. "If you think I'm sitting there by myself waiting—"

She didn't finish the sentence. Inside the elevator there were a couple of men in suits, clearly on their way downstairs for breakfast. They gave Shelby's disheveled costume a sidelong stare, but she didn't seem to notice. She was as taut as a harp string, Jack thought, vibrating to the same awful possibilities that were zinging through his own nervous system.

They were out of the elevator before the doors were even half-open at the ground floor. Jack had seized Shelby's hand without realizing it, and he wasn't sure which of them was urging the other along as they pelted through the lobby and out into the parking lot.

The sidewalk was covered with bright green artificial lawn. Jack knew the hard plastic must be hurting Shelby's bare feet, but she didn't slow down even slightly.

"There."

Her voice was husky with strain as she pointed to a long white car with tinted windows pulling smoothly across the middle of the parking lot.

"Got it." Jack dropped her hand and decided the only way to do this was to cut straight through the rows of cars between him and the white sedan.

If he could keep out of sight—

If he didn't have to think about Shelby at the same time—

If the men in the car hadn't spotted them already—

There were still too many "ifs" in this case, he thought savagely. And not enough time to do anything about them.

"Keep out of sight," he growled at Shelby. "I'm going to see if I can get the plate number."

There was no time to make sure she was listening. Ducking low, Jack headed for the first row of cars.

"Jack, be careful—"

He wished Shelby Henderson was a million miles away.

Or safe in his arms.

Having her so close to such danger made his head spin. He felt as though he were running across a minefield as he crossed the open space of the parking lot, and he was sweating by the time he'd taken cover behind a boxy green Volvo.

The white car was cruising slowly, clearly not wanting to attract undue attention. But even at that speed, it had almost reached the exit. There was no time to plan, no time for subtlety. Cursing inaudibly, Jack sprinted across the next open space and ended up with a clear view of the exit lane.

If it wasn't for that damned bush—

He could feel his gut telling him it was too risky, that he shouldn't stand up. But he overrode his own good sense, desperate to get at least one small piece of information that might let them get a step ahead of Jerry Lawrence. It would only take two seconds—all he had to do was get a clear view past those branches . . .

He could feel the muscles in his legs protesting as he pushed himself upright.

The license number of the white sedan seemed to sear itself instantly on his memory.

It was crystal clear—so clear that he didn't notice the rear window sliding open until it was too late.

His mind knew what was going to happen before his body felt the impact of it. It wasn't the silenced .44 this time, his brain told him—it was something with a longer barrel, something that would fire with more accuracy over this range.

It caught him before he could move, slamming into his right side and spinning him around. He could hear the squeal of tires as the white sedan raced away. A moment later the hard black surface of the parking lot came rushing up to meet him.

Chapter 11

He hung on to consciousness because he couldn't afford to let go—not yet, anyway.

His thoughts were starting to scatter on him. Only about half of them made sense, and he wasn't sure which half it was.

Shelby, get over here—

Get yourself someplace safe—

His entire right side felt numb. He wasn't sure where the bullet had hit him, but he knew it was going to start hurting like hell in a minute or two.

There were things he had to tell her before then.

If only he could keep them straight—

"Jack—oh, my God..."

The pure terror in Shelby's voice was enough to drag Jack's thoughts into some kind of order. He opened his eyes—he hadn't been aware of closing them—and saw her pale, frightened face looking down at him.

"You're bleeding—they shot you—"

For an excruciating moment all Jack could think about were the official police shots of Emilio Sabinal's body, and his own mental images of Shelby cradling her dead husband in her arms.

He didn't want her to have to do this all over again.

"It's all right—it's not as bad as it looks."

He knew he sounded like the hero of some cut-rate action movie. But he couldn't stand to see the panic in Shelby's eyes, or to think of how she must be feeling—what agonizing memories she must be reliving right now.

And it couldn't be that bad, anyway, if he was still conscious. Jack clung to that thought, and fixed his eyes on Shelby's. He could hear voices yelling in the background. He knew they didn't have a lot of time.

"Shelby, listen to me." Somehow he'd closed his fingers around hers. He could feel the strength in her grip, and he hung on to it as if it could keep him in one piece. "Get my wallet out of my hip pocket."

"Why—"

"Just do it, all right?" He closed his eyes again. Pain was starting to stab at him from somewhere low down in his rib cage. "You're going to need to play dumb, sweetheart. Can you do that?"

"I don't understand."

Jack winced as he tried to ease his weight off his left hip so Shelby could pull his wallet free. "Get the keys, too," he muttered.

He heard the faint jingle of his car keys as she dropped them into the breast pocket of her shirt.

"You need help, Jack. You need an ambulance. I've got to go—"

"*No.*" He told himself it wasn't just the idea of Shelby leaving him that made him feel so panicked. There were things they needed to get straight, damn it.

He forced his eyes open again and wondered why the car bodies above him had developed those bright, hazy edges.

He frowned, and clasped Shelby's hands again, and said as clearly as he could, "As far as you're concerned, you don't know who I am, all right? You came running when you heard the shot. You don't know who the shooter was. You don't know anything at all. And you don't mention Emi to anybody—no matter how hard it is to stay quiet about it. Have you got that?"

Her face looked blank for a moment, or maybe it was just the red-hot pain that was making everything seem suddenly distant. When Jack got the world back into focus again, Shelby was nodding.

"We don't want the police involved," she was saying.

"Right. The less anybody knows about this, the happier Jerry Lawrence will be."

And the happier Jerry Lawrence was, the better their chances were of getting Emi back alive. He didn't have to spell it out—he could see the awareness of it in Shelby's intelligent eyes.

"Should I call the FBI?"

"No." The word came out more faintly than he'd intended, but it still sounded strong enough to surprise her.

"But you need—"

"That's how they found us, Shelby." He was having a hell of a time keeping his eyes open. His body was demanding all his attention, stabbing at him with shards of pain that were getting harder and harder to ignore. The simple act of breathing was suddenly almost more than he could manage.

He didn't know how Shelby was reacting to his words. And he couldn't get his mind focused enough to spell out any of the details—how the only way to trace his car license number and the credit card he'd used was through the FBI itself. Jack wasn't sure how Jerry Lawrence had managed it, but someone at the Bureau had to be on the bastard's payroll.

And it had cost Emi's freedom.

''Call my brothers.'' His own voice sounded far away. ''Cotter Investigations. In Austin. Tell them what happened. Tell them—''

There were other people around now. Jack could hear voices, sharp and anxious.

''Get a doctor!''

''Put some pressure on that wound.''

''What the hell is going on?''

What *was* going on? Jack fought to hold on to what he'd been about to say, and felt it slipping away on him.

The number. Tell her the number.

He pulled Shelby's hand closer to him and felt her leaning over him. Even now, even when he was half-consumed with the pain in his ribs and the weakness that he knew had to be from shock and loss of blood, Jack could feel her warmth, her perfume, the spirited, feminine essence of Shelby Henderson that seemed to have become a part of him in some impossible way.

He wanted desperately to tell her what last night's lovemaking had meant to him.

He wanted to say *You make me feel things I've never felt with any other woman.*

He was pretty certain he wasn't dying.

But just in case he was, he wanted Shelby Henderson to know how she made him feel, how she'd somehow altered and illuminated the landscape of his heart so that he barely recognized it.

''There's an ambulance coming.''

''Give the man some air, will you?''

Jack almost smiled.

Every time somebody got hurt, there was a voice in the crowd saying *Give him air.* Sometimes it had been Jack's own voice mouthing the words.

''Jack—hold on, all right? There's an ambulance on the way.''

"I know." He wasn't sure whether his words were audible. He tightened his grip on Shelby's hand, and tried to pull himself a little closer to her.

The scent of her skin swirled around him, and he clung to it as he felt the darkness reaching up to surround him. He couldn't find the words he wanted to say, and he wasn't sure there were words for it, anyway. He had no right to ask anything of Shelby Henderson, and no right to promise her anything beyond simple safety.

His own safety seemed more and more precarious as the pavement started to tilt underneath him. He could feel himself losing his grip, and even the thought of Shelby's face was starting to recede into the dim light around him. There were futile phrases of longing and passion beating at his ears, demanding to be said, but Jack knew that even without a bullet hole in him, he didn't have what it took to shape those vague intuitions into words.

And there wasn't time anyway.

With the last of his energy, he managed to murmur the license number he could still see behind his closed eyelids. And then he felt the edges of his concentration ebbing, and everything around him slid into blackness.

It was almost midnight when the phone finally rang.

The day had felt endless. In some ways it had been even worse than the day following Emilio's death.

Shelby had spent a good deal of that day, too, answering questions for the police. But at least then she'd been able to tell the truth. The police and the FBI had seemed like allies then.

And she'd been dealing with certainties.

Emilio was dead.

She was pregnant with his child.

And she was a danger to the two men she'd seen in her kitchen half an hour before Emilio was killed.

Those facts had been stark but unchangeable. And so she'd had to deal with them—slowly, painfully, but imperatively.

Now she wasn't sure which way to turn.

For her own sanity she had to believe that Emi was still alive. Why else would Jerry Lawrence have gone to the trouble of kidnapping her, if not to use her as a bargaining chip in some horribly mercenary way?

But she had no idea where her daughter was.

And Jack—

She hadn't begun to sort out her thoughts about Jack Cotter, even after a whole day of trying.

She'd waited until she'd seen him safely bundled into the back of the ambulance, and then she'd hightailed it back into the lobby, ignoring people's curious stares at her mismatched outfit and bare feet. It hadn't been easy to come up with a believable story for the desk clerk, but she'd finally managed, and she'd kept her voice almost level as she'd told it.

She'd been wakened by the sound of Jack arguing with a pair of strangers, she said. No, she didn't know him well. He'd picked her up yesterday when she'd been hitchhiking with her daughter, and he'd been kind enough to pay for her hotel room last night. Yes, she knew it sounded unusual. But he'd been . . . an unusual sort of man.

And tantalizing, and baffling, and so achingly sexy that Shelby had let her heart race miles ahead of her brain, and had spent the night in his bed instead of sleeping next to Emi, where she belonged.

She didn't say that part to the desk clerk. She pretended not to see the young woman's raised eyebrows, and went on to explain that she'd stepped outside her room to see what all the shouting was about, and had inadvertently locked herself out. She'd seen Jack chasing the two men, and had been watching when he was shot. Beyond that, she didn't really know anything. Luckily, the pair of businessmen who'd been in the elevator with her and Jack seemed to have disappeared from the scene, so there was no one to contradict her story. It was hard to keep her voice steady when the shock of watching Jack's big body spun around by the shot from the car was still reverberating through Shelby's whole frame. But she couldn't let the desk clerk see that.

Or the police.

She managed to get up to her own room before the squad cars arrived. She buried Jack's wallet and keys in the depths of her padded bag, nearly choking over the familiar scent of talcum powder that met her when she undid the zipper.

Emi's toys were still scattered around the room, but Shelby couldn't bring herself to pick them up. It was all she could do to lift Jack's gun off the table where he'd set it down, and to hide it, too, under the diapers and rompers that were neatly folded and waiting for another day of caring for her baby daughter.

She was on the edge of helpless, hysterical tears by the time the police knocked on her door. She managed to push her feelings deep down inside—would there ever be a time when she didn't have to clamp down on her fears like this?—and to meet them with a composed face and the request that they stay out in the hall so they didn't wake her daughter, who was still sleeping.

And then she'd told her story again.

And again.

And again.

The local police seemed to sense that there was something she was leaving out, but as interrogators they weren't terribly skillful, and Shelby was able to keep sidestepping their questions. No, she didn't know Jack had signed the register under another name. She'd known him only as Jack. She didn't know where he was from. No, she had no idea why his license number didn't appear in the registry's list. Or why he'd been carrying no ID when he'd been shot.

It didn't all happen at once. Between bouts of questioning, Shelby was able to get herself cleaned up and dressed, and to place a call to Cotter Investigations in Austin. She used the phone at the back of the lobby, because she didn't want the police to be able to trace the call to her room in case they turned out to be more enterprising than she'd thought.

And she wasn't sure she'd actually accomplished anything, even when she'd gotten through to Jack's brothers' agency. Neither Wiley nor Sam was around at the moment, a young man's voice informed her. Did she want to leave a message?

Shelby hesitated. Telling her story to a stranger went against every instinct she had. Look at the mess her life had turned into since she'd let Jack Cotter into it. Was she making an even bigger mistake by confiding in his brothers?

She was tempted just to hang up, but something stopped her.

Emi was gone.

Jack was in the hospital.

The FBI couldn't be trusted.

For all practical purposes, Shelby was completely alone in the world right now, cut off from any kind of support.

And somehow it didn't seem wise to burn the one single bridge she had left.

So she gave the man at Cotter Investigations the bare bones of her story, including the fact that Jack had been shot and the license number of the vehicle that had carried her daughter away. Her hands were shaking as she hung up the phone.

And then she'd waited.

It had taken hours for the police to stop buzzing around the hotel. She recalled this, too, from the day of Emilio's death. When you lived in a quiet little place, it didn't take much of an event to create a big stir.

When they'd finally gone, Shelby went out to the parking lot and took a look at Jack's car. Both tires on the driver's side were flat, and when she examined them closely, she could see the clean, round mark of a bullet hole in each one.

The sight threatened to crumble her resolve all over again. She thought about the two shots that had taken Emilio's life—those ridiculously neat bullet holes in his chest. She remembered staring down at them, unable to believe at first that anything so precise and small could be so deadly.

If the bullet that hit Jack had been a couple of inches to the right—

If the man holding that damned gun to Emi's forehead had decided to squeeze the trigger—

You can't think about those things, or you'll go crazy.

How many times had she repeated that phrase to herself over the past couple of years? She'd clung to it in the middle of some very dark, very lonely nights. Repeating it to herself now made her feel bleak and alone. But at least it was familiar. And it gave her just enough strength to focus on the immediate task at hand.

Luckily the local police hadn't decided to impound Jack's car. Just as luckily, Shelby hadn't lost all her cash to those three drifters at the bus station yesterday. Finding a repair service that was willing to come out and replace the two flat tires took some time and a few phone calls, but the offer of an extremely generous fee—in cash—finally did it. By late afternoon the car was in operating condition again.

By early evening she'd called the hospital in the nearest town, thirty miles away, and discovered that Jack was out of danger but still sleeping off the anesthetic after minor surgery to repair a shattered rib.

By eight o'clock she was climbing the walls.

And the phone didn't ring until midnight.

Why hadn't Jerry Lawrence or one of his henchmen called her? Were they afraid the phone line might be tapped? In that case, how was she ever going to find out where Emi was? How would she know what she had to do to get her baby back?

When the phone by her bed finally rang, Shelby grabbed it immediately. But it wasn't the call she'd been hoping for.

"Are you Shelby Henderson?"

The man's voice was a slow drawl, deep and low and unexpectedly familiar.

It wasn't Jack. But it was close.

"Who is this?" she demanded.

"Sam Cotter. I'm Jack's brother. Are you okay?"

The question caught her off guard. She'd gotten through the day by focusing on other things—on Emi, on Jack's car, on the facade she had to keep up for the police's benefit. She *wasn't* okay—not even close—but she'd been coping by shoving her own feelings out of sight, down deep where they wouldn't spill over and blot out everything else.

Sam Cotter's simple query threatened to take the lid off all of that, and Shelby had to clamp down hard to keep her voice from trembling as she answered him.

"I'm in one piece, if that's what you mean," she said.

There was something ridiculously comforting about the way he chuckled in reply. He sounded cynical and sympathetic and as unerringly perceptive as his brother. "Fair enough," he said, and added, "I've had days like that myself," as though he knew exactly how much she was refusing to tell him.

This is a bad idea. Shelby held the receiver a little harder and tried to remind herself what a disaster it had been to let herself give in to Jack Cotter's dangerously seductive charms. It had been momentarily comforting to let herself dissolve into Jack's embrace, to let the undiluted passion of their lovemaking block out everything that was wrong in her life.

But she was paying the price for that passion now. And she didn't want to let herself weaken again, just because another one of the Cotter brothers seemed to know instinctively what was going on in her mind.

"Why are you calling me?" she asked briskly.

"To let you know we traced that plate number. I don't know what Jack's planning to do with it—"

Shelby didn't know either. And Jack wouldn't be planning much for the immediate future, anyway. Damn it, she'd been hoping this call would bring her some definite information at last, and instead it was just presenting her with more questions.

But at least the Cotters had traced the number of the car that had made off with Emi. "Tell me what you found out," she said to Sam Cotter.

"Car belongs to a guy in Fredericksburg." Fredericksburg was in the heart of the hill country, Shelby knew, roughly halfway between Austin and the quiet spot where she was now. "We couldn't find anything much about him—he seems to have plenty of money, although it's not clear where it comes from. Anyway, we have a name and an address, for what it's worth."

Shelby copied down the information on a sheet of hotel stationery. She was trying her best to keep thoughts of Jack out of her mind, but Sam's deep voice, so reminiscent of his brother's, was making it difficult to do.

"Are you—have you called the hospital?" she asked him.

"Yeah. In fact, Wiley's on his way down there right now."

So Jack wouldn't be alone when he woke up. For some reason that had been weighing on Shelby's mind ever since she'd looked down into his handsome, immobile face against the white sheet on the stretcher this morning.

Now, if she could just do something to make sure Emi, too, woke up to a familiar face tomorrow morning.

"Thanks," she said to Sam Cotter. "I appreciate the information."

"Hold on a minute. What are you—"

She didn't wait for him to finish. Tempting though it was to share her thoughts and her worries with Jack's brother, she didn't want to let herself do it.

Her padded bag was next to her on the bed, and she was already reaching into it, delving for Jack's car keys, as she said a hasty good-night and hung up the phone.

"This is the worst." Jack winced as he tried to turn around. He couldn't see over the counter in front of him, and he didn't like the feeling that he was being left out of what was going on.

"No, little brother, this is not the worst."

Wiley was busy scribbling his signature on something—no doubt the stack of forms the hospital wanted to have signed before they would allow Jack to check out against their recommendations. Jack had signed a bunch of them already, and he was impatient to get moving.

Except that he couldn't.

"The worst is that I get a phone call saying I have to come out to the middle of nowhere and identify your body." Wiley sounded as smooth as he always did, but Jack could hear an undercurrent in his voice that meant he was very serious about what he was saying. "Compared with that, finding you shot full of holes and fuming because you're stuck in a wheelchair is relatively pleasant."

"One hole," Jack reminded him. "I've only got one hole in me, and it—"

"Only hurts when you breathe, right?" Wiley finished for him.

It was regrettably true. Jack felt all right—a bit woozy, but clear enough—as long as he stayed perfectly still. As soon as he tried to move, or talk, or breathe, though, his right side lit up like an overloaded switchboard.

But he still hated having to ride in this damn chair. "Makes no sense," he muttered. "They don't care what you do as soon as you're out in the parking lot, but until then they insist on treating you like an invalid."

Wiley finished signing the last form with a quick flourish, and nodded to the orderly to indicate that Jack was officially ready to be sprung. "You're lucky to be leaving here on any terms," Wiley said. "Quit complaining about it."

Jack didn't feel lucky.

He felt like hell.

And the bullet that had redesigned one of his ribs was the least of his worries.

Shelby Henderson had trusted him to help her.

And he'd unwittingly led her husband's killer right to her door.

She'd opened up to him in a way that still had Jack's head spinning.

And that openness—that long-denied moment of passion—had cost her the thing she valued most in the world.

Jack had blown it, in every possible way.

In spite of his confident words, he had a couple of rough moments when it was time to step out of the wheelchair and climb into the cab of the black pickup truck. It was Sam's truck, and Jack had never noticed before just how high off the ground it was.

Wiley watched him without comment and without offering to help, which Jack was grateful for. Once he'd eased himself painfully into the passenger seat, though, there was no mistaking the concern in Wiley's deep voice.

"I'm not so sure we're doing the right thing here," he said.

Jack closed his eyes.

And saw Shelby's frightened, beautiful face.

"It's the right thing," he growled. "It's just not the *easy* thing." He could tell Wiley was getting ready to argue with him, and he didn't want to hear it. "You owe me this, Wiley," he said. "The FBI gave you a lot of backup when you were trying to get Rae-Anne away from that guy she was going to marry. And we helped you wrap up that case of Sam and Kelley's down in Cairo, too."

"I know it." Wiley started to put the truck in gear. "What I don't understand is why you called me and Sam, instead of your own buddies. This is a kidnapping case, Jack—it's the FBI's own bailiwick. Not to mention that you guys have resources we can't even imagine."

So Shelby hadn't told his brothers that part of the story. Jack sighed, and immediately regretted it.

"Unfortunately, Jerry Lawrence seems to have access to each and every one of those resources," he said stiffly. "Somebody's been leaking information to him. That's how he found us."

Wiley's short expletive was caustic and heartfelt. Jack couldn't have agreed more.

Nothing in his world was quite the way it had been just a few days before.

The agency he'd worked so hard for had let him down at the moment when he'd needed its help the most. Until he knew who was responsible for the information leak at the FBI, he couldn't risk letting any of his colleagues in on his whereabouts or his plans.

And even if he *had* been able to trust them, how could he have explained to them why this case had suddenly become so important to him?

He'd broken one of the cardinal rules of investigative work. He'd gotten emotionally involved with a subject.

And his involvement—the fact that he'd refused to let Shelby Henderson just disappear when she'd wanted to, not to mention the fact that she'd been sleeping in his bed when Jerry Lawrence's men had come to grab her daughter—had nearly ended in disaster.

There was still time to keep the ultimate disaster from happening. But Jack needed his head clear and his emotions firmly in check if he was going to fix what had gone wrong.

Yesterday, in a confused, panicky moment, he'd wanted to tell Shelby that he wanted desperately to hold on to the fragile beginnings of the trust and hope he'd felt every time they held each other close.

Today it was easy to see that those hopes hadn't been just fragile.

They'd been downright absurd.

If he'd listened to Shelby when she'd tried to tell him they simply weren't right for each other, Emi might still be safe. Jack might not have been shot. And Shelby herself wouldn't have been hurt so devastatingly.

Again.

Jack knew his older brother well enough to know that Wiley was probably getting ready to ask a whole raft of questions that Jack really didn't want to answer. What he wanted to do—what he needed to do—was to finish this case as quickly and as professionally as he could manage, under the circumstances. And that meant keeping his heart out of it.

"Mind if we get this show on the road?" he asked, nodding curtly at the windshield. "The sooner we wrap this up, the happier I'm going to be."

An hour later he was drumming all ten fingers impatiently on the knees of his jeans while he waited for Wiley to come back out of the hotel.

They'd agreed it made more sense for Jack to wait in the truck. There were too many variables—the police might still be around, or Jerry Lawrence's spies, or the hotel staff might raise an alarm if they saw Jack.

"Especially since you look like you died a week ago," Wiley told him, with a quick grin.

''Thanks.'' Jack's eyes were scanning the parking lot. ''My car's gone,'' he added.

''Police, you think?''

Jack hoped that was what it meant. He didn't like the alternative that was presenting itself to him, but he couldn't put it out of his thoughts. It made his stomach even tighter and his fingers restless as he waited for Wiley to return. And it made his voice sharp when Wiley finally slid back into the driver's seat after almost half an hour's absence.

''What's the story?'' he demanded.

''She's gone.''

Wiley's answer was blunt and to the point. And it didn't hurt *quite* as much as the bullet Jack had taken yesterday morning.

''She leave anything? A note, maybe?''

Wiley sounded sympathetic. ''Just this,'' he said, and handed Jack a yellow plastic duck.

Jack squeezed it. It quacked forlornly.

''*Damn* it,'' he said.

Wiley was pulling a sheet of paper out of his jacket pocket. ''I thought it might be worth checking over the room,'' he said, ''so I had a word or two with one of the chambermaids.''

''I'll reimburse you,'' Jack said.

Wiley waved the offer away. ''Somebody'd been scribbling notes on the pad of hotel stationery,'' he said. ''It was still in the drawer. Want to look?''

Jack had to admit he couldn't have pulled it off any more neatly himself. There, emerging from the pencil shading Wiley had rubbed over the blank page, was the impression of the words Shelby had written on the page over it: an address in Fredericksburg.

''It's the one Sam and I dug up last night,'' Wiley said. ''Sam must have called her after I left to come get you.''

''I'll throttle him.''

"Don't do that, little brother." Wiley was already turning the key in the ignition. "There aren't that many of us left on your side. It's in your best interests to keep us healthy."

They hadn't reached the hotel until midafternoon. It took a couple of hours to get to Fredericksburg, by the time they jogged from one little hill country town to the next, zigzagging northwest across territory where all the roads seemed to go in the wrong direction.

Wiley had brought a street finder map with him from the investigation agency he'd once run. Fredericksburg was a busy place by hill country standards, but it wasn't large, and it was easy to find the house they were looking for.

It was barely a block away from the wide main street. It was one of the town's old-style homes, a gracious limestone structure with a tall, square front and the kind of wrought iron balcony that made many of Fredericksburg's buildings look as though they couldn't decide whether they really belonged in San Antonio or New Orleans.

The late afternoon rush hour traffic made it easy to blend into the crowd as Jack and Wiley cruised the street a couple of times, getting a good look at the house.

"That guy in the maroon station wagon is just sitting there," Jack pointed out. "Think he's up to something?"

"'Course he is," Wiley said. "That's Grant. Sam sent him up here as soon as we got hold of the address."

"Oh." Jack turned to face the windshield again, holding his ribs carefully still as he moved. "I take back what I said about throttling Sam, then."

"'Course you do." Wiley spun the wheel and they came around for another pass.

The house looked quiet, although as the light dimmed outside someone switched on a couple of lamps in the front rooms. Was Emi there? Jack wondered restlessly. Was she all right? Did the people who'd nabbed her have any idea how to treat a baby? Would they care that you couldn't leave her alone in the bath, that she sometimes cried when she first woke up, that she hated creamed peas but loved squash?

Wiley found an unobtrusive parking spot and sauntered out to contact the Cotter Investigations agent who'd had the house under surveillance since early this morning. "He says there's not much going on," Wiley reported, when he came back to the truck. "A woman from a nanny service showed up early on—Grant overheard her at the door."

Jack's sigh of relief was so pronounced it nearly cracked his rib all over again.

"Other than that they seem to be laying low. The nanny's a definite sign the baby's in there, though, I'd say."

Jack agreed. He wished they could get closer to the place—they were parked down at the end of the block, where their view was blocked by an ancient wisteria vine that grew between the house and a big old sycamore tree in the garden. The vine spilled over the garden gate, its gnarled branches standing out against the black paint of the wooden fence. It was a pretty sight, but not the one Jack had come in search of.

As it turned out, if he hadn't been gazing at the wisteria vine he might have missed her.

They'd been sitting for about an hour when he saw something rustling in the branches. Probably a squirrel, or a cat, or both, he thought, and went back to trying to figure out how much backup a person would reasonably need to have before storming a fortress like that thick-walled limestone house.

The branches stopped rustling abruptly. And then Jack thought he heard shouting from inside the fence.

"Wiley—"

"I hear them." Wiley was already half out of the cab.

Jack stayed where he was. He couldn't run, and he didn't know yet what was going on. But his nerves, already tense, were jumping now, telling him something was happening and he needed to pay attention to it.

Wiley was too far along the street to see the side garden, but Jack still had a clear view of it. Something else was rustling now. It almost looked like—

It was. He could see a head—dark, he thought, and wearing some kind of hat, or maybe a kerchief—poking through the shrubbery between the limestone house and its neighbor. The person was moving awkwardly, as though he or she—definitely she, Jack saw, as she pushed a little farther through the undergrowth—was carrying something.

Something like a baby?

Jack leaned forward, ignoring the stab of pain from his rib.

He saw her stoop down to get clear of the overhanging branches. The figure was stout, her hair jet-black, nothing like Shelby's golden blond.

But she *was* holding a baby in her arms.

He hesitated, wondering if Jerry Lawrence had realized the house was being watched from the front, and had sent this woman out the side exit with Emi. But that didn't explain the shouting.

On the whole, this looked a lot like an escape.

He slid over into the driver's seat and turned the key in the ignition. His stitched and bandaged rib yowled in protest, but Jack clenched his teeth. *Later,* he told his body. *There'll be plenty of time to hurt later.*

There was barely time enough to switch the headlights on before he heard a shot being fired from the direction of the house.

And in the sudden glare of the lights, he recognized Shelby Henderson.

He couldn't imagine what she'd done to conceal her hair and her slender figure so completely. But as the beam of the headlights caught her, he saw the look of combined fear and determination in the quick flash of her eyes.

He'd have known it anywhere.

Grunting with the effort, he got the truck into gear and steered it away from the curb. Shelby had gotten free of the clinging hedge by now. She was starting to sprint across the lawn next to the house she'd just escaped from. Jack leaned over, wondering whether his whole rib cage had just caught on fire or whether it just felt that way.

"Shelby, get in!" He yelled the words at her as he pushed the passenger door open. The truck was still rolling, and he didn't quite have the coordination to deal with the brake and the door handle at the same time.

It didn't matter. Shelby was quick on her feet, despite the padding she'd obviously used to disguise herself. She was climbing into the truck cab in seconds flat, and by the time two chillingly familiar-looking men had come crashing through the shrubs after her, Jack had the truck in reverse and it was screaming backward down the quiet street and away from danger.

Chapter 12

Half the people in the room looked like Jack. It was very disconcerting.

Shelby had lost track of what time it was. It felt late, but maybe that was only because she'd had so little sleep last night. Emi had drifted off in her lap some time ago, and even the trip into the big Victorian-style house and the buzz of voices all around hadn't wakened her. It was as if being restored to her mother felt so safe and natural that even the strangeness of the situation wasn't going to keep the baby awake.

And Shelby wasn't about to let her daughter go, not even when someone suggested putting Emi down in a crib in one of the other rooms. Even if Emi had been wide-awake and crying, instead of sleeping contentedly, Shelby would have insisted on keeping that warm, familiar weight in her arms. After the awful uncertainties of the past thirty-six hours, she knew it would take a while before she took Emi's presence for granted again.

She still wasn't exactly sure where they were.

Or what they were doing there.

But the bigger of the two men who looked like Jack—the one who'd introduced himself to her as Wiley Cotter—seemed to be trying to sort things out.

Shelby leaned back in the corner of the big padded sofa and pulled Emi a little closer to her. She'd shed her wig and most of her padding in the truck cab, and left her clunky nanny-style shoes at the door. Her black dress was loose on her frame and she felt badly in need of a shower and some clean clothes that fit her. But just at the moment she was happy enough to tuck her feet up under her and to listen to Wiley Cotter's deep voice cutting through the other conversations going on around her.

"I think we might all benefit from an exchange of information," he was saying, as he dragged one of the Queen Anne chairs around from the long dining room table behind him. "At least, I know I would. Shelby, did you meet everybody?"

Shelby looked around the room. She'd spotted Sam Cotter immediately—somehow his long-boned, loose-jointed style went perfectly with the slow, cynical drawl she'd heard on the telephone late last night. Sam was leaning one lean hip against the end of the other sofa in the room, with a hand resting possessively on the shoulder of the serene-looking, elegantly blond woman seated next to him.

"I'm Kelley Landis," the woman said, as Shelby's gaze met hers. "And if I'd had any idea you and Jack were in such a bind, Shelby, I'd have been in the office to take your call yesterday, instead of out picking up wedding decorations."

Kelley was marrying Sam on Saturday, Shelby remembered. And Wiley was marrying—

The vivacious red-haired woman who'd just reentered the big drawing room. "My fiancée, Rae-Anne Blackburn," Wiley said, with obvious affection.

"Pleased to meet you." Something about Rae-Anne's bright blue gaze made Shelby think there was a good proportion of curiosity mixed up with Rae-Anne's pleasure in meeting her. How much did these people know about what had happened between her and Jack? she wondered.

And what *had* happened between them, anyway? Shelby still wasn't certain, and there'd been no chance to sort it out this evening.

Rae-Anne was continuing briskly, "At the risk of sounding like your dear old mom, Shelby, I really think you should have some of this. You look absolutely wrung out."

"This" was a cup of steaming hot chili, clearly homemade and aromatic enough to make Shelby realize how long it had been since she'd eaten.

"My dear old mom tended more toward canned soup," she said. "This smells wonderful."

"Good. Eat it all up, then. I tried to make Jack have some, but apparently he's such a tough guy he doesn't need food like the rest of us do."

Sam snorted. "He doesn't need to rest, either, even with a bullet hole in him," he said. "Do you, big brother?"

Shelby paused with her first bite of chili halfway to her lips, and looked across the room at Jack.

He'd taken a seat in a straight-backed wooden chair, and from the way he was holding himself, she knew he had to be in pain. The jolting ride from Fredericksburg to Austin couldn't have done him any good, and his face was almost gray with fatigue or soreness or both.

He looked so tired...

And so remote...

Those handsome features glaring at her through the windshield of the black pickup truck earlier this evening had been one of the most beautiful sights Shelby had ever seen. She'd swung aboard with her heart slamming in sudden relief, sudden exhilaration.

Jack was all right.

He'd come looking for her.

Somehow, miraculously, he'd offered a way out of a situation that was rapidly turning uglier than Shelby could cope with on her own.

In the confused moments after he'd called her name and before they'd left their pursuers behind, there'd still been time for Shelby to feel amazed at how much had changed since he'd come to her rescue at the bus station.

Then, she'd wanted him out of her life—or so she'd told herself.

Now, everything felt different. She had no idea where she and Jack were headed, but she was past denying that he had somehow pushed past her careful defenses and found a way to stir the very depths of her soul.

Of course, she also couldn't deny that he'd barely spoken to her all the way to Austin.

He met Shelby's eyes across the drawing room, but there was no warmth in the brief flicker of his gaze. "I'm waiting for those explanations Wiley mentioned," he said. "And then I'll be more than happy to go to bed."

He'd barricaded himself more firmly than ever behind the professional facade Shelby had disliked so much when they'd first met. There was no trace of the man who'd played so guilelessly with Emi, or of the tender lover who'd stirred Shelby so deeply, so powerfully.

A couple of days ago, she would have been relieved.

Now she wasn't.

She was hurt, and puzzled. And she was grateful for the distraction of the chili Rae-Anne had handed her, and the introduction of the final occupant of the room.

"This is Grant," Kelley Landis was saying. "He works for us at Cotter Investigations."

The bright-looking young man at the other end of the sofa from Kelley sketched a wave in Shelby's direction. "I was listening in when you showed up this morning in that uniform," he said. "That was good work."

"It's not really a uniform." Shelby swallowed a mouthful of the chili, savoring its welcome warmth. "It was just—"

"Hold on." Wiley swung the Queen Anne chair around and planted himself on it, his strong forearms resting on the curved wood and his long legs stretched out on either side. "Why don't you start at the beginning, and bring the rest of us up to speed?"

Shelby glanced at Jack again, but he looked the way she imagined he always looked at official briefings: concentrated, serious and very definitely detached.

Well, fine, Shelby thought. If he could insulate himself from everything that had happened over the past few days, then she'd clearly been badly mistaken about what she thought she'd been seeing in those smoldering dark eyes of his, and what she'd imagined the passion in his touch had meant. Personally, Shelby didn't think she would ever be quite the same after the highs and lows she'd experienced since meeting Jack Cotter.

And unlike Jack, she wasn't about to distance herself from the friendly, interested faces in the room around her. It was an unexpected relief to feel surrounded and supported like this.

"After I got Sam's call," she said, "I decided it couldn't hurt to check out the address that the white car was registered to. I was just going to take a look at it, but then when I got there—I heard Emi crying inside."

She looked down at her daughter, nestled so snugly in her lap, and recalled the wave of relief and urgency and helplessness that had rolled through her when she'd heard Emi's unhappy cries coming from behind that imposing limestone facade.

"I couldn't imagine how to get in, but I couldn't imagine turning around and leaving her there, either," she went on. "It was 2:00 a.m. by then, and there didn't seem to be much I could do. But I did manage to get into the garden behind the house, and by the time it got light I could see people moving around inside.''

She didn't mention how cold she'd gotten, or how many times she'd wondered if she was really doing the right thing. She'd been utterly unable to leave her daughter—that had been the one thought that had kept her in place through the dark hours before dawn.

''At about seven a couple of men came out onto the porch at the back of the house,'' she said. ''They seemed to be trying to have some kind of a meeting, although I couldn't hear everything they were saying. Emi was crying again by then, and—well, she can make a pretty impressive noise when she gets cranked up.''

She twirled a gentle finger into the blond curl at Emi's temple, and smiled. Her baby was the picture of contentment now, with her full eyelids drooping shut and her little mouth pursed into a tight bud. But back at that house in Fredericksburg, Emi had had the volume turned up as high as it would go, almost as though she'd wanted to let the whole world know something was wrong.

''I got underneath the porch in time to hear one of the men—I think it was Jerry Lawrence himself—''

''Tall guy?'' Jack asked. ''Looks like he's lost a lot of weight recently?''

''Yes. That's him. Anyway, he was complaining about the baby. 'As soon as that agency's open for business,' he called to somebody inside the house, 'get on the phone and get somebody over here to look after that kid. Tell them we'll pay double whatever nannies usually get.'''

''So you decided to be the nanny.'' There was admiration in Kelley's voice.

''It seemed like too good an opportunity to pass up. I found a thrift store that was open early, and bought myself some clothes and a wig—''

''And some padding.'' Jack growled the words from his corner.

"And some padding. Those men knew what I looked like, after all. Fortunately, I speak pretty fluent Spanish— it was something I learned while I was teaching down in Lafayette. So it was easy for me to pretend my English wasn't very good. I looked in the Fredericksburg phone book and only found one nanny service listed, so I figured that would be the one Lawrence's men would call. I just showed up at his house a little after nine, saying the agency had sent me."

"And they never blinked." Wiley, too, seemed impressed.

"No. The accent seemed to fool them."

"Good thing the agency didn't send somebody else to do the job," Sam said.

"I know. I was worried about that all day. But apparently the agency had said they couldn't promise anyone at such short notice, but that they'd send the first nanny who was available. And those men were desperate. They didn't know the first thing about babies, and Emi made them pretty nervous. They were just so glad to have somebody to deal with her that I probably could have shown up dressed like Mary Poppins and they wouldn't have questioned it."

She told the rest of the story quickly—how she'd carefully checked out the building, but discovered that whenever she got too close to an exit, either Lawrence or one of his henchmen would remind her that the baby had to stay indoors. The man Lawrence had been meeting with early in the morning had been gone by the time Shelby had come back in her disguise, but there were three or four others who came and went during the day, and all of them had been equally watchful. It had been early evening by the time she'd seen a real chance for escape.

"And that was only because they were busy arguing about whose turn it was to go out and get food," she said. "I managed to get out the ground floor door with Emi, but the garden gate seemed to be padlocked when I reached it.

We had to shove our way through the hedge, and by that time the men knew we were gone.''

"And Jack was sitting in Sam's truck waiting for you," Rae-Anne finished.

"Waiting for *something*." Jack sounded almost angry about it. "I wasn't exactly expecting Shelby herself, with Lawrence's boys in hot pursuit all over again."

"Lighten up, Jack." Sam grinned at his brother. "Our own people couldn't have done a better job of infiltrating the place, and you know it."

"We probably couldn't have done as *good* a job," Kelley added. "I'm sure Emi was a thousand percent quieter because it was her own mother looking after her."

It was true. Emi had calmed down the instant Shelby had plucked her out of the makeshift crib Lawrence's aides had set up for her. And the sudden peace and quiet in the house had seemed to make everyone more relaxed, less suspicious.

"*And* Grant and I were right at the end of the street, with our eyes on the house," Wiley put in. "I'll admit that was more good luck than good planning, but sometimes you need both in this business."

A maroon station wagon had come barreling along the street at just the right moment to cut Jerry Lawrence's men off from a clear shot at the disappearing pickup truck, but Shelby hadn't realized until afterward that it hadn't been just a lucky accident. Emi's rescue had been a joint effort, and it had needed all of their combined skills and bravado to make it work.

If only it was finished—

She felt exhaustion starting to claim her as she finished the rest of her chili and listened to the Cotter brothers talk. Emi was safe, for the moment, but Jerry Lawrence was still on the loose, and she felt certain he was vengeful enough and frustrated enough to come after her again if she was foolish enough to try to lead anything like a normal life.

"We're still trying to track down your dead witness's widow," Sam was saying. "Trouble is, your people hid her pretty thoroughly. If we had access to the FBI files—"

Jack shook his head adamantly. "Too risky," he said. "I have no idea who's been leaking information to Jerry Lawrence, but whoever it is, I don't want them getting wind of where we are, or what we're doing."

"Where *are* we, anyway?" Shelby couldn't help asking the question.

Wiley flashed a smile at her. The oldest and youngest Cotters seemed so open, so at ease, Shelby thought. Jack's coolness seemed even more pronounced in comparison.

Had it always been this way? Or did the two other women in the room have something to do with the way Sam and Wiley seemed so different from their brother?

It was Rae-Anne who answered Shelby's question. "We're just outside Austin, near the lake. This place is an inn," she explained. "It's run by friends of friends, and they agreed to let us have the run of this wing of it for the whole week. We'll be stashing most of the out-of-town guests here, but they're not arriving for another couple of days."

"Won't Jerry Lawrence look—"

Wiley shook his head. "The Cotter name isn't on anything official like a booking list or a credit card bill," he said. "The whole arrangement is informal. Unlike Jack's FBI card, this transaction really *can't* be traced. And anyway—"

He got to his feet and strode over to the tall windows overlooking the lawn. Pulling back the heavy green velvet curtain, Wiley nodded at the driveway that curved around in front of the house.

"Sam's got people posted out there," he said. "And at the back of the house. All the approaches are secured. And I've had a word with the local police chief, who's an old buddy of mine. At the first sign of anything wrong up here, the place'll be crawling with cops. You can sleep tight tonight, Shelby. And speaking of which—''

He seemed to have noticed her efforts to hide the jaw-cracking yawn that suddenly overtook her. Or maybe it was Jack's gray, drawn face he was looking at.

She let herself be shepherded into a low wing of the house that seemed to be an annex devoted to comfortable bedrooms furnished in ornate Victorian style. She was almost too tired to take in the flowery patterns of the wallpaper and comforter in her room, or the fact that someone had provided diapering supplies and even a teddy bear in the small room next to hers where a crib had been set up for Emi.

''My bag—'' She'd forgotten all about the bag until this moment. ''It's still in Jack's car in Fredericksburg.''

''Give me the keys.'' Kelley held out a hand as she stepped into the little room. ''If you tell us where you left it, we'll get somebody to drive it back here.''

How long had it been, Shelby wondered, since she'd had a circle of people around her that she could trust as instinctively as she trusted the extended Cotter family? How long had it been since she'd been willing to share her troubles with people who seemed so intuitively to understand?

It occurred to her that she'd *never* really felt this way. For so much of her life she'd been unsure of exactly who she was and where she fit in. Even during her years of teaching, and her brief marriage, she'd never felt the immediate sense of connection and community that she'd sensed with Jack's brothers and soon-to-be sisters-in-law this evening.

As she drifted into almost instantaneous sleep in the big canopied bed, she found herself wishing that she could find some way to make this last.

Emi's cranky cries reached her through a thick fog of sleep. It took a moment before she was awake enough to respond to the sound.

Diaper change, her mind told her groggily.

And then, as the events of the past couple of days came back to her, she felt relief crowding into her all over again at the thought that Emi was here at all. Compared with losing her daughter, being wakened far too early to change a dirty diaper was a positive pleasure.

Still, it took her a moment to get her eyes open. Everything seemed strange, from the dim glow of the night-light in the adjoining room to the soft white flannel nightgown she was wearing. Rae-Anne had lent it to her, along with a whole selection of other blessedly clean clothes. Seeing the array of shirts and sweaters draped over the divan at the foot of her bed brought back the details of the night's events a little more clearly, and by the time Shelby padded into Emi's room she was feeling almost fully awake.

But Jack had beaten her to it.

At first she thought she was dreaming it. His room adjoined Emi's, too, on the other side, and they shared a bathroom as well, but they'd managed to avoid each other while getting ready for bed. Now, though, Emi's crying seemed to have stirred him out of sleep even before it had penetrated Shelby's dreaming mind.

Or maybe he hadn't been sleeping. He had his jeans on, but no shirt, and against the broad, tanned expanse of his chest, the white bandage around his ribs stood out in glaring contrast. Had the pain of his bullet wound kept him awake?

If it had, it wasn't enough to prevent him from lifting Emi out of her crib. He was moving stiffly and slowly, but his voice was steady as he settled Emi against his shoulder.

"All right," he said. "What seems to be the problem here?"

The baby kept crying, and Shelby found herself smiling in amused surprise as Jack peered experimentally under the edge of Emi's diaper.

"It's got to be either diaper or food, right?" he asked. "Or it's 'none of the above,' in which case we might as well go ask your mom for help right now. I'm definitely the B team, sweet pea, but—" He stopped abruptly, and cleared his throat. "Well, at least I know a dirty diaper when I run into one. Let's see what we can do about this."

He laid Emi onto the changing table next to the crib, and Shelby watched in growing amazement as he navigated the mysteries of the diapering process. Clearly he'd never tried it before, but just as clearly he was willing to learn.

"So diaper pins are a thing of the past, huh?" His deep voice seemed to lull Emi, calming her into silence. "Just as well. I suspect they're beyond my skill anyway. Long live disposables, I say."

Leaning against the doorframe with her arms crossed, Shelby found herself reaching a hand up to smother her almost audible smile as Jack encountered the source of the problem.

"Whew," he said to Emi. "No wonder you sounded annoyed."

Sometimes Emi refused to go back to sleep once she'd wakened in the night, in which case Shelby knew they could be in for a replay of the first night they'd spent together, desperately trying to induce Emi to feel drowsy. Tonight, though, she seemed tired enough that a clean diaper was all it took to do the trick.

But even after Emi seemed to have drifted off again, Jack didn't settle her back into her crib. Shelby watched, her amusement mellowing into a soft ache as Jack held the baby against his broad shoulder, spreading one strong hand across Emi's tiny back.

There was such tenderness in his pose, such silent wonder in the way he lowered his dark head and rested one cheek against Emi's hair. He seemed tentative at first, almost as though he were afraid the gesture might wake her, or that the black stubble along his jawline might be too rough for her velvety baby skin.

But Emi never moved, and Shelby had to blink away sudden tears as she watched Jack raise one hand and trace the plump curve of Emi's cheek with the back of his knuckles.

He needs this, she thought. He needed the simple joys that babies could bring, the everyday miracles that made up a child's life. He'd lived his own life in a climate of uncertainty and deception, but somewhere deep down, in spite of it all, Jack Cotter had managed to hang on to a vision of something warmer, something more human than guns and raids and distrust and the constant, unending threat of danger. He couldn't possibly be holding Emi so gently now if he'd surrendered himself body and soul to the grim realities of his working world.

"Jack."

She waited until he'd lowered the baby back into her crib before she spoke.

Jack turned around too quickly and winced as the pain caught at his rib cage. Damn it, how long had Shelby been standing there?

"Her diaper needed changing." He spoke quickly, quietly, stepping away from the crib and toward his own doorway.

"I know. Thank you."

He didn't understand the look in her eyes, and it made him uneasy.

She looked intent and hesitant and concerned.

Concerned about Emi? It made no sense. Emi was sleeping like an angel, her little ribs barely rising and falling as she lay in her crib.

Jack's ribs, on the other hand, felt as if someone had performed a clog dance on them. And his breathing, unlike Emi's, had quickened as he watched Shelby standing there in that pure white nightgown in the dim light.

Was it *Jack* she was concerned about?

"I—guess I should get back to bed," he said, and tried to make his body turn and leave the little room.

It wouldn't go.

And Shelby was stepping closer to him, frowning a little as she held out a hand toward his bandaged ribs.

"Wiley told me they didn't want to let you out of the hospital," she said.

Jack tensed when her palm met his skin. *You were going to keep your distance, Cotter,* he reminded himself. But how was he supposed to do that when Shelby had crept up on him without warning?

"Hospitals always think they know best," he muttered.

"And so do you."

Her light, husky voice had that note of amusement in it that drove Jack half-crazy. He closed his eyes and felt his arms quivering with the effort of not reaching for Shelby Henderson.

"I listen to orders if they make sense to me," he said tightly.

He was doing his best—he really was—to keep from sliding back into the seductive spell that always seemed to wrap itself around him whenever he was close to Shelby. But even the curt tone of his voice didn't seem to have deterred Shelby from whatever she thought she was up to.

She smoothed her palm over the flat skin of his belly, almost as though she knew exactly how tight and hungry he felt in exactly that spot.

"Would you follow *my* orders," she asked softly, "if I asked you to kiss me right now?"

Jack squeezed his eyes tighter shut and felt the quiver in his arms spreading through his entire body.

He tried to think about Jerry Lawrence, but he could barely remember the man's name.

He tried to gather clues in his mind, to recall what had happened to Jessie, to conjure up some of his earlier fury at his unknown FBI colleague who'd put them all in such danger.

But all he could think about was the way Shelby yielded so eagerly to his kisses, inviting him into a world of such sensuality and promise that it was more than he could do to refuse it.

He groaned wordlessly as she stepped closer to him. The feeling of her belly against his hips deepened the sound a little. Her hair felt like sun-warmed satin when Jack reached up to clasp the back of her neck. And her mouth—

Her mouth was unimaginably welcoming, indescribably sweet. It was impossible to remember why he'd been working so hard at holding aloof from her all evening, impossible to think of anything at all besides the way her lips met his and instantly seemed to smooth away all the rough edges he'd been grappling with just a few minutes ago.

She was moving intimately but cautiously against him, resting her hands on his bare shoulders, tunneling her fingers up into his disordered hair. Jack knew he looked like a bear—he hadn't shaved in far too long—but Shelby didn't seem to mind. He could feel her raising herself on tiptoe to meet him, touching him so gently and yet so arousingly that Jack groaned again, and felt his own voice reverberating against the softness of her mouth.

And then, as easily as she'd initiated the kiss, she ended it again, and stood half a step away from him.

Watching him.

Waiting.

She'd asked him to kiss her. Nothing more. And now that he'd done it, she was letting him make the next move.

Jack knew there shouldn't *be* a next move, except for the logical one of stepping back into his own room and getting what fractured sleep he could manage for whatever was left of the night.

He closed his eyes again and tried to will himself to do just that.

It's a mistake, Cotter, his conscience was telling him. *Remember what happened before.*

"I think—you want more from me than I can give you." He ground the words out, not quite meeting Shelby's level gaze.

"I don't know what I want from you." Her quick reply told him how impatiently she'd been waiting for him to speak. "We just—seem to want each other. Isn't that enough, Jack?"

He didn't know. Hell, he barely knew which way was up at the moment. He only knew that Shelby was standing close to him, breathing as quickly as he was himself, and that the longer they stood that way, the more difficult it was getting to think of anything beyond his own overwhelming desire for this woman who touched him, stirred him, as no one else had ever done.

It might be the last time.

The thought spun jaggedly into his mind. Once he wrapped this case up—once Shelby came to her senses and realized that a jaded, danger-prone FBI agent was no kind of partner, much less a fitting parent for a child—

He might never have this chance again. And Shelby was still waiting, still offering him the solace and solidarity he'd wanted for so many years without even knowing what he was hungering for.

Suddenly he didn't care if this was a mistake. He wanted Shelby Henderson, and she wanted him. She'd said it herself, in that slightly breathless voice that seemed to connect directly to Jack's libido.

Without speaking, without taking a chance that words might break the spell that was increasing its hold on him, Jack reached out and slid his palms upward over the downy-soft flannel that covered Shelby's arms.

He could feel her trembling, feel her starting to melt toward him even before he took a step.

Her kiss was hungrier this time, matching the fierce longing that was taking over Jack's whole body, blocking out even the pain in his ribs. He felt himself giving in to it, letting it carry him miles away from rational thought and into the realm of pure pleasure.

They moved together into his bedroom without a word being spoken, as though this magical moment in the depths of the night had been there all along, just waiting for Jack's resistance to crumble.

"Are you really all right?" Shelby didn't miss the careful way he lowered himself onto the edge of the bed.

"No." It was an effort to get the word out. He wanted to be kissing every inch of her—her hair, her breasts, the crook of her elbow. "No, I'm not really all right—but at the moment I don't really give a damn."

Her smile was wide and sudden. It seemed to light up the whole room, and Jack felt his loins contract with almost painful need as he looked up at her.

He wasn't prepared for the suddenness of the way she reached down and pulled the white flannel nightgown over her head, exposing the white, slender perfection of her body.

Or for the slow, erotic way she settled herself astride his hips, carefully taking her weight on her knees while she circled her arms around his neck.

She was offering him this as a gift, he realized.

He couldn't imagine why she thought he deserved it.

But he accepted it eagerly, ravenously.

He bent his head and swirled his tongue around the hidden curve of her breast. The feeling of her nipple hardening under his lips was electrifyingly sweet.

He moaned her name on a note of raw need when she slid off his lap to undo his jeans. Her eyes were bright in the low light from Emi's room next door, her lips parted slightly, her breathing quick and erratic. Still, she seemed to be considering something, weighing some set of options Jack couldn't begin to imagine.

It was only after she'd come to a decision that he realized what she'd been thinking about.

"Come on," she said, and took his hand to lead him to the big overstuffed armchair that took up one whole corner of his room. He closed his eyes as he eased himself into it, already half-lost in deliriously erotic images of himself and Shelby twined together in the chair's upholstered depths.

His imagination, it turned out, wasn't nearly up to the task. The reality of Shelby's body wrapping itself around him made his head spin wildly and his body ache for release. She was so daring. So open. So inventively sensuous.

He'd known this side of her was there, hidden beneath layers of caution and uncertainty, since the moment he'd first seen her. He'd recognized her intensity, her spirit, her defiant strength. And now she was turning that strength into passion.

And lavishing it all on him.

He had no clear idea whether their lovemaking this time was slow or fast, endlessly prolonged or as searingly quick as lightning.

Maybe it was all of those things. Jack plunged into Shelby's soft, welcoming depths as though finally, just for this moment, and against all the odds, he'd decided to listen to some message being drummed into him from deep inside his own body. It was telling him to hold on to this instant if he could, to push his fears beyond arm's length just for tonight, to capture in feelings all the dreams he didn't dare put into words.

And there were no words, anyway, for the euphoria that surged through him as he and Shelby reached a glittering pinnacle together and tumbled headlong down the other side, still locked in each other's arms.

There was no way to tell her what he'd just felt, or the visions that had dazzled him behind his closed eyes. This wasn't the time to remind either of them of what they both already knew—that this kind of longing could be a dangerous thing. It opened you up to the kind of pain Jack had felt too much of in his thirty-eight years. The kind of pain he didn't want Shelby ever to have to feel again.

He couldn't stand to think about that now—couldn't make his mind face the reality that his life and Shelby's just didn't mesh, no matter how brightly passion might flare between them. So he stayed silent, and just pulled his arms more tightly around her, kissing the honey-scented softness of her hair as the night's darkness closed around both of them again.

Chapter 13

Somehow—Jack wasn't sure how—they'd gotten themselves from the chair into the bed.

And now there was someone tapping on his door.

"Jack." It was Sam's voice, gravelly as always. "You decent, brother? I've got some news."

Decent... Jack wasn't even sure he was awake. He pushed himself up on one elbow and felt his rib cage twanging like an out-of-tune guitar.

That helped chase away the sleep. But the fact that he was lying next to Shelby's soft, warm body didn't make it easy to focus on what Sam was saying.

News...

"What the hell time is it?" he muttered.

Shelby raised her tousled blond head from the pillow and looked at the bedside clock. "Early," she said. "Doesn't Sam ever sleep?"

"Not to my knowledge." Jack grunted as he eased himself into a sitting position and reached for his jeans. "I'll see what he wants."

He didn't repeat what Sam himself had once told him—that Sam had picked up the habit of staying up all night while trying to recover from a bullet wound he'd picked up in the line of duty. He'd been working with Kelley at the time, and the whole thing—the case, the screwup, Sam's injury—had nearly blown their relationship to bits. They'd put it back together, but it had taken them awhile.

He growled as he pulled on the dark brown trousers and light crewneck sweater Wiley had dug up for him to wear. The remnants of last night's loving—and last night's extravagant, impossible dreams—were still with him, making it difficult to concentrate on Sam and whatever he'd come to say. And now the thought of Sam and Kelley—the thought that "happily ever after" might not be just an empty phrase after all—was tugging at him, too.

It was still a brand-new notion to Jack.

And he had no clear idea what he was going to do with it.

He stepped out into the hall, carefully closing the door after himself. Sam raised an eloquent eyebrow, but didn't comment on the possible reasons why Jack hadn't wanted his brother to see into the room.

"We found your witness's widow," he said. "Only problem is, she won't talk."

"Won't talk at all, or won't talk to you?"

Sam shrugged. "Hard to tell," he said. "I'd have taken Kelley with me to interview her—her Spanish is better than mine—but she and Grant were getting your car back while I was visiting the woman."

"She speak any English?"

"Hard to tell that, too. My guess is she's mostly just scared."

Jack didn't blame her. Like Shelby, the woman had good reason to know what happened to people who went up against Jerry Lawrence.

"Shoot," he said, and rubbed a hand over his unshaven jaw. "Well, I appreciate you tracking her down. Guess I'll have a try at her myself."

Maybe he could convince the woman, he thought. Maybe, if he could convey to her how much it would mean for Shelby, for Shelby's baby, for Jack himself, the frightened widow might be willing to help put an end to this whole dangerous business.

"Jack?" Sam's voice caught him as he was turning around.

"Yeah?"

"You might want to shave first." Sam rubbed his own jaw in an imitation of Jack's gesture. "If she's already scared, seeing you in that state isn't going to calm her down any."

The room was empty when he stepped back into it. He could hear Shelby in Emi's room, speaking quietly to her daughter, and he decided not to interrupt them. Last night's encounter had been explosive and unnerving in a whole variety of ways, and he needed to regain his perspective on the world this morning, if he could.

And he needed to wrap this case up. If he was going to do that successfully, he needed his mind clear and undistracted.

He'd told himself the same thing yesterday, and it hadn't worked.

He thought he was doing better today, right up until he pulled away from the big Victorian inn in his company car.

Kelley and Grant had carefully checked the vehicle for tracking devices, Kelley had told him. And for bombs. And hidden tape recorders. They hadn't found anything, which meant that even in the unlikely case that Jerry Lawrence's boys *had* found the spot where Shelby had parked the car in Fredericksburg, they hadn't deemed it important enough to keep track of.

That was good. And it was heartening to know that his brothers' efforts had turned up the crucial information about the dead witness's wife. Now, if the woman had just seen or heard something that might lead Jack to some of the answers he was looking for—

He was so busy thinking about that, that at first he didn't register the face in the rearview mirror.

He was getting used to seeing wide, intelligent hazel eyes and flyaway blond hair whenever he let his mind drift even slightly. It took a few seconds to realize that he was seeing them now because Shelby was in the back seat of his car, looking at him in the mirror.

Jack swore loudly and tromped on the brake pedal. The sudden movement set off a whole clanging symphony in his ribs, and by the time he'd wrestled the car to a stop on the side of the road, his palms were sticky with sweat.

"What the *hell* are you doing here?" He was too startled to sugarcoat the question.

She was wearing different clothes—a loose-fitting tan-and-white check blouse with the collar turned up, and a pair of tan trousers that matched the shirt. They were Rae-Anne's, Jack guessed. The two women were about the same size.

And despite some basic differences in their characters— Rae-Anne was exuberant where Shelby tended to be understated—he guessed they had a few more things in common besides their size. He remembered how furiously Wiley had complained when Rae-Anne had refused to stay out of the way of danger in the case the two of them had been involved in.

At the time, Jack had been bemused by Wiley's fury. Now he was more inclined to see his brother in a more sympathetic light.

"I heard you talking to Sam," Shelby was saying matter-of-factly. "I thought you might be able to use a translator. A sympathetic translator."

Shelby, like the woman they were heading in search of, had lost her husband because of Jerry Lawrence's orders.

Which only meant, in Jack's view, that she should want to stay as far away as possible from what was happening right now.

"I thought you wanted to be left out of this," he muttered.

"It's too late for that." Quickly, she relocated herself on the front seat next to Jack. She looked fresher and lovelier than he'd seen her yet, and it didn't do anything to improve his powers of concentration. "I'm involved whether I want to be or not, Jack. And since I am, I want to get this wrapped up quickly. For everybody's sake."

It was what Jack wanted, too. But he hated like hell to have to be worrying about Shelby while that was going on.

"I'm taking you straight back to the house," he told her.

"You can try."

She tilted her chin up, and Jack knew he wasn't going to get her out of the car without a physical struggle. He wasn't sure he was up to that, even if he *had* wanted to get into a wrestling match with Shelby Henderson.

"This is a mistake, Shelby," he told her.

"Why?"

The single word stopped him for a moment. Jack rested his wrists on the steering wheel and searched the hilly landscape around them for answers that just weren't there, no matter how hard he looked.

"You're acting—as though we're partners in some way." He chose the words carefully, picking from the thousand different disjointed phrases that had bombarded him in the moments between sleep early this morning. "And we're not. We're just not."

He wondered if he was repeating the words to convince himself as well as Shelby. He couldn't tell what she was thinking behind the sudden frown that creased her forehead.

"We are—*some* kind of partners."

She was speaking slowly, too. Both of them knew they were navigating across an emotional minefield here, Jack thought. The difference was that he was trying to get back to safety, while Shelby—for some reason he didn't understand—seemed determined to press forward.

He shook his head. "It's too soon even to think about that," he told her.

"After last night? After—how we feel about each other?"

Jack didn't know how they felt about each other. Hell, he wasn't sure how he felt about himself at the moment.

All he knew was that he had a job to finish, and once he'd done that, assuming he was still alive, there would be a chance to start figuring out what to do about all the feelings Shelby had stirred in him—the feelings she was stirring in him now, without even trying.

He fought against the dangerous longings that were pulsing in his fingertips at the thought of reaching out and pulling her close to him, and glared out at the scenery again.

"When this is over, you may see things differently," he said. "You may decide you were right in the first place when you said we weren't suited to each other."

He waited for the kind of concise question she was so fond of tossing at him, but this time she stayed silent. He met her eyes briefly, and saw what looked like the beginnings of hurt in their hazel depths. He looked away again before he could lose his resolve.

"You have Emi to think about," he reminded her.

"Emi adores you."

"She probably adores Big Bird, too, sweetheart, but that doesn't mean he would make a good father for her."

There, Jack thought. He'd said it. He'd raised the subject they'd both been dancing around—love, and marriage, and the baby carriage and all that stuff.

And surely she would see now that this momentary passion they shared—or whatever the hell it was—couldn't possibly fit with the part that ended "happily ever after."

She was shaking her head, looking puzzled as much as anything else. "You're not giving this a chance," she told him.

"Shelby." Jack gripped the wheel hard, although the car was still idling on the shoulder. "What chance do we have? I can't provide the kind of home you and Emi want—and need—and deserve."

"Are you sure about that?" Her voice had gotten soft all of a sudden.

Jack couldn't let himself look at her this time. He tried to picture himself as a father—tried to push past all those memories of all those promises that had come to nothing in his own childhood.

What if he couldn't measure up? What if he couldn't give Emi what she needed? How would he ever live with himself if someday he had to watch that gleeful baby smile turn to hurt and puzzlement, exactly the way Shelby's beautiful face was doing right now?

The risk was unthinkable.

And so he refused to think about it.

Even now, last night's passion was still singing in his veins, reminding him how instinctively he and Shelby seemed to know each other, to touch the depths of each other's hearts.

But that couldn't guarantee happiness.

Shelby had offered him a gift last night, and Jack had grabbed it—eagerly, greedily, thoughtlessly.

And now, with a regret so strong it made his gut tighten into a knot, he was handing it back to her.

"Let's just get this case out of the way, all right?" He heard the roughness in his own voice, but there didn't seem to be anything he could do to moderate it. "Once that's done, my bet is that you'll see that you and Emi are a lot better off without me.''

He put the car in gear, but didn't take his foot off the brake. Somehow he knew Shelby was working on an answer, and he wanted to hear what it was.

It seemed to be a long time coming. By the time she finally spoke, Jack's whole frame was tense from struggling with his own hungers, his own bitter memories, his own impossible hopes.

"If you don't want to risk this, then say so, all right, Jack?" The wary edge had come back into her voice. All of a sudden she sounded the way she had when they'd first met, and a knot of remorse tightened inside Jack at the sound of it. "But you can't make my decisions for me. Don't tell me I'm going to dump you before I've done it."

"You will." Jack gritted his teeth and eased the car away from the shoulder.

"Maybe." The word had a soft, melancholy sound to it. "But I haven't done it yet."

Damn it, he didn't want this. He wanted clarity, not more confusion. He wanted to keep his mind on his work, and not on the puzzle that Shelby and Emi Henderson had become in his life.

With an effort that jangled his patched-up rib all over again, he forced his attention onto the road and ahead to the interview they were on their way to conduct.

"She says she can't remember."

Jack was getting tired of hearing the same answer.

They'd found the woman easily enough, although after Sam's early morning visit she'd been leery of more strangers knocking on her door. At first, in fact, she'd refused to speak to them at all.

He still wasn't sure how Shelby had won her over. It had been startling to hear Shelby's fluent, musical Spanish, and even more startling to see the two women exchanging a smile after several minutes of rapid-fire conversation that Jack could follow only partially.

"What's up?" he'd demanded, when the woman finally opened the door to her apartment in the low brick complex an hour away from Austin.

"I told her about Emilio." Jack had already gathered that. It didn't explain the smile, though.

"And?" he prompted her.

"And about Emi. She has kids, too. For their sake, she'd like this cleared up."

"So what's so amusing about that?"

"Nothing. We were just—comparing notes."

"About—"

"You and Sam. She wanted to know if there were any more of you in the family, and if you all looked like there was a thundercloud over your heads all the time."

Jack wasn't wild about the satisfaction he could see in Shelby's eyes as she translated the comment. "What did you tell her?" he asked.

"That there were, and you all do, and that I wouldn't be risking standing around next to a thunderstorm if I wasn't pretty desperate to hear what she has to say. That's when she decided to let us in."

The problem was that the woman didn't seem to have much to tell them. She didn't know who had visited her husband on the morning of his death. Someone had come to the door while she'd been getting the children ready for school, but she hadn't seen who it was. Her husband had gone out with the man—she had the impression it was a man, from the way her husband's voice had sounded—and he hadn't come back again. A couple of days later his body had been discovered in a Dumpster two towns away.

Jack found himself clenching his back teeth when Shelby reached out a sympathetic hand and squeezed the woman's trembling fingers. *Think, Jack,* he ordered himself. *That's what you're supposed to be good at.*

Had there been any unusual mail? Any out-of-the-way phone calls?

She didn't remember.

Had her husband done anything out of his usual routine? Had he seemed nervous, or excited?

No. She didn't think so.

Had he been in contact with the FBI recently, did she know?

She didn't.

After almost an hour Jack sighed and shook his head. "I think we're wasting our time," he said.

The woman was young, with bright, intelligent-looking eyes. She was turning her gaze first to Jack's face and then to Shelby's, as though she truly wanted to help but she wasn't certain how to do it.

She said something too hasty for Jack to pick up. "What's that?" he asked Shelby.

"She says Anglos always want a single answer in a hurry," Shelby translated. "I think she thinks life isn't quite that simple."

It wasn't a comforting idea. Jack stood and eased his rib cage into action again. His own Spanish was good enough to thank the woman, but when he and Shelby had reached the door, he had to ask her to translate the thought that had just occurred to him.

"Ask her what other Anglos have been wanting simple answers lately," he said.

Shelby translated, then waited.

"Her husband was complaining about it, one night after he'd been out at the bar," she said.

"He used to go out drinking with Anglos?"

Another pause while the woman answered. "He had one Anglo friend who used to visit him. She doesn't know his name."

A little alarm was going off in Jack's brain, something that seemed to signal the beginning of what he'd been looking for. "Does she know what he looked like?" he asked.

He saw Shelby's eyes widen and brighten as she listened to the woman's reply. "She said he was a tall man with brown hair, a bit on the heavy side. He had a ring with a ruby in it—that's the only thing she remembers positively about him. But, Jack—"

It was starting to click into place, the way it did sometimes when you finally stumbled on the one small fact that held the key to a much larger puzzle. Jack almost wasn't surprised to hear Shelby's next words.

"The man I saw meeting with Jerry Lawrence on the back porch of that house in Fredericksburg yesterday morning—I couldn't get a look at his face, but when he waved his hand, I could see the sun glinting in a ruby on his finger."

Jack was nodding grimly, and heading for the telephone he could see on the woman's kitchen wall. "It's a college ring," he said tersely. "Rice University, class of '75."

"How do you know that?"

He picked up the receiver and quickly punched in the number of the inn where his brothers were staying. "Because, sweetheart," he said, "I look at that ring across the office almost every morning. It belongs to a man named Mack MacGuire, who just happens to be a Special Agent and a good buddy of mine."

There were a couple of basic rules in Jack's business.

One was not to go into a confrontation too soon. If you rushed things, you risked losing everything you'd worked for.

The other was not to leave things so late that your target had a chance to get away on you.

He thought the tension between the two might just pull him apart by the time he pulled his car into a parking space around the corner from Mack's small house in suburban Houston.

"I'm coming in with you." Shelby's voice was nervous but determined.

"Don't even think about it." Jack frowned at her. "You're staying right here, and you're not leaving this car for any reason except to save your own life. Got that?"

She started to argue, but something in his eyes seemed to change her mind. Jack patted the gun he'd slid into Sam's shoulder holster under his sweater and pointed a forefinger at the keys he'd left in the ignition.

"If anything goes wrong, I want you to get the hell out of here," he told her.

"I wish you would wait for Sam and Wiley."

Jack shook his head. Urgency was eating at him—and a sense of fury and betrayal so strong he thought he might explode if he didn't vent some of it soon. Mack was home—he could see his colleague's fancy little sports car in the driveway. Jerry Lawrence was gone from the house in Fredericksburg, but Mack—who was on Jerry's payroll— would most likely know where to find him.

Jack had known the car in the driveway was pricey, and the house hadn't been cheap, either. Mack had bought it when real estate was expensive a few years ago, and he'd been complaining about it ever since, and about what it cost to run his big new boat, on top of the alimony and child support payments he had to carry every month. But Jack had had no idea Mack's life-style was being funded by Jerry Lawrence's dirty money.

Or that Mack had passed FBI information along to Lawrence—information that had almost led to Jessie's death, and Shelby's and Emi's. And Jack's.

There was as much anger as passion in his quick kiss as he left Shelby in the front seat of the car.

While Shelby had been borrowing clothes from Rae-Anne and arranging for Jack's two prospective sisters-in-law to keep an eye on Emi, Jack himself had been accepting the loan of Sam's .38 revolver and a spare five-round cartridge. He hoped like hell he didn't have to use it—Mack MacGuire had been a colleague for a lot of years, and Jack hated the thought of firing on his former friend. But if he had to...

At first he thought he was going to be able to mop this up without using force.

He scouted around both sides of Mack's house, but saw no signs of visitors. He knocked on the kitchen door and waited until Mack came to answer it. The smile on his associate's face faded quickly when he opened the door and saw the gun in Jack's hand, but although Mack blanched, he didn't run or lunge at Jack or do any of the other stupid things Jack had half expected.

"You figured it out." He said the words dully, as though he'd been waiting for this moment.

"Yeah, I did." Jack stepped inside, gun still leveled at Mack's midriff. "And I'd just as soon not hear any excuses about it, if it's all the same to you."

Mack spread his big, fleshy hands. "There is no excuse," he said simply. "I was strapped for the money. I couldn't stand the thought of having anybody know how broke I was. Lawrence was paying big bucks, and at first I thought nobody was going to get hurt—that he just wanted to keep tabs on that witness in Hays County."

"Kind of naive, weren't you, Mack, for a seasoned FBI agent?"

"I didn't want to see it, Jack. I kept looking the other way—kept pretending it wasn't connected to anything worse than information tampering. I didn't think Jerry would risk having the guy actually killed. And then he did—"

"And then I mentioned that Jessie wanted me to put Shelby Henderson wise to the danger she was in."

Mack nodded unhappily. "I saw Jessie pull that address out of her date book when she was talking to you," he said. "And then you mentioned the errand you were going on. I managed to get word to Lawrence what was happening—that was part of our deal, that I would let him know about anything that affected the case against him—but I had no idea he would go as far as running Jessie down. My God—there were less drastic ways of getting the damn address."

But Lawrence's way had not only given his men a chance to grab Jessie's date book—they must have blended into the crowd around her car when she'd been run down, Jack thought—but it had put Jessie out of action at the same time.

Which had left only Shelby.

And Jack.

"The timing of that attack at the hotel should have tipped me off," he said grimly. "You were away all weekend, so Jerry couldn't find out where Shelby and I were. It wasn't until Monday morning, when you were back at the office, that you could feed him the information about where the company credit card had been used. And sure enough, on Monday morning, a couple of shooters came looking for us."

"I swear to God, Jack, that was the final straw. I hated the idea of ratting on colleagues—hated putting you and Jessie in danger. I told Lawrence that was it, that I wouldn't do any more. But I should have known he wouldn't let me just beg off."

At first Jack couldn't figure out what Mack's words meant.

By the time he did, it was too late.

The first man stepped out of the cellar doorway in the same moment that the second one kicked open the kitchen door at Jack's back. Jack managed to hang on to his gun as he was propelled forward, but the searing pain in his ribs as he hit the edge of the counter loosened his grip, and the quick chop from the man behind him finished it off. The gun clattered over the linoleum floor, out of reach, and the bleak, defeated look on Mack's face seemed to sag into utter hopelessness.

"It's no good, Jack," he said. "The bastards were here waiting."

And then the third man appeared in the open cellar door. He was tall and heavyset, and in spite of the fact that his skin hung loosely on his frame—he'd been ill in prison, Jack had heard—Jerry Lawrence was wearing one of his trademark designer suits, still dapper in spite of his obvious poor health.

And Jack had walked right into Lawrence's hands, with his mind only half-focused on the job because the other half of it was thinking about Shelby Henderson and her baby.

He cursed himself, but it didn't help.

"Morning, Jerry." He nodded curtly as Jerry Lawrence stepped into the kitchen and took a chair at the table. One of the gunmen was gesturing for Jack to raise his hands, and he finally did, but without taking his eyes off the principal felon. "You have any idea how much grief you're going to cause by icing a pair of federal agents?" he added, as calmly as he could manage.

"It's a good try, Mr. Cotter." Jerry's voice sounded wheezy and asthmatic. "But I'm afraid it's too late. I'm on my way out of the country—in fact, I have my ticket right here." He patted the breast pocket of his expensive-looking olive suit. "I just wanted to tie up what loose ends I could before I left. Having you stumble in here is a nice little bonus, I must say."

"You coulda done this the easy way." It was the first shooter who spoke, the one who'd grabbed Emi out of the crib while his partner had held the gun on her. "Jerry was willing to trade the baby in exchange for you two erasing all the files on his case at the FBI. But that broad screwed everything up. And now Jerry just wants this done. So get closer together, the two of you.''

Jack closed his eyes and prayed that ''that broad'' had the sense to start the car and get out of here once she'd figured out he wasn't coming back anytime soon. He hated—even more than he let himself think about it—the idea of Shelby having another man in her life killed by Jerry Lawrence's bozos.

At least this time she wouldn't be an eyewitness.

And at least he hadn't made her any promises he wouldn't be around to keep. They'd stopped short of actually discussing the future, and Jack knew he should feel grateful about that.

Somehow, though, it only made everything seem bleaker.

Behind his closed lids he could see the soft tilt of Shelby's smile.

And the dimples in Emi's baby fingers.

He couldn't quite bring himself to believe he would never see those things again. He clenched his hands over his head, forcing his eyes open.

And saw Shelby looking at him through the living room window.

Chapter 14

It was like every nightmare he'd ever had all rolled into one. He hadn't had time to absorb the fact that she was there before she raised her right hand and aimed the gun in it through the big picture window.

How the hell had she gotten a gun?

Jack saw her reinforcing her right arm with her left hand, compensating for that still-healing sprain. She looked pale. And determined. And frightened. And at least halfway competent with the weapon, although the reluctance in her eyes told him exactly how much she hated to have to use it.

She didn't hesitate, though. Jack saw her finger squeeze the trigger, and he launched himself forward toward Sam's discarded .38 in the same moment that Shelby's shot shattered the big window and the two gunmen whirled to see who was firing on them.

For a moment after he hit the kitchen floor, he couldn't get air into his lungs past the agony in his ribs. But he managed to curl his fingers around the handle of the revolver, and as the gunman closest to him turned back in

Jack's direction, Jack fired two shots in quick succession, spinning the man around and landing him on his back, moaning, in the living room doorway. His .44—the same gun that he'd held to Emi's forehead that morning in the hotel—had clattered to the other side of the kitchen floor, well away from the action.

Jerry Lawrence would be armed, Jack was certain. And there was the other shooter to consider.

But in the same moment that Jack had lunged for the loose gun, Mack MacGuire had taken advantage of the brief moment of chaos and had hurled himself at the second gunman. Jack heard them grunting as they struggled with each other, each trying to get control of the sawed-off shotgun in the shooter's hand.

"Shelby, get out of here!" His fear for her safety was jabbing at him even more sharply than the pain in his rib cage. He forced himself to his knees, trying to push past the pain, wishing he could keep Shelby and Jerry Lawrence in his vision at the same time, wishing their two images didn't keep blurring every time he fought to get a breath past the stabbing sensation in his right side.

He could see Shelby stepping tentatively through the frame of the window she'd demolished. At the same time Jerry was getting to his feet, his hand sliding smoothly under the lapel of his suit jacket.

There was a muffled roar to Jack's right, followed by a long, gurgling gasp. Jack had no idea whether it was Mack or the other man who'd been hit—they were both staggering, and he thought he heard the shotgun hit the floor.

There wasn't time to make sure. Jerry Lawrence was pulling out his own weapon—a little Colt pistol, Jack noticed fleetingly. It looked small in Jerry's big palm, but Jack knew it was plenty powerful enough to do some damage. And Shelby was getting closer to the danger instead of farther away.

"Get to a neighbor's phone—call 9-1-1." He met and held her terrified gaze for one brief second.

And then Jerry Lawrence was moving, and Jack lost track of where Shelby was. He rolled himself painfully to one side as Jerry leveled the pistol at him and fired.

The bullet went wide, but only barely. Jack loosed off a poorly aimed shot of his own and heard the ceiling light fixture shatter.

As an offensive maneuver, it was rotten. But it worked well enough as a distraction. Jerry raised both arms to shield himself from the sudden shower of glass fragments, and it gave Jack enough time to aim his next shot.

It stung Jerry's right hand and knocked the Colt pistol flying. The sight of it was enough to get Jack moving past his own pain, pushing himself upward into a flying tackle.

"Go!" he roared at Shelby.

He saw the quick blur of her tan-and-white outfit heading for the front door.

And felt the solid impact of Jerry Lawrence's body staggering off-balance, careening against the open cellar door and then disappearing in a tangle of windmilling arms and legs down the yawning staircase below.

Jack had never felt such fury.

Or such fear.

He'd never had to fight so hard for simple comprehension. It seemed to take forever for the facts to sink in.

He'd shoved Jerry down the cellar steps, and the big man was lying on the concrete floor below him, unconscious.

The first gunman was clutching his kneecap and moaning in the living room, oblivious to everything but his own agony.

Mack and the second gunmen were both out cold on the kitchen floor. There was a lot of blood, and Jack still wasn't certain whose it was.

It wasn't until the police and the paramedics showed up that he realized his ex-friend and the other man had jointly

taken the blast from the sawed-off shotgun, and that neither of them had survived the point-blank impact of it.

It wasn't until much later—until he was finally able to
breathe again, thanks to a paramedic who took pity on him
and slipped him a few painkillers while everybody else was
still asking questions—that Jack realized it was really over.

He'd done what he set out to do.

He'd won.

And it didn't matter anymore.

Nothing mattered except the way Shelby had looked at
him through the splintered picture window.

He'd seen the truth in her terrified hazel eyes just before
Jerry Lawrence had raised his gun to fire at Jack.

She could never love him, not after this.

Suddenly—now that it was too late—he realized that was
what had been tantalizing him everytime he looked into her
perceptive hazel eyes. It was the possibility of Shelby's love
that had been dancing at the edges of his dreams since he'd
met her.

And now it was gone.

The life Jack led wasn't the life Shelby wanted.

And he couldn't blame her for feeling that way.

He didn't see her again after she'd fled to call for help.
He didn't expect to.

And when his brothers showed up about an hour later,
they found him still sitting in a corner of Mack's living
room sofa, looking blankly at the place where the picture
window had been and wondering how the hell he'd managed to find the woman of his dreams and lose her again in
such a short space of time.

He'd fastened the cummerbund a little too tightly. The
edge of it kept digging into the bandage around Jack's ribs,
reminding him that under his tuxedo and crisp white shirt
he was still more or less a wreck.

"You about ready to go, little brother?"

Wiley was standing by the low door that led into the main body of the church. He had one hand on the velvet curtain that covered the door, as though he, like the minister standing to one side, were impatient to get this show on the road.

Sam was slouching against the counter that ran along one wall, hands deep in the pockets of his dress pants. As far as Jack could tell, Sam had never shown impatience about anything in his life.

But beneath Sam's surface nonchalance, Jack could sense the quiet buzz of anticipation. Sam had never shown much affection, or concern, or warmth, either, until Kelley Landis had come back into his life.

He'd shown all three only today, when Jack had eased himself slowly into the back seat of Wiley's car at the big Victorian inn. After an enforced one-night stay in an Austin hospital, Jack was back on his feet again, but the new damage to his rib in the struggle with Jerry Lawrence seemed to be mending slowly, and getting around wasn't easy.

At least Sam hadn't suggested the theory that had been kicking around in Jack's own mind—that he'd be healing a hell of a lot quicker if his heart hadn't been so bruised as well.

Sam *had* remarked on Jack's creaky pace, and he'd gone a step farther, commenting, "Mothers-in-law aside, Jack, you really should consider trying this sometime. It's a lot more fun than you'd think."

Of course it was fun, if you found a woman who loved you, Jack wanted to reply. No wonder Wiley and Sam looked so pleased with themselves as Wiley pulled away from the inn's front door. Unlike Jack, they'd managed to hang on to the happiness that had shown up in their lives.

Jack hadn't even recognized it until it was already walking away from him.

He refused to be drawn into that angle of the conversation, and said instead, "Kelley's mother still fidgeting about things?"

Sam rolled his eyes. "Big-time," he confirmed. "Rae-Anne and Kelley decided on some last minute change in the ceremony, and Mom's having kittens about it."

"As I understand it, the main function of the bride's mother is to be nervous." Wiley sounded amused by the whole thing. "Don't sweat it, Sam."

"I'm not." Sam grinned, and Jack could see an uncharacteristic gleam in his brother's slate blue eyes. "I'm just hoping Jack doesn't keel over, that's all."

Jack wasn't worried about keeling over.

He was worried about keeping his act together in other ways, though.

The best man was supposed to look as though he knew what he was doing, as though he'd remembered all the last minute details even if the nervous bridegrooms hadn't.

In this case, it was the bridegrooms who were calm. And Jack was having a hell of a hard time keeping his thoughts in one place.

He hadn't seen or heard from Shelby since the fiasco at Mack MacGuire's house three days earlier. He told himself he wasn't surprised. Shelby had made it plain from the beginning how much she disliked the life he led. Now that she'd had some time away from him, no doubt she'd decided there was no point in prolonging what had been nothing more than a brief affair fueled by adrenaline and coincidence.

It was nothing more than coincidence that their lives seemed to have suited them to understand one another with an intimacy that Jack could barely stand to think about.

No doubt it was nothing but coincidence that had made him jump every time a phone had rung in his vicinity for the past three days, too. He knew it wouldn't be Shelby's soft, husky voice on the other end of the line, but still—

There had been enough other people wanting to talk to him that there should have been no time left over to think about Shelby and Emi. He'd been up to his eyeballs in FBI business, in briefings with the border authorities and the police in Hays County and Houston and Lafayette, Shelby's old hometown. He'd visited Jessie in the hospital, too, just as soon as he'd gotten out of the Austin hospital himself.

"You heard from Washington yet?" she'd asked him, once he'd filled her in on everything that had happened since she'd asked him such a seemingly simple favor a week earlier.

"Washington? What are you talking about?"

The gleam in her eye told Jack she'd already known his whole story before he'd laid it out for her. And she knew more than just that, apparently.

"I've had a call," she said. "Some people at the main office are impressed by the fact that you mopped up Jerry Lawrence on your own when the whole Bureau hadn't been able to do it despite our best efforts. I'm pretty sure there's a promotion in the offing for you, Jack. A major-league one, if you want it."

Did he want it? Jack still hadn't decided by the time he'd left Jessie's hospital room.

He *did* want—and was gratified to learn that he would probably get—the satisfaction of knowing that Jerry Lawrence would be behind bars for a very long stretch this time. One of Lawrence's henchmen was dead, the other one talking eagerly to the authorities, happy to point fingers at his former buddies if it meant a lighter sentence for himself.

It had been hard for Jack to mourn Mack's death too bitterly. His former colleague had done too much damage for that. He'd attended Mack's funeral just the same, and then he'd stayed up far too late afterward drinking with Annette and Garry, neither of whom had quite been able to believe a member of their own team could turn traitor the way Mack had done.

"I heard a rumor you're up for a new job," Annette said.

Jack shrugged. "Could be just a rumor," he replied.

Garry snorted. "Yeah, right," he said. "And I'm J. Edgar Hoover. Come on, Jack—this is the break we all look for. Finally you'll get your hands on some real authority around here."

A month ago, he'd have been pleased about that.

A month ago, though, Jack Cotter had been a different man.

He'd answered all the questions that had plagued him since he'd found himself in the middle of the Lawrence case, including the mystery of how Shelby had managed to come up with a gun at exactly the right moment.

It was his own gun, it turned out—the one he'd left in the hotel room after Emi had been kidnapped. Shelby had hidden it away in that bag she'd been carrying with her all along. When Kelley returned the car, the bag—with the gun—was in it.

If it hadn't been for that piece of dumb luck—and Shelby's willingness to use the weapon—Jack would probably not be around to be climbing the steps at the front of the church with his two brothers now.

And still, none of it really mattered.

Even if Jack *had* had the time to track Shelby down, or any idea where to start looking for her, he still didn't have the faintest idea what he could say to her.

It was Shelby's doing—and Emi's—that Jack was at such loose ends now, not certain what he wanted or where he was headed.

Shelby had offered him a new beginning, a new way to look at life.

And he hadn't known what to do with it.

The thought of it churned in his gut as he listened to the organist starting into the wedding march and saw the congregation turning in their seats, rustling and jostling each other as they tried to catch the first glimpse of the two brides making their way up the aisle.

Rae-Anne came first, glowing and beautiful in a dress so simple and elegant that Jack almost couldn't believe she was the same woman he usually saw slinging beers at the barbecue restaurant. There'd been some reason—although he couldn't recall just what it was—that she'd insisted on a simple dress instead of an elaborate one. To Jack's eyes, the natural beauty of her own dazzling smile was all the ornament he could imagine wanting.

Kelley, a few steps behind, was tall and serene in a frothy white dress that made her look like Venus rising from the waves. She was smiling, too, not as broadly as Rae-Anne, but with such tranquil love and certainty that it brought an unexpected catch to Jack's throat.

Suddenly, the only thing he wanted in the entire world was to have a woman looking at him with that kind of love.

And not just any woman.

One woman.

The woman he'd lost.

He heard a ripple of laughter running through the congregation, and realized someone else was following in Rae-Anne and Kelley's wake. He'd thought they'd decided not to have any attendants, but clearly they'd changed their minds—that must be what Kelley's mother had been flustered about.

The moment he saw who it was, he completely forgot about Kelley's mother, and everyone else on the planet with him.

Shelby Henderson was coming up the aisle behind the two brides, looking so ethereally beautiful that for a moment Jack was sure she was a hallucination brought on by pain and sleeplessness and regret.

Somehow she'd managed to find a dress that fitted her perfectly, a yellow-and-rose floral print closely fitted in the waist with a flaring skirt and extravagantly full sleeves. It accented Shelby's slender, womanly body as though it had been made for her, and set off the pale gold of her hair and the pink softness of her lips so exquisitely that even in his bruised and battered state Jack could feel his own body responding to the beauty of hers.

She'd pulled back the front strands of her hair—he could see the pink petals of the flowers that covered the clasp at the back of her head. But her face was half-veiled by the rest of her hair as she dipped her head toward the small, unsteady person who was accompanying her.

That was what the spectators were laughing at, and Jack heard his brothers chuckling, too, as Emi's baby legs carried her erratically toward the front of the church.

Jack couldn't laugh. He couldn't muster so much as a faint smile past the tightness in his chest.

Emi was walking.

Just a few days ago she'd still been hanging on to things, wobbling a lot and sitting down suddenly whenever she tried to look up. And now she was navigating under her own steam—slowly, unsteadily, but with a look in her velvet brown eyes that said she knew where she was going and she was determined to get there by herself.

They grew so quickly.

The thought tugged at Jack, making it suddenly hard to breathe. In no time at all, Emi's garbled syllables would turn into actual words. And then into sentences. And then into requests to borrow the car keys.

He could see it all suddenly as though her future—with all its promise and heartache and joy—were spread out ahead of her on the rich red carpet of the church aisle.

And he'd already missed a piece of it. He'd missed the moment when she'd taken her first step.

He looked at Shelby again and saw that she was watching him under that gold curtain of hair. Her hands were guiding Emi's wavering steps, making sure her daughter didn't let go of the little white satin bag that no doubt held the two weddings rings that would match the ones in Jack's inner pocket.

But her eyes were on Jack's face, searching, seeking.

He'd been to the wedding rehearsal yesterday evening, but the ceremony as it was unfolding now felt utterly foreign, almost as though he'd never been to a wedding before. He watched Emi totter to the railing, watched Shelby scoop her daughter up, listened to the minister's voice and the renewed murmur of amusement as Emi held out the bag containing the rings at just the right moment.

He heard his brothers and their brides exchanging vows. Saw them slipping the wedding rings on their fingers.

Found himself feeling very much on the sidelines as Wiley and Rae-Anne, Sam and Kelley sealed their pledges with a kiss.

He felt that clutch of longing down low in his body all over again as Shelby's eyes met his own.

And then, suddenly, as he let himself gaze into those hazel depths, he figured it out.

He'd been leaving out the most important piece.

He'd been focusing all his thoughts on safety, and practicality, and professionalism. On wrestling with his own unhappy memories and trying to guarantee that nothing bad ever happened to Shelby or Emi again.

He'd been so busy doing all of that that he'd never stopped to think about love.

Suddenly he knew—with a certainty that made him tremble from the toes of his polished dress shoes to the top of his carefully combed head—that it was love that had been beckoning to him from the depths of Shelby's eyes all along.

It was love—the first faint possibility of love—that had wakened him from a sound sleep and sent him in search of Shelby and her baby when they'd given him the slip the first time.

And maybe it had been love, too, that had prompted Shelby to follow him into such deadly danger at Mack's house three days ago.

When he looked at it that way, everything that had been so confusing and unnerving began to make sense at last.

What if love came first?

What of love was the piece that made the rest of the puzzle fit together?

Suddenly he was sure it was.

And he hadn't even recognized it.

Maybe he'd been working too hard at answering all the wrong questions.

Maybe the only one that really mattered was the one that could be answered with a simple "I do."

The organ blared out triumphantly as the two newly married couples strode back down the aisle. The congregation was a lively one—"Between the private-eye types and the barbecue types, this could be quite a party," Rae-Anne had confessed to Shelby—and people broke into spontaneous applause as Wiley and Sam led their brides out into the clear winter sunshine.

Rae-Anne had talked about a lot more than just wedding arrangements to Shelby over the past couple of days.

It had been both frightening and exhilarating for Shelby to discover that Jack's brothers, too, had hidden from love for a very long time. "It's just the Cotter way, Shelby," Rae-Anne had said. "All three of them like to think they can manage perfectly well on their own."

Wiley and Sam had obviously changed their minds about that, Shelby thought. But Jack—

She'd gratefully accepted the keys to Kelley's apartment, because she felt uncomfortable being in the midst of the wedding guests who'd started to fill up the Victorian inn immediately after the finale of the Jerry Lawrence adventure. She liked Jack's family and family-to-be immensely, but she wasn't exactly certain where she stood in the flurry of last minute preparations.

Rae-Anne and Kelley had quickly made it clear that as far as they were concerned, she was a part of the family, too. "There's time to get dresses for you and Emi," Rae-Anne had said. "Come on, Shelby. It'll be a great way of declaring that you're really back in the world again."

It was startling to realize how quickly Rae-Anne and Kelley had seemed to understand what Shelby had gone through—how she'd tried to hide herself away and cut herself off from everything that had gone wrong in her life.

It hadn't worked, not in the long run. Once she'd met Jack Cotter, she'd been forced into contact with all the things she'd been trying so hard to avoid.

Like danger.

And passion.

And love.

Sometimes, she'd come to realize, you couldn't just turn your back and pretend life's dangers didn't exist. To live fully—sometimes just to live at all—you had to grapple with threats, and with ugliness. Running away wasn't the answer.

She'd learned that from Jack. He was willing to do a dangerous job so that other people—like herself and Emi—could be safe. The realization of just how necessary that dangerous job really was had given Shelby the strength to step into the confrontation with Jerry Lawrence at that house in Houston a few days earlier.

She'd done it because she loved Jack—because she couldn't stand to see him killed.

The problem was that now that it was all over—now that Jerry Lawrence was in jail and she and Emi out of danger—it was beginning to seem as though the danger had been the *easy* part.

Love, she was discovering, could be a lot harder to figure out.

Did Jack love her at all? Was there any chance that the two of them—no, the three of them—might be able to find a future together?

She'd accepted Rae-Anne and Kelley's invitation to join their wedding party mostly because she wanted so desperately to see Jack again, to find the answers to those questions if she could.

And judging by the turbulent look in his dark eyes during the ceremony, he wasn't happy that she'd done it.

Well, Shelby thought, fighting her own plunging spirits as the wedding came to a close, *at least I've accomplished something.* As Rae-Anne had said, she'd gotten back into the real world again. She was ready to face the future squarely, instead of hiding from it.

And if the future meant she had to put Jack Cotter behind her—

Her heart twisted in protest as she carried Emi down the aisle after the two happy couples. She knew now that she was stronger than she'd let herself believe—that she would survive whatever she had to face. But if she never felt the all-encompassing warmth of Jack Cotter's embrace again...

She found herself blinking back tears as she paused by the back of the church, letting the guests stream out around her. Several people paused to smile at Emi, and Shelby did her best to smile, too, hoping people would assume she was just one of those people who always cried at weddings.

"Fow-wow," Emi said, poking her mother in the nose.

"I know. They were pretty flowers, weren't they?"

"Fow-wow." Emi waggled her hand up and down.

"Did you want some flowers of your own, sweetie?" That seemed to be the point Emi was trying to make. Shelby reached around and started to pull the pink roses out of her hair. She'd already decided to skip the reception—she wasn't in the mood for the raucous party Rae-Anne had predicted, and anyway, she'd already learned what she'd come here to learn.

Jack *didn't* want all the things she'd hoped they were coming to share—didn't want to be a part of her life, or her daughter's. She felt her spirits sinking as she tried to twist the little rosebuds free. If he'd cared, wouldn't he have smiled at her, or at Emi, or done *something* besides just look at her with that unreadable expression in his eyes?

"Here. Let me help."

His hands were in her hair before she'd even known he was stepping up behind her. Shelby jumped a little at the sound of Jack's rich voice at her ear, and saw her daughter's face crease into a smile as she pointed one stubby finger and pronounced her own version of his name.

"Dja!"

"Same to you, sweet pea." Jack had managed to pull one of the rosebuds loose, and he handed it to Emi, who promptly tried to eat it.

"Bad idea," Shelby said, as she took the rosebud away again.

Emi's smile trembled and disappeared, but Jack was already taking steps to head off the tears that threatened to overtake her. Deftly, he pulled the arrangement of white ribbons and baby's breath off the end of the closest pew and presented it to Emi with a little bow.

"There," he said. "That one's too big to eat."

The tiny flowers seemed to captivate her. "Ooo," she said, and promptly forgot all about her mother and Jack as she began counting the little white blossoms according to some system of her own.

Shelby waited.

She wasn't sure what was behind Jack's change in manner. He seemed excited about something, but maybe that was just a natural aftermath of the wedding ceremony. He seemed hesitant, too, although she couldn't figure out why.

Last Tuesday night, when they'd encountered each other in Emi's room in the middle of the night, Shelby had taken the initiative, refusing to let Jack pretend the powerful attraction between them didn't exist. And she'd proved her point, too, in lovemaking so vivid and intense that even now, days later, her knees trembled slightly at the recollection of it.

But despite all her openness, despite the mind-numbing danger they'd shared and survived the next day, Jack had kept his distance.

At first she thought he was still doing the same thing now.

But then—

"Shelby—" His voice sounded as tentative as he looked. "I... When did Emi start walking?"

"Two days ago. It just happened all of a sudden." She frowned up at him, and wished she could run her fingers over the tired-looking lines in his handsome face. He'd endured a lot over the past few days, and it broke her heart that he didn't seem to be able to let himself enjoy the good things that had come out of it all.

"It's kind of scary, actually," she went on, uncomfortable with the silence that threatened to stretch between them. "All of a sudden it's as though most of the world is within grabbing distance. And so of course she—"

"Shelby." This time he sounded a little more forceful. "I—can we talk about Emi later?"

"You asked the question," she pointed out.

"I know," he growled at her, and suddenly Shelby could see that what she'd thought was hesitation was in fact plain, old-fashioned nervousness. "And I'm sorry I did. I love Emi, but I don't want to talk about her right now. I want to talk about *us*."

He loved Emi?

The admission was the last thing Shelby had expected.

Except for the next thing he said.

"Do you think—is there any way you might see your way to disregarding the way I've been behaving since I met you?"

Shelby frowned. "How exactly is that?" she asked.

Jack looked at the ornate wooden ceiling of the church, then back at her. "Like a stubborn fool who doesn't know a good thing when he sees one," he said. "I've been running in the wrong direction this whole time. And I didn't see it until just now."

Shelby shifted Emi to her other hip. The move didn't so much as dent her daughter's concentration.

"What—exactly did you see just now?" she asked slowly.

Jack drew in a deep breath, catching himself when it obviously touched off the pain in his ribs. "I saw my brothers and their brides looking at each other as though nothing but love mattered in the entire world," he said. "And it suddenly occurred to me that they were right."

"Jack—"

The tension of the past two years seemed to be churning around inside her now, like an ice floe starting to break up. Shelby felt herself trembling at the feeling of it, not sure whether it was a comfortable sensation or not.

Comfortable or not, there was still a certain amount of caution ingrained in her, and she could hear the wariness in her voice as she said, "We've never mentioned love. Not once."

"I know." He took a step closer, and Shelby could tell that it genuinely surprised him—and it seemed to hurt him, too—to have to admit it. "Lord knows, we've talked about nearly everything else."

It was true, Shelby realized. She'd shared things about herself with Jack Cotter that she'd kept hidden from everyone else she'd ever met.

They'd talked about her childhood, and his—about her dreams for Emi's future—about Jack's difficult, demanding job—

Speaking of which—

"I've been wanting to tell you this," she said. "I just haven't had a chance. I know I've said a lot of things about not wanting anything to do with the world of law enforcement, Jack, but I also know that Emi and I wouldn't be free to live our lives the way we want to if it hadn't been for the way you solved this case. I just—" How could she phrase this? "Rae-Anne mentioned something about you taking some higher-up job with the FBI, and I just wanted you to know that I'm happy for you. You're good at what you do, Jack. You deserve success at it."

It was the truth—although not quite the whole truth.

The whole truth was that this new job of Jack's was likely to be just one more reason that he was likely to disappear from her life after today.

Something had flared in his eyes at her words, as though her changed attitude surprised him.

Or maybe that dark gleam meant something else.

"I was trying to talk about love," he said slowly. "Not about my damn job."

He sounded impatient, almost angry. Shelby frowned again and adjusted her grip on Emi's hips.

"Aren't you taking that promotion?" she said. "I thought—"

He waved one big palm in the air. "I just had a better idea," he said.

"'Just'?" She repeated the word, growing more puzzled. "When did you have this idea?"

"About ten minutes ago."

"Ten minutes ago your brothers were kissing their brides up at the front of the church," she said.

"I know. That's what made me think—I've been a fool about you and me since the very beginning."

Shelby was out of questions, or answers. She just looked at him, trying to block out the soft murmur of Emi's voice at her ear.

"If I leave the FBI—which I'll probably do anyway—but if I do, and if I take a job with Sam, at Cotter Investigations..."

The sentence sounded unfinished. "Does Sam know about this?" Shelby asked.

"No—as you pointed out, he's had other things on his mind for the past ten minutes."

"What kind of job are you talking about?"

He waved his hand more broadly. "Routine stuff—bread-and-butter investigative work. Missing persons, maybe. Missing kids. I could find people's kids for them, Shelby." His sudden grin made Shelby's knees weak all over again. "Maybe it would restore my confidence after the way you got the jump on me in finding Emi."

Shelby felt her heart beating faster as he stepped even closer to her and slid his hands along her forearms. "Do you think... it's too late to start talking about this... and about love?"

"Too late?" She shook her head, and felt her fine, silky hair pulling free of the clasp Jack had loosened. "If you really love me..."

They were like two dancers trying to overcome the pain of old injuries long enough to start moving in step, Shelby thought. They were both awkward at this. If either of them had ever known a time when love was easy and straightforward and trust was something as natural as breath, it had been a long time ago.

But not for Emi, it hadn't.

Shelby was still looking into Jack's serious, tentative face, still wondering why the simple, natural words wouldn't quite form themselves on her lips or his. Did they *not* love each other, after all? Or didn't they love each other enough? Was that why this was so difficult?

And Emi, when she'd finally finished whatever she'd been doing with the bouquet of baby's breath, decided to set them both straight.

She did it without words, without planning, without apparently thinking at all. Something—the excitement of the wedding, maybe, or her pleasure with the flowers Jack had given her, or some sense that her mother and Jack weren't quite getting on with the program—made her look up all of a sudden, meeting first Shelby's gaze and then Jack's.

She stretched her little arms out straight, one in either direction. Shelby could see the dimples at her elbows just below the pink-and-yellow sleeves.

Emi clasped Shelby's neck with one fat hand, and Jack's with the other.

And she smiled.

Sweetly, calmly, beatifically. As though nothing could have been more natural than for the three of them to be standing close together like this. Like a family.

Shelby laughed. She couldn't help it. So did Jack.

"She's right," he growled. "We're both beating around the bush here." He cleared his throat and pulled Shelby all the way into his arms, encompassing Emi in his grip as well.

"I love you, Shelby Henderson," he told her. "And I love this baby of yours, too. Do you think the two of you might consider marrying me?" He looked down at his sharp black tuxedo and Shelby's fairy-tale dress. "I mean, we've already got the clothes."

"You're right." She laughed again. "And yes, I do—and I do love you, Jack."

He was already lowering his head to kiss her, but before his lips reached hers, the wedding crowd seemed to surge back into the church from the steps outside.

It was only a few people, but their boisterous, happy voices seemed to fill the quiet place. The two new couples were in the forefront.

"Come on, Shelby!" It was Rae-Anne, calling to her. "How can we throw our bouquets at you if you're hiding in here?"

They threw them anyway, and Shelby found herself with her arms suddenly full of flowers, and Emi, and Jack. People were applauding again, and Jack was kissing her, and Emi was beginning to pull the pink-and-yellow freesias off their stems. Shelby felt the flowery perfume surrounding her, and her eyes filled with happy tears, as though the lighthearted "whoever catches the bouquet gets married next" ritual had been an actual ceremony, uniting her and Jack and Emi into a family.

Love had already done that, she thought, looking into Jack's eyes. Love didn't care about ritual, or about danger, either. Wholehearted, trusting, instinctive love—the kind Emi's baby heart already knew so much about—had a power all its own. And it had finally found a way past all the stubborn fears Shelby and Jack had tried so hard to put in its way.

As Jack had pointed out, they were halfway equipped for a wedding of their own. The clothing part of it was well in hand, and Emi had been fully checked out on the duties of ring bearer.

All that was left, really, was to set a date, and to announce to the rest of the world that Jack Cotter, like his brothers, had just embarked on an assignment that he hoped to be working on for the rest of his life.

* * * * *

The first book in the exciting new
Fortune's Children series is

HIRED HUSBAND

by *New York Times* bestselling writer
Rebecca Brandewyne

Beginning in July 1996
Only from Silhouette Books

Here's an exciting sneak preview....

Minneapolis, Minnesota

As Caroline Fortune wheeled her dark blue Volvo into the underground parking lot of the towering, glass-and-steel structure that housed the global headquarters of Fortune Cosmetics, she glanced anxiously at her gold Piaget wristwatch. An accident on the snowy freeway had caused rush-hour traffic to be a nightmare this morning. As a result, she was running late for her 9:00 a.m. meeting—and if there was one thing her grandmother, Kate Winfield Fortune, simply couldn't abide, it was slack, unprofessional behavior on the job. And lateness was the sign of a sloppy, disorganized schedule.

Involuntarily, Caroline shuddered at the thought of her grandmother's infamous wrath being unleashed upon her. The stern rebuke would be precise, apropos, scathing and delivered with coolly raised, condemnatory eyebrows and in icy tones of haughty grandeur that had in the past reduced many an executive—even the male ones—at Fortune Cosmetics not only to obsequious apologies, but even to tears. Caroline had seen it happen on more than one occasion, although, much to her gratitude and relief, she herself was seldom a target of her grandmother's anger. And she wouldn't be this morning, either, not if she could help it. That would be a disastrous way to start out the new year.

Grabbing her Louis Vuitton totebag and her black leather portfolio from the front passenger seat, Caroline stepped gracefully from the Volvo and slammed the door. The heels of her Maud Frizon pumps clicked briskly on the concrete floor as she hurried toward the bank of elevators that would take her up into the skyscraper owned by her family. As the elevator doors slid open, she rushed down the long, plushly carpeted corridors of one of the hushed upper floors toward the conference room.

By now Caroline had her portfolio open and was leafing through it as she hastened along, reviewing her notes she had prepared for her presentation. So she didn't see Dr. Nicolai Valkov until she literally ran right into him. Like her, he had his head bent over his own portfolio, not watching where he was going. As the two of them collided, both their portfolios and the papers inside went flying. At the unexpected impact, Caroline lost her balance, stumbled, and would have fallen had not Nick's strong, sure hands abruptly shot out, grabbing hold of her and pulling her to him to steady her. She gasped, startled and stricken, as she came up hard against his broad chest, lean hips and corded thighs, her face just inches from his own—as though they were lovers about to kiss.

Caroline had never been so close to Nick Valkov before, and, in that instant, she was acutely aware of him—not just as a fellow employee of Fortune Cosmetics but also as a man. Of how tall and ruggedly handsome he was, dressed in an elegant, pin-striped black suit cut in the European fashion, a crisp white shirt, a foulard tie and a pair of Cole Haan loafers. Of how dark his thick, glossy hair and his deep-set eyes framed by raven-wing brows were—so dark that they were almost black, despite the bright, fluorescent lights that blazed overhead. Of the whiteness of his straight teeth against his bronzed skin as a brazen, mocking grin slowly curved his wide, sensual mouth.

"Actually, I *was* hoping for a sweet roll this morning—but I daresay you would prove even tastier, Ms. Fortune," Nick drawled impertinently, his low, silky voice tinged with a faint accent born of the fact that Russian, not English, was his native language.

At his words, Caroline flushed painfully, embarrassed and annoyed. If there was one person she always attempted to avoid at Fortune Cosmetics, it was Nick Valkov. Following the breakup of the Soviet Union, he had emigrated to the United States, where her grandmother had hired him to direct the company's research and development department. Since that time, Nick had constantly demonstrated marked, traditional, Old World tendencies that had led Caroline to believe he not only had no use for equal rights but also would actually have been more than happy to turn back the clock several centuries where females were concerned. She thought his remark was typical of his attitude toward women: insolent, arrogant and domineering. Really, the man was simply insufferable!

Caroline couldn't imagine what had ever prompted her grandmother to hire him—and at a highly generous salary, too—except that Nick Valkov was considered one of the foremost chemists anywhere on the planet. Deep down inside Caroline knew that no matter how he behaved, Fortune Cosmetics was extremely lucky to have him. Still, that didn't give him the right to manhandle and insult her!

"I assure you that you would find me more bitter than a cup of the strongest black coffee, Dr. Valkov," she insisted, attempting without success to free her trembling body from his steely grip, while he continued to hold her so near that she could feel his heart beating steadily in his chest—and knew he must be equally able to feel the erratic hammering of her own.

"Oh, I'm willing to wager there's more sugar and cream to you than you let on, Ms. Fortune." To her utter mortification and outrage, she felt one of Nick's hands slide insidiously up her back and nape to her luxuriant mass of sable hair, done up in a stylish French twist.

"You know so much about fashion," he murmured, eyeing her assessingly, pointedly ignoring her indignation and efforts to escape from him. "So why do you always wear your hair like this...so tightly wrapped and severe? I've never seen it down. Still, that's the way it needs to be worn, you know...soft, loose, tangled about your face. As it is, your hair fairly cries out for a man to take the pins from it, so he can see how long it is. Does it fall past your shoulders?" He quirked one eyebrow inquisitively, a mocking half smile still twisting his lips, letting her know he was enjoying her obvious discomfiture. "You aren't going to tell me, are you? What a pity. Because my guess is that it does—and I'd like to know if I'm right. And these glasses." He indicated the large, square, tortoiseshell frames perched on her slender, classic nose. "I think you use them to hide behind more than you do to see. I'll bet you don't actually even need them at all."

Caroline felt the blush that had yet to leave her cheeks deepen, its heat seeming to spread throughout her entire quivering body. Damn the man! Why must he be so infuriatingly perceptive?

Because everything that Nick suspected was true.

* * * * *

To read more, don't miss
HIRED HUSBAND
by Rebecca Brandewyne,
Book One in the new
FORTUNE'S CHILDREN series,
beginning this month and available only from
Silhouette Books!

This exciting new cross-line continuity series unites
five of your favorite authors as they weave five
connected novels about love, marriage—and
Daddy's unexpected need for a baby carriage!

Get ready for

THE BABY NOTION by Dixie Browning (SD#1011, 7/96)
Single gal Priscilla Barrington would do anything for a
baby—even visit the local sperm bank. Until cowboy
Jake Spencer set out to convince her to have a family
the natural—and much more exciting—way!

And the romance in New Hope, Texas, continues with:

BABY IN A BASKET
by Helen R. Myers (SR#1169, 8/96)

MARRIED...WITH TWINS!
by Jennifer Mikels (SSE#1054, 9/96)

HOW TO HOOK A HUSBAND (AND A BABY)
by Carolyn Zane (YT#29, 10/96)

DISCOVERED: DADDY
by Marilyn Pappano (IM#746, 11/96)

DADDY KNOWS LAST arrives in July...only from

DKL-D

MILLION DOLLAR SWEEPSTAKES

SWP-M96

The dynasty begins.

LINDA HOWARD
The Mackenzies

Now available for the first time, Mackenzie's Mountain and Mackenzie's Mission, together in one affordable, trade-size edition. Don't miss out on the two stories that started it all!

Mackenzie's Mountain: Wolf Mackenzie is a loner. All he cares about is his ranch and his son. Labeled a half-breed by the townspeople, he chooses to stay up on his mountain—that is, until the spunky new schoolteacher decides to pay the Mackenzies a visit. And that's when all hell breaks loose.

Mackenzie's Misson: Joe "Breed" Mackenzie is a colonel in the U.S. Air Force. All he cares about is flying. He is the best of the best and determined never to let down his country—even for love. But that was before he met a beautiful civilian engineer, who turns his life upside down.

Available this August, at your favorite retail outlet.

Who can resist a Texan...or a Calloway?

This September, award-winning author
ANNETTE BROADRICK
returns to Texas, with a brand-new
story about the Calloways...

SONS OF TEXAS

Rogues and Ranchers

CLINT: The brave leader. Used to keeping secrets.

CADE: The Lone Star Stud. Used to having women
fall at his feet...

MATT: The family guardian. Used to handling
trouble...

They must discover the identity of the mystery
woman with Calloway eyes—and uncover a
conspiracy that threatens their family...

Look for **SONS OF TEXAS:** Rogues and Ranchers
in September 1996!

Only from Silhouette...where passion lives.

FORTUNE'S Children™

New York Times Bestselling Author
REBECCA BRANDEWYNE

Launches a new twelve-book series—FORTUNE'S CHILDREN
beginning in July 1996 with Book One

Hired Husband

Caroline Fortune knew her marriage to Nick Valkov was in name only. She would help save the family business, Nick would get a green card, and a paper marriage would suit both of them. Until Caroline could no longer deny the feelings Nick stirred in her and the practical union turned passionate.

MEET THE FORTUNES—a family whose legacy is greater than riches. Because where there's a will...there's a wedding!

Look for Book Two, *The Millionaire and the Cowgirl*, by Lisa Jackson. Available in August 1996 wherever Silhouette books are sold.

Silhouette®

SILHOUETTE... Where Passion Lives

Add these Silhouette favorites to your collection today!
Now you can receive a discount by ordering two or more titles!

SD#05819	WILD MIDNIGHT by Ann Major	$2.99	☐
SD#05878	THE UNFORGIVING BRIDE	$2.99 U.S.	☐
	by Joan Johnston	$3.50 CAN.	☐
IM#07568	MIRANDA'S VIKING by Maggie Shayne	$3.50	☐
SSE#09896	SWEETBRIAR SUMMIT	$3.50 U.S.	☐
	by Christine Rimmer	$3.99 CAN.	☐
SSE#09944	A ROSE AND A WEDDING VOW	$3.75 U.S.	☐
	by Andrea Edwards	$4.25 CAN.	☐
SR#19002	A FATHER'S PROMISE	$2.75	☐
	by Helen R. Myers		

(limited quantities available on certain titles)

TOTAL AMOUNT	$_____
DEDUCT: 10% DISCOUNT FOR 2+ BOOKS	$_____
POSTAGE & HANDLING	$_____
($1.00 for one book, 50¢ for each additional)	
APPLICABLE TAXES**	$_____
TOTAL PAYABLE	$_____
(check or money order—please do not send cash)	

To order, send the completed form with your name, address, zip or postal code, along with a check or money order for the total above, payable to Silhouette Books, to: **In the U.S.:** 3010 Walden Avenue, P.O. Box 9077, Buffalo, NY 14269-9077; **In Canada:** P.O. Box 636, Fort Erie, Ontario, L2A 5X3.

Name:_____

Address:_____ City:_____

State/Prov.:_____ Zip/Postal Code:_____

**New York residents remit applicable sales taxes.
  Canadian residents remit applicable GST and provincial taxes.

Silhouette®

™

SBACK-JA2

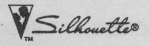